The Indian Cowboy
Part 1

The night of the wolfes

The Author:
Brita Rose Billert was born 1966 in Erfurt, Germany. She is a specialized nurse of critical care and respiratory care. A fact that also competes well in her novels. She spends her spare time with her horse in the Kyffhäuserland, Thüringen. She has made many friendships with Native Americans in Utah, South Dakota and British Columbia through her trips to the United States. This fact, the love for the horses and her job inspires her to write. Twelf novels have already been published.
Home page of the Autor:
www.brita-rose-billert.de

Brita Rose-Billert

The Indian Cowboy

The night of the wolves

Novel

Bibliographische Informationen der Deutschen Nationalbibliothek: Deie Deutsche Nationalbibliothek verzeichnet diese Publikation in der Deutschen Nationalbibliographie; detaillierte bibliographische Daten sind im Internet über dnb.d-nb.de abrufbar.

© 2021 Brita Rose Billert, Seitenweise Voraus
The Indian Cowboy 1

TWENTYSIX
Eine Marke der Books on Demand GmbH

Herstellung und Verlag:
BoD - Books on Demand, Norderstedt

ISBN: 9783740785369

Übersetzung: Bruno Winkler, Swiss
Korrektur: Natasha Lynn Anderson Wallace, Utha USA
Satz und Layout: Holger Scheidemantel
Coverdesign: Robert Billert

Indian Rodeo

Life is a Rodeo and a Rodeo is the constant up and down in life.

You struggle to stay on top, to be sure you will fall. It is not the question of whether you stay up, but for how long.

And if you find yourself rubbing your face in the mud, it is not the question of how long, but if you get up again.

It's on you, to get up again.

Silence is the center of the universe.
Silence is the center of our souls.
It is the great mystery.

We may never experience it´s origins, but we must pay attention to it.
We must listen to it and we must learn to be quiet.
Every morning we must experience the silence, because it makes us think of all the things.
We must pray to the power that stands above all the humans in the universe:

  The Great Spirit, that has no beginning and no end.

That´s everywhere, in all things and in all human beings."

  (Lakota Moon by Christopher Cain)

This page is written by my friend and translator Bruno

Chapter 1   The night of the Wolves (15)

Chapter 2   The other world (68)

Chapter 3   Endurance test (111)

Chapter 4   Inuk, the white Bear (171)

Chapter 5   Betrayal (223)

Lead-In

Like a lantern, the full moon sent its cool light over the land. Dark clouds passing by and let spooky shadows wander across the grassy plain. The Northwind blew rough over the Land. The breath of the North Pole drifted teeny ice crystals deep in to the Mid-West, in to the Great Plains. The almost treeless grassy plains did not stop him. In one of the valleys people found shelter. The old wooden house defied storm, cold and rain for more than seventy years. Weathering had gnawed at it. But the house had remained steadfast. On the slope behind the house creaked a few pines. They looked like black giants and defy the storm, upright and crooked. In a creek crossing the valley reflected the glittering Moonlight. Close crowded stood five horses' bodies together and dozing on their feet. Not far from the crowded horses fine white ice crystals thrown up to a black stallion. He had lowered his head and his back showed against the icy wind. The wind sang his monotone song across the night, as if he wanted to put everything to sleep. Even the coyotes were silent. The creatures of darkness seemed to have found a protective shelter.

The noise of an engine mingled rudely with the deceptive sound.

Increasingly louder, an old Buick drove over the gravel road that led to the valley. It stopped in front of the old wooden house. Two young men stepped off and pulled a third out of the car. They dragged him up to the porch steps. Then they turned him off at the door. Swaying, he leaned against it. The white shirt had slipped out of his pants. His long black hair was in a mess. The wind played

with it. One of the men hung a furlined denim jacket over the swaying figure's shoulder and tapped it with his hand.

"Keep your pecker up!", he said.

His tongue barely obeyed him. He chuckled to himself.

"Get out of here!" the guy lolled.

He leaned against the door so as not to fall over. He raised his hand in greeting.

"Thank you, Scott."

The two young men got a grip on oneself and toddled straight to the car. The Buicks spinning wheels threw up dirt and pebbles. The car turned at a rapid pace and sprinted away, as if he feared being pursued. The hiss of the wind finally swallowed the engine noise.

Slowly the stars faded at dawn. Several times the young Indian stroked the hair from his face. He took a deep breath and tried to open the door. With a jerk, the door was suddenly torn open, so that the guy stumbled into the house. A tall, sturdy man caught him in his arms. He had long hair, parted in the middle and braided in two braids. It shimmered silver gray.

"Good evening, Dad", the young man lolled in surprise. Actually, it should have been called 'Good morning' for a long time.

The face of the addressed seemed to be petrified. With no emotion he revealed his thoughts. He did not answer his son either. Nevertheless, he repressed his anger with difficulty. With a hard grip, he grabbed his own flesh and blood. Then he dragged the drunken son behind him, out the door. The denim jacket remained lying on the ground.

The sixteen-year-old made no attempt to fight it. He did not make a sound either. Only when his father had dragged him to the creek and pressed his head under the icy water, he began to fight back. Vain. The firm grip of his father did not diminish. He held his son for a long time until he thought his resistance would subside. Then he pulled him up. The horses had lifted their heads and watched the action.

The young man gasped for breath, before he found himself submerged again. His senses were suddenly wide awake and he realized what was happening to him. When his father pulled him out of the water again by the neck, he had swallowed and coughed suffocatingly. He could not have said a word. Again, he felt his head, his entire upper body under the floods of the creek. The gentle flow played with his hair as if she wanted to wash it away.

"John! Let him alive. John! Stop it! You will kill him!" , a female voice called. She sounded desperate.

John pulled the seemingly lifeless body out of the water and left it lying on the shore. A soft rattle was the only sign of his son's life. John still did not speak. But his face twisted as if someone had stabbed him in his heart. He turned away from his eldest son. Silently passed his wife and went in to the house and left the door ajar.

The advancing dawn completely faded the stars.

Only the yellowish white lunar disk and the morning star stood in the sky. Fine ice crystals hovered gently on the seemingly lifeless body, which did not obey the will of its owner. The limbs were stiff with cold, the muscles weak and the head wanted to shatter. Everything turned around. With the dizziness, the nausea came like an overwhelming force that could no longer be restrained, not controlled, and no longer suppressed. With his last strength, the sixteen-year-old propped up on his hands

and throwed up. He crawled to the stream to rinse his mouth with clear water. The wet shirt stuck to his skin. Only then did he feel the cold creeping up on him. Involuntarily his body began to tremble. His inner voice forced in: 'Get up! Get up!'
He tried.
Crawling, he moved forward, finally he came staggering on his own feet and to the house. Only when he had reached the stairs to the porch did he notice the woman standing there wrapped in a blanket. His mother's worried look met his. He averted her eyes in embarrassment and went inside. She silently followed him and closed the door.

*****

The sun was already high up when the tribal police came down the gravel road into the valley. Then the car stopped in front of the log house. An officer got out and knocked on the front door. The owner opened.
"Hau, John Black Hawk. Is your son at home?", asked the Officer with an apprehension in his voice. A deep wrinkle was formed over the nose of the man, who could be about John's age.
"I have three sons. Which one do you mean?", John asks with an untouched voice.
"Your oldest one, Ryan."
"Is he in trouble again?"
"This morning we had a heavy car accident, just around the corner. A drunken driver crashed with another car. The car, an old Buick, after a flashover, went up in flam-

es and burned out. The car belonged to Scott Waci Tate. Ryan was seen with him, yesterday evening. Two charred human remains were found in the wreck. We do not know who else was in the car with Scott. But we found a buckle who could belong to your oldest one..."
The officer was silent, awaiting.
"What did they do?"
"Illegally car race. Drunk driving and maybe some drugs. Well, unfortunately. The boys are not to bring to reason. Two of them had paid with their lives."
John nodded.
"They brought Ryan back at dawn and drove away. He lies up in bed and is sleeping off his drinking spree."
"Who was with Scott in the car?"
"I don't know the boozing companions of my....", John hesitated before continuing: "....my son. Ask him by yourself."
The Officer nodded, went in to the house. After going up the stairs, he banged his fist against the door.
No answer.
He pushed the door open and pulled the blanket off the bed. The rascal lay like dead on the bed, wearing only black boxer shorts. When the officer shook him rudely, Ryan blinked his eyes. With a questioning look, he looked around as if he did not know where he was.
"You've been blasting yourself again. With drugs too?"
With contempt Ryan deflated air through his lips and closed his eyes again.
"Did you drive with Scott yesterday?"
Ryan don't answer.
"Scott brought you home drunk. The right train of your buddy. He gets brandy and a bad pot for a minor. Who was the other one in Scotts car?"

Ryan remained silent. He had opened his eyes narrowly again. His eyes went to his own bare chest and the corners of his mouth defiantly bent down.

"Alright. Then I want to tell you that your two friends have caused a serious accident. They burnt in Scott's car this morning. Two charred humans remained in the wreck. Maybe you had more luck than mind.

Ryan jumped up from the bed and suddenly seemed wide awake.

"Was Scott just as drunk as you", the Officer asked.

"Scott has always taken more than me", Ryan answered with a heavy tongue.

"Scott was twenty-one. You're just sixteen."

Ryan remained silent.

"Who sat next to Scott?"

"I don't know."

"You could save us a great deal of work, Ryan."

The officer took a deep breath before continuing. "Maybe we can identify him. An analysis is too expensive for one who is missed from nobody."

Ryan nodded.

"I can't remember anything"

"Think about it, Ryan!"

Ryan propped up his still too heavy head on his hands. Then he shook it very slowly. "No. I do not know anything anymore. Absolutely nothing."

Chapter 1
Night of the wolves

Since that night, two years ago, Ryan hasn't touched Alcohol anymore. He struggled with self-indulgent hardness to regain his lost face. Before his father and himself. When he first joined the sundance last summer, he felt his father's pride and his own. Ryan was eighteen now.
Together with his fifteen-year-old Brother Robert, Ryan pulled the wire taut from post to post and rebuilt broken patches.
"Shit!", he cursed.
He injured his fingers with the barbed wire.
"Let it be, Robert. I will do the rest by myself."
"An Indian knows no pain", Robert grinned braving.
Ryan laughed.
"I know."
Then he looked at the eleven-year-old Andy. His youngest brother worked unremitting with a pinto foal.
"He really believe, he can keep this foal", Robert said.
"A Horse Ranch without Horses is no Ranch. I'm trying to come up with an idea", Ryan answered.
Not only the horses were emaciated over the last winter. Ryan put his hand on Robert's shoulder and smiled. Robert's eyes were filled with worry.
"Father has given away two great brood mares. Far below the price."
"We have three foals."
"Right."
Robert looked at Andy and the foal. He grinned. "Just look at them. They get along great. Soon Andy starts neighing."
Ryan laughed.

"Do you really think we can keep the ranch and the horses, Ryan?"

"And what do you think about that?"

Ryan stared at his boot tips, shrugged his shoulders, and said nothing.

"I try to get my old Pontiac back on the road. Then I teach you to drive", Ryan finally said.

Robert nodded.

How often he wished to do that. He stayed with Ryan to finish the necessary patchwork on the fence. Ryan gripped hammer and pincers with one hand as the work came to an end. He said: "It's done. Let's go for dinner. I'm hungry like a Wolfe".

Robert picked up the packet of nails with his bloody fingers.

"Me too!", he replied.

When Robert asked her to look at the injuries, the old woman smiled at her grandson. Lucy Black Hawk was very experienced in medicine. She never needed a doctor in her whole life. Many of the people visited likely her than a white doctor. The Lakota called them Wasicu Wakan, White Spirits, and they did not trust them. When Unci had bandaged Roberts hands, she sent a scrutinizing look at Ryan's hands. Ryan noticed that.

"Everything OK. I just looked", he grinned.

Lucy shook her head and smiled.

"Chiseler", she said gentle.

Mother, Anny Black Hawk, set the table. The dishes rattled softly. There was a smell of bean stew. The door opened. John and Andy were entering the room.

"Hm. Smells good, Anny", John raved.

They were all hungry. Anny distributed the bean stew on the plates of the four men. As she scratched the rest out of the pot for herself and Lucy, Ryan and Robert looked at each other. For weeks there was this bean stew that Anny certainly knew how to prepare tasty and nobody had complained. It was filling people up.

After dinner, John lit his pipe. He sucked it with pleasure. Deep worry lines had dug into his features. He seemed to think. After old tradition Ryan asked the father to speak. John nodded to him.

"Will you give me your hunting rifle? I want to get out with Two Moon."

Two Moon was Ryan's friend since he was a little boy.

John sucked two three times on his pipe, before he looked straight in Ryan's eyes. Then a smile played around the corners of his mouth.

"I do not have much ammo left. Part it well. Make sure you catch at least an elk. You know where the gun is". John's eyes glittered in amusement.

"An elk... okay", Ryan smiled amusedly.

His eyes seemed to shine as he stood up. He quickly got everything he needed to hunt. He disappeared with the words: "Toksa, the road is long."

*****

The rifle in his hand and the ammunition packet in his dark blue shirts breast pocket, he set off on foot. In continuous running he went along the gravel road. The evening was still young and at some point a car would come along here.

As Ryan reached the main road, he slowed down. It was about seven miles to the next town, Kyle. Near Kyle lived his friend, whose father was trading in wood and building supplies. The shouting of playing children came through his ears. Dog bark occasionally mingled with it. As far as the eye could see, the hilly grassland lay before him. He called it: *The land where heaven touches the earth.*

Ryan held the hunting rifle firmly in his hand and continued on the roadside. The distances did not frighten him. He never knew it differently. When his old Pontiac finally broke down a few months ago, he also walked that route. There were enough people in the reservation he had picked up. Therefore, he did not doubt that a car would stop and he could jump in. After about three miles, Ryan thought he heard an engine sound. He looked around. His senses had not deceived him. He stopped and turned to the red car. Ryan hoisted his right arm. An unmistakable sign that he was looking for a ride. The red Ford past him fast and braked sharply. A cloud of dust enveloped Ryan. He narrowed his eyes to slits as he walked to the stopped car. The passenger door opened. Ryan pulled her up completely.

"Hi Sam. Do you pick me up?"

"My name is Samantha! You should know this, Ryan Black Hawk! Where do you wanna go, great warrior?"

"Two Moon", Ryan grinned.

"If you don't shoot me into my knee with your gun", Samantha smiled. "What are you waiting for. Jump in."

Ryan put the hunting rifle behind the seat, got in and closed the door.

Samantha shook slowly her head and put the pedal.

"Where did you learn to drive?", Ryan asked skeptically.

"I have three brothers, all belonged to your bunch. The rest is creative work."

Ryan chuckled.

"That you would ever let me drive you ..."

"What a coincidence", Ryan grinned cheekily and watched her.

Blood rushed into her head. Her cheeks turned telltale red. She had tied the upper part of her hair with a red rubber. The tight, pink shirt marked off all body contours. Ryan's eyes wandered over the short denim skirt, along her slender, hazel legs to the leader boots. On the right arm, with every movement, two bangles rattled against each other. They sparkled as silvery as the earrings.

"You should not do that, Ryan!"

"What?"

"Look at me like that."

Ryan raised his hands defensively, put them back on his legs and looked out the window.

"Where do you want to go, Sam?"

Samantha grimaced her face.

"Two Moon", she answered curtly.

Ryan did not ask further. If Two Moon had a date with Samantha Crying Crow, then he probably had bad cards. They had all gone to school together. Samantha was seventeen. She was pretty, that was undeniable. She always liked to dress up. Some of the guys took a closer look at this woman. Why not Two Moon? Shortly before Kyle Samantha turned left. The paved road dissolved into dust. At some point a few trailers appeared, then two of the usual Rez houses and finally piles of wood.

"Okay. Here we are", Samantha said and stopped the car.

She waited, but made no move to get out. So Ryan got out and pulled the rifle behind the seat.

"Didn't you say you want to go to Two Moon?"
"Yes, I said."
"You do not get out the car?"
"No. I wanna go home. It just seemed safer to drop you off at the finish. It is evening."
Ryan smiled and narrowed his eyes.
"Thanks Samantha."
She smiled too.
Ever since they met, he had said that to her for the first time. She narrowed her eyes while she said: "Do not hurt yourself with that thing."
Then she laughed.
Quickly and unexpectedly, Ryan leaned toward her in the car and pressed his lip against hers. Samantha opened them and let their tongues touch. She closed her eyes. Ryan seemed uncontrollable and withdrew from her after a few moves of his tongue. He hastily slammed the passenger door. Breathing fast, as if he had run all the way, he turned and walked to the house. Several times he wiped his lips with the back of his hand. It tasted strange. Lipstick probably. Behind him, he heard the car start.
Before him, Ojeda Two Moon appeared.
"Hello Ryan! Were you hunting?"
"I want to do that."
Ojeda grinned smugly.
"Wasn't it Sam's car that just left?"
"Yes."
Ojeda Two Moon whistled softly through his teeth. "Is there something going on?"
"Dumbass. I drove hitchhiking. How else should I have come here?"
Ojeda laughed.

"Come on in my friend!"
Ryan followed his friend into the house and closed the door behind him.

*****

A short time later, the friends drove with 's fathers GMC truck direction Scenic. The sun sets to the west and dipped the land in a golden yellow aura. After leaving the old ghost town behind, turned east. The paved road went into a dirty road. The gravel road led through the middle of the prairie and miles straight ahead. A cloud of dust followed the truck.
"Sunglasses are in the glove compartment", Ojeda Two Moon said finally.
Ryan reached in and gave his friend one of the glasses. The other one he set on his own nose. Lost in thought, he looked out the window. Two lonely farmhouses appeared in the distance of the largely uninhabited area. It was already outside the reservation.
"Hey! Are you sick? So taciturn I haven't experienced you for a long time", Ojeda broke the silence.
Ryan smiled tiredly.
"Did Sam turned your head upside down?"
"Let's talk about something else. I urgently need some spare parts for the Pontiac so I can drive it again. If I'm lucky, only the starter is broken or the battery. He does not move anymore. I have been praying that the engine itself is still okay. I need the car."
"Maybe the car is running out of fuel", Ojeda laughed.
"How stupid do you think am I?", hissed Ryan.

Shaking his head, he grinned finally.

"I'll help you, my friend. You do not have to hitchhike anymore .... with Sam."

Ojeda did not stop scoffing.

Ryan jokingly slapped his friend's arm.

Ojeda Two Moon laughed.

The road now led through valleys and lay in front of them. Like a flat snake. At some point a road crossed its way. Nothing but gravel and dust. turned right, direction southeast. The path led gently downhill.

"Maybe we should go buffalo hunting. I can almost see the buffaloes", Ojeda enthused .

"Hunting ban", Ryan mumbled.

"I know. Maybe one will get lost", Ojeda said .

"A beautiful dream, my friend. But I'm looking for an elk."

Ojeda laughed amused.

"Here I often went with my father. There is plenty of game here. Deer and antelopes, turkeys, rabbits were playing at dusk at the Waterhole. Wildcats, foxes and lynxes I have already met there. But there is no trace of the wolves."

Ryan just smiled.

The two young men got out of the car and put on their quilted jackets. The air was clear and cold. The sun had already lost power. The shadows slowly wandered into the valleys. The two friends drank coffee while they talked quietly. Ojeda Two Moon get out salt pretzels from a torn bag. Then they left. Each of them carried his hunting rifle and a knife. With fast steps and alert eyes, so as not to drive off the game, they approached the waterhole. The two friends were silent, communicating only with looks and hand signals. Countless tracks crossed their path. Ryan smiled confidently and nodded. The hunters remained motionless in the high bank grass, which covered them. There was a smell of wet grass and mud. Turkey vultures circled at high altitudes. On the opposite side of the lake, something was stirring. A deer appeared in the high reeds, stopped for a long time, and eyed suspiciously. At some point it seemed calm. It sensed no danger. The animal was reluctant to drink. A cub followed. Ojeda and Ryan smiled. The rifles remained firmly in their hands. When the animals had left the shore, it remained calm. The oblique rays of the setting sun glittered on the water surface. Insects were buzzing around. A raccoon couple ran playfully along the riverside covered with tall grass. Just as the sun disappeared on the horizon and dusk dominated the land a white-tailed deer stepped through the tall grass and cautiously followed the path down to the water. Ryan's eyes flashed. His heart pounded faster as he set the rifle. The animal eyed attentively before bent his head and slowly began to drink. The rifle clicked softly. Ryan held his breath. Suddenly the proud animal lifted its head and looked exactly in his direction. So the deer remained a few moments.

*****

Both, Ryan and Ojeda, had heard the murmuring of the reed. Ryan barely dared to breathe. He had set up his hunting rifle. Ready for a shot, he remained paralyzed. A second animal stepped out of the reeds into the glade. The other white-tailed deer stalked toward the waterhole and began to gesture aggressively. With lowered heads, the struggle for the privilege of the fittest and over the water started. The clash of their antlers echoed widely through the dusk. The hunters agreed with a look and a nod of their heads. The opportunity was favorable. They could not miss them, even if the animals provided a gripping show. Two shots were fired at the same time sounded like a single one. Seconds later, the animals dropped to their knees and remained motionless on the ground.

There fell a deep silence. No bird was near anymore. Only the faint buzzing of insects hit Ryan's ears. Carefully, the hunters left their cover and ran along the shore to the spot where the animals lay. Satisfied, they looked at the animals. They had been hit with one shot and died instantly. Both hunters touched the animals they had killed. Sacrificed sage and thanked the white-tailed deer people for sending their brothers. Then Ryan and Ojeda Two Moon sent their souls on the journey.

"Good shot", Ryan broke the silence.

"Yes. But now we have a problem", Ojeda laughed.

"Or maybe two", Ryan laughed.

Ojeda raised his head, looked up at the dark sky where the first stars were blinking, and inhaled the fresh air deep into his lungs.

"We have to be faster than the hunters of the night if we do not want to leave them our prey. They smell the fresh blood for miles", he finally said.

"And quickly it gets so dark that we hardly see our hands in front of our eyes anymore. It promises to be an interesting evening."

"You must have had better evenings", Ojeda quipped.

"What could be better than spending a summer night

with his best friend in the wild and being surrounded by predators?"

Ryan laughed and pulled out his hunting knife.

Immediately he began to examine the prey and disassemble. Fresh blood ran down to the ground, colored the grass and was absorbed by the earth. Meanwhile, Ojeda went to the truck to get the boxes in load area. The moonless night had come quickly.

Ryan listened attentively. He actually got a visit. Threatening hissing announced him. Ryan looked at his rifle, which was right next to him. The hiss was repeated, this time quieter. Ryan was pretty sure he was dealing with a Bobcat. The animal crept through the tall grass and seemed to observe the human hunter closely.

Ryan listened.

Behind him, the reeds rustled softly. Then silence. Would the shy hunter flee from the human being? Or was hunger stronger? Ryan did not dare move. The animal was lying in ambush behind him. Lynxes usually beat their prey themselves. Like his big brothers Wolf and Cougar, he avoided people. Surely Ryan and had invaded his hunting grounds. Lynxes also hunted in the dusk. Their paths had crossed. The Bobcat was brave. He jumped the kneeling Ryan directly in the neck. Although Ryan was prepared for it, the animal's weight threw him to the ground. Ryan rolled over his shoulders. The lynx was unable to bite. He too rolled over the ground. After a short time they tried to concentrate they was eyeball to eyeball. The brave Bobcat appeared to be terrified when he recognized a dreaded human being in his prey. A shot banged. The Bobcat startled and fled. His will to survive was stronger than hunger. Ryan heard the laugh of his friend.

"The lynx probably thought you were an easy prey. Maybe also for a marriage-willing female."

Ryan straightened and looked in the direction the Bobcat had disappeared.

"I think he needs glasses. And since when do I smell like a bobcat female"?, Ryan replied.

"A magnificent animal. Pity that I missed him", Ojeda Two Moon regretted .

"If you were such a bad hunter, then I'm glad you did not hit me off."

Ojeda slapped Ryan's arm and laughed.

Then he put up two lamps so that the hunters could finish their work in the dark. Shadows and light played with every movement. When the animal was cut, light steam rose into the cold night. Ryan was sweating at work. Together, the friends packed their hunting booty in the boxes and carried them to the truck. The boxes were big enough to stow both animals. They were heavy, so the young men had to carry them in twos. The night was black and the stars were pale and blurry. Carefully, the two groped forward. The light of the flashlight dangling from 's belt was hardly an aid.

Ojeda handed the car keys to his friend.

"Would you like to drive?"

Ryan gave him a questioning look.

"Well, before you lose it completely ..."

"I almost got used to being driven", he countered.

"Okay", Ojeda said. "Then give me the key back."

"You could find a taste for it!", Ryan hissed and immediately placed himself in the driver's seat.

Ojeda Two Moon laughed and got into the car.

Ryan let the GMC roll back and turned on the gravel road. He turned down the radio while spoke to him.

Ryan laughed now and then. He had always been the more restrained Person. That was already the case at school. But he had always thought up nonsense and persuaded to take part. If one of them appeared, the other one was quite near-by. When Scott Waci Tate crossed Ryan's path, her inseparable friendship had been severely tested. Scott was five years older than Ryan and one who literally walked over dead bodies. That must have impressed a fourteen-year-old strongly. Especially when Scott left Ryan at the wheel of his sports car. Ryan had to drink like a man and drive like the devil to subsist in the groupe. Ryan did that and became a respected gang member himself. Although he was the youngest, he had gained respect in no time. Only a few months later, by bet stakes and dealing with Marihuana, he had purchased an old Pontiac.

Ojeda Two Moon had withdrawn. Only once, when he caught Ryan alone, had he tried to bring his friend to his senses. In vain. At that time, Ryan had thrown all his frustration at him. What would be the purpose of completing the school well? Then to run the streets with a piece of paper in hand cockamamy. No chance to get an education. To find a job that would pay well enough to feed a family. blamed randomly after his head he should stop complaining and start fighting for a better future. Ryan had answered him uncalled-for. Ojeda did not understand Ryan anymore and said every word was superfluous.

In spring, two years ago, the spook finally had an end. The evil spirit Ryan had seized had left him. Two Moon had thanked Wakan Tanka for that. Ojeda was the only one who had visited Ryan in the sobering-up cell of the tribal police. The bad part was that Ryan was sober when he had to spend the three days in prison. The good part the friends talked to each other again. For the first time in his life, Ryan had asked someone for forgiveness. His remorse for his regained, never lost friend, Ojeda Two Moon, confessed. Nobody could destroy this bond.

*****

The two young men reached the Black Hawk Ranch about one hour past midnight. The joy of the hunting success was great. Ryan got out of the car, pushed the door closed and headed for the house. A candle burned in the living room. Grandmother Lucy Black Hawk sat alone in the living room. She looked worriedly into Ryan's eyes. His beaming smile gave way to a serious facial expression and the question: "Unci, what's going on?"
"Anny had to be admitted to the hospital. It's her heart. Your dad is with her. Things are looking bad for her. Your brothers are outside in the barn. They are afraid. I pray for everyone, but I dreamed of wolfes creeping around our house."
Ryan swallowed.
The queasy feeling in his throat remained. He lowered his eyes and nodded.
" Ojeda Two Moon is waiting outside. We bring the kill, a whitetailed deer, into the house, before the wolves snatch it," Ryan said softly.
Then he crouched in front of the little old woman and looked her in the eye. They sparkled like black sapphires in the dim light of a candle. The warm light illuminated

hardly more than her face and gave the old woman a mysterious aura. Ryan knew that his grandmother was a medicine woman. He felt the touch of fear that was handed over him. But Ryan also felt the power of the old woman, who gave him safety.

"I'll help you," Grandmother said softly.

Lucy stepped out of the door with her grandson. Robert and Andy Black Hawk must have heard the truck. They stood next to and talked quietly.

Ojeda looked into Ryan's serious face. He greeted his brothers and finally said only: "Let's unload."

When the work was finally done and the fresh meat was stored in the freezer, Ryan, Robert and Ojeda stood on the porch and smoked.

"Can I do something for you?", Ojeda asked.

"Can you take me to the hospital?", Ryan asked back.

"Of course, it's a serious matter", Ojeda replied without hesitation.

Ryan nodded.

"Mother's heart. I'm scared", he said softly.

He stubbed out the cigarette after three or four puffs. noticed well the inner restlessness of his friend. He understood.

"Okay, let's go."

It was already at three forty-five in the morning when Ryan entered the emergency room at the Indian Hospital at Pine Ridge. The light of dawn was already penetrating through the window into the room where his mother lay. Next to one of the two beds sat a stooped figure. His father did not move. He did not turn around either as Ryan quictly closed the door and stepped beside him. Anny seemed to be deep in sleep. An infusion bottle and a small box hung above her bed.

Lights danced on the monitor.
"How is she doing?", Ryan asked slightly.
John raised his head and looked at him with tired eyes.
"Better", he murmured. "Doctor Ethan said she got past its worst moments. She will have to stay for some time.
Relieved, Ryan nodded.
Carefully he sat down on the edge of the bed and put his hand on his mother's. She must have felt it. She blinked at him.
"Hi Mom".
Weakly she smiled and closed her eyes again.

Only around nine o'clock father and son left the hospital. Doctor Ethan had assured he would take good care for Anny. John got into his old pickup truck. Ryan sat in the passenger seat and slammed the door.
"Hopefully, the engine will start."
John looked at his son, raised his eyebrows and smiled barely noticeable. Ryan crossed his arms and waited. It sounded as if the truck would start up again out of sheer defiance. As if the engine understood John's words. Ryan too, twisted his mouth into a grin. They left the place in a westerly direction, left Interstate 18 and followed the bumpy dust track towards Manderson. The rolling Prairie spread in front of them. Scattered pine trees lined the way. From time to time, Ryan looked at John. He had no intention of saying anything.
They were silent for a long time.
When they reached Manderson, John began to talk again.
"We will sell the horses. Anny needs the expensive medications the Indian Health Service won't give to us. Doctor Ethan said she can't survive without this

medicine."

His words sounded level-headed and matter of fact. It was his decision. Ryan breathed air into his lungs. It was like a stabbing pain in his heart. He knew this decision was very difficult for his Father. The horses were her life. Ryan, who had never contradicted his father in the last two years, didn't dare now either. He struggled for breath. The horses were also his life, his future, the future of his brothers and the ranch. Ryan kept quiet. His thoughts worked at full speed. He had also made a decision and the idea had been there for a long time. Now the time had come to talk about to his father.

Ryan asked, "What happens when the money we get from the sale of the horses is used up? What if mother needs surgery? Then she has to go to Rapid City or a special clinic."

John kept an embarrassed silence.

Ryan noticed that his father was totally helpless and at a loss.

"Father, I'm thinking about leaving the ranch. I go to see the tribal council. Maybe Chief Red Eagle can help me to find a job."

John was still silent. He seemed to consider.

"We have to tell Lucy, Robert and Andy", he finally said dejectedly.

Ryan took a deep breath.

He knew only too well that his father's decision was very difficult.

*****

After John had talked to everyone, no one dared to contradict his decision. Her thoughts and pain were hard to hide. Andy let his anger run free and finally slammed the door behind him as he left the room. When Ryan stepped on the porch to light a cigarette, he looked at his youngest brother who led the piebald foal through the paddock. The little stallion followed him wherever he went. It almost looked like they were talking to each other. The little stallion behaved more like a dog.
Ryan grinned.
When he had smoked the cigarette, he went towards them. Andy had noticed Ryan and turned to him. The boy's traits were open, expressing all his anger, despair and fear. He could not hold back his tears.
"It's hard to tell his little brother, Nishunkala, that he has to leave", Ryan said softly, stroking the little piebald who nibbled cheekily on his hand.
"Did you already tell your friend, your Kolà?"
"No", Ryan replied and swallowed hard.
He did not avert his gaze from the black stallion.
"I'm looking for a job. Maybe I can preserve something."
"You want to leave"?, Andy asked horrified.
Ryan avoided.
"I will visit Red Eagle. Maybe he can help me."
It didn't sound very confident. Andy also knew how jobs had been affected in the reservation. He sensed that his brother had little chance. Also Andy knew what possibilities existed to get a job in the reservation. Ryan had only learned ranch work, nothing else. A smile flitted Ryan's face. The small pinto tickled on his neck with his velvety lips. Ryan gently fondled his nostrils.
"I will ask father to give me his truck. We'll win through in the end, Mishunkala, my little brother", Ryan softly

said. He patted Andy's arm in confidence. Then he got up and went back to the house.

*****

Early the next morning, Ryan drove with his father's truck to Pine Ridge and parked right in front of the red brick house. With a glimmer of hope for a job, he entered the tribal building.
Ryan was told Chief Red Eagle wasn't in the house. He took a seat in front of the chief's office and waited patiently. Hours passed without anything happening.
Ryan had read the Lakota Country Times from the first to the last page. Now he rummaged through a thick dog-eared magazine. It looked like someone had pulled it out of the trash. Gossip of the white world wasn't from interest for the young Lakota. He kept flicking through and grinning as a naked blonde smiled at him. Slowly he further turned the pages. A few pages with test results from different types of cars appeared. He dealt with it in more detail. After looking at a few men's fashion pages, he came across a US Air Force ad. The photo showed a fighter plane, a helicopter, a Jeep and an aircraft carrier. At the bottom a phone number with bold letters was listed. Ryan teared out the page and put it in his pocket. He knew that the Army was always looking for good people. If there was no other possibility for him, he would have to make friends with this thought.
Without paying attention to the rest, Ryan leafed through the pages lost in thought. At some point he put the magazine back, leaned his head against the wall and

crossed his arms. A long time later, he startled from his thoughts. The door had opened and Red Eagle entered with a tribal member. The two men were engrossed in their conversation and hardly noticed the young man. Ryan got up.

He greeted Old Raven and Red Eagle courteous.

"What do you want?", Red Eagle asked.

"We have to talk."

"What about?"

"At the office", Ryan answered defiantly.

Old Raven grinned barely noticeable.

The seventy-nine-year-old man knew Ryan from the first day of his birth. He was one of the most distinguished men in the reservation. Old Raven was a secret man, a Wicasa Wakan. He was a medicine man to whom many Lakota still came for medical advice. Especially the old people still did not trust the white doctors at the Indian Hospital. They only went there when there was no other option and Old Raven urged them to do so.

The old man's gray braids were mixed by white strands. Above the red shirt he wore a black leather vest, the fringes reaching almost to his knees. His eyes lit up from his wrinkled face. He was silent.

Chief Red Eagle barely knew Ryan. Maybe he only knew that he was the son of his former school friend, John Black Hawks. Since Leonard Red Eagle was elected as tribal chief, this friendship had suffered in various circumstances. The white's called him chief.

The chief scrutinized Ryan skeptically.

"Wait here. I still have to talk to Old Raven."

Ryan nodded and sat down on the chair next to the office door, where he'd spent hours.

The two men went into the office. If the two had to talk

to each other, it could last for hours. For four hours Ryan had already sat here and he slowly got hungry. He jumped up quickly and came back a little later with a large bottle of coke and a sandwich, which he had brought from the gas station. Another hour passed without anything changing. Some people came, greeted and left.

A stocky white man entered. He was dressed like a typical rancher and wore a cowboy hat. Straight and without greetings, he headed for the door to Red Eagle's office. He cast a grim look at Ryan. Then the White knocked loudly against the door and entered immediately.

Ryan knew the man. McLaughleen had leased the property next to them and bred cattle. They had no relation to each other. Neither good nor bad. Ryan did not worry about why McLaughleen had been given immediate admission. It had to be very important. Ryan finished the coke and put the empty bottle next to the chair. The door opened and a petite, young woman entered the room. She kept a big briefcase in front of her chest. She smiled when she saw Ryan and walked over to him.

"Hi Sam, Samantha", Ryan sneered.

"Hello Ryan. I saw your father's truck and thought ... do you want to see Red Eagle?"

"Yes"

"Me too. I should give him this from my grandfather." She pointed to the briefcase.

"Is there somebody in?"

"Old Raven and McLaughleen."

"McLaughleen?"

"Yes."

Samantha morosely twisted her face.

Ryan didn't ask.

She sighed low.

"His lease expires at the end of the year", Samantha whispered.

Then she looked around. Nobody was present except the two. "Red Eagle is well-intentioned towards him. But the council wants back the land", Samantha whispered and looked around again. "On this map there is the plan for a project to breed Bisons. The property should only get to a Lakota who can and wants to carry out the project."

Ryan nodded.

"Are there any applicants?"

"Yes, there are. Charles Windcoock. He's thirty-three years old and the only one at the moment."

"Where do you get that from?"

"I have an apprenticeship at the post-office. I took a look at the papers in the briefcase...", Samantha smiled triumphant.

Ryan grinned.

"And why are you telling me all this?"

"Because I thought you might be interested. After all, you are neighbors."

"You bet. that's interesting", Ryan confirmed.

"Wouldn't that be something for you?"

"You must dreaming, Charles is thirtyfor years and almost twice my age. He has much more experience in this issue then me."

Samantha remained silent.

Also Ryan didn't say anything.

The door was flung open. Without a greeting, McLaughleen passed Ryan and Samantha. He left the building with long strides.

"Go first", Ryan said to Samantha. "It might take a longer

time on my part."

Samantha stud up and nocked at the door. She was invited to step in. Ryan waited. Barely five minutes later she came out again.

"You can go in there", Samantha said.

Ryan entered and silently closed the door. Red Eagle was just saying goodbye to Old Raven. Ryan also courteous said goodbye to the Elder.

"Toksa, Ryan", replied Old Raven and left the Office. Red Eagle offered Ryan the seat in front of his desk.

"Speak!", he was requested.

"I urgently need a job."

Red Eagle grinned.

"You've caught the wrong man, Black Hawk. Go to the Bureau of Indian affairs. Maybe they can find something for you."

"I do not intend to cleanse in Rapid City for the city government or to fold cartons as a laborer in the packaging industry."

Red Eagle's face darkened over so much arrogance. "What are you up to?"

"Build something up here. I'm a rancher, horse breeder and if necessary cowboy", Ryan challenged.

"You're dreaming!", Red Eagle snapped at him.

"Do not mock me, Read Eagle! I came to you because I hoped you could help me. My father is about to sell all the horses. Mother is seriously ill and is in hospital."

"I'm sorry, Ryan. I did not know that", said Red Eagle, much friendlier.

He seemed to cogitate.

Ryan waited.

"McLaughleen could need for use another cowboy. He pays well."

"Hm! For how long?", Ryan asked, making no effort to hide the sharp undertone.
Red Eagle winced barely noticably.
"You have to take that up with him", he coldly replied.
Ryan got up and politely said goodbye. Silently, the door closed behind him. His hard facial features immediately gave way to a smile when he saw Samantha.
"You're still here."
"May I have a ride with you? My father needs his car today."
"Okay. But first I have to go to the Hospital."
"No Problem. I will wait."
"Just as you like."
Ryan shrugged his shoulders.
After about seven hours he left the tribal building together with Samantha Crying Crow.

*****

Anny was awake and smiled as her son entered the room.
"Hello Mom. How are you?"
"I feel like a herd of Buffalo trampled over me."
She smiled.
Ryan shook his head with a grin. "At least they haven't trampled your humor."
He sat down beside her.
"Be careful that your father does not do anything stupid while I'm away. Do you hear! He must not sell the horses!"
"I pay attention." Ryan nodded.

She closed her eyes and paused. She looked tired and it seemed speaking was difficult.

"I'm much tougher than you think", Anny finally said. "Just don't think you're gonna have your peace because I'm here".

"I believe that. Don't think you just can turn your back on this problem. We still need you", replied Ryan and grinned.

"Do you need anything?"

"The prairie wind and my horse. That's enough", she whispered.

Ryan touched her hand. "Soon!"

Anny seemed to have fallen asleep again. She looked weak and vulnerable. Ryan looked at her for a while. Memories made him think back. Finally, Ryan said goodbye to his mother and left.

Samantha had been waiting for him in the truck for more than an hour. She smiled as he got in.

"How is your Mom?"

"Better than before", he answered while he left.

Ryan pulled a cigarette out of the box and lit it. Samantha shoved a book into her purse and looked directly at him. Ryan pretended not to notice.

"How was your hunt?", Samantha asked.

"We've killed two white-tailed deer."

Ryan wrapped in silence.

Samantha waited before continuing. She knew the fact that he was quite sensitive being questioned.

"Something bothers you. Don't you wanna talk to me?", She finally asked.

Ryan didn't react at first, as if he hadn't heard Samantha. "I'll ask McLaughleen if he might need a cowboy", he said after a while.

"Are you sure?", Samantha asked skeptically, as if she had read his thoughts.

Ryan turned his head and looked straight into her eyes.

"I could marry you. You seem to me a good solution." Then he grinned from ear to ear.

"Why are you mocking at me, Ryan Black Hawk?"

"Well, that would not solve my problem."

"Do you need money?"

"Who does not?"

Samantha did not ask further. Ryan had already said more than she expected. She knew he was ashamed of it.

It had been early evening when the truck stopped in front of Crying Crows' house. Her parents' car was not there.

"Can you open the door for me? The lock is stuck. It looks like no one is home", Samantha asked.

Without a word Ryan got out of the car and went to the house with Samantha. The lock was actually difficult to move. He dug a wire out of his jeans and with a jolt he opened the door in a few seconds. Ryan stood in the mouth of the entrance and Samantha right in front of him.

"Thank you, Ryan", she whispered, putting her arms around his neck and pulling him close.

He let it happen and got carried away by her kiss. Again he felt how hard it was to control himself. When he separated his lips from hers, he gasped for air.

"You play with fire, Sam."

"I am on fire"

"I should better go. You're still underage."

"But I'm not a virgin anymore", she whispered in his ear. Again she merged with his lips. Ryan struggled for air again, then he dropped the door into the lock.

"I'm not either", he grinned significant and took Samantha's jacket off. Silently she slid to the ground. Then he grabbed the young woman and lifted her on the same level so they could look each other in the eye. Samantha immediately wrapped her legs around his waist. Ryan carried her to the dining table and set her down. Samantha slowly reached for Ryan's shirt buttons and opened them. She still had her legs wrapped around Ryan's hips. She had felt his arousal immediately. Ryan's chest went up and down with every breath. His heart beat faster as he felt her fingers on his bare chest. Ryan pulled the shirt over her head. His eyes touched her breasts, which were in a black bra. He felt a slight shiver as he reached for the straps. With skillful hands he opened the hooks. He didn't do it for the first time. With one hand Ryan covered her breast. The other one he put behind Samantha's head and pulled her towards him. She sighed softly. They kissed each other intensively. They felt their tongues, the heat and their throbbing hearts. The desire rose with every breath.

"Come on!", she finally asked Ryan and took her legs off his hips.

Ryan didn't hesitate for a moment. He stripped off his shirt and threw it to the ground. Then he opened his leather belt and jeans and undressed completely. Samantha had done the same.

Completely naked they faced each other in the dim room. Only a few seconds. Ryan lifted Samantha up again. Her skin slipped over his. Again Samantha wrapped her legs around Ryan's hips. He heard her soft moan. Their tongues played together. Ryan sat Samantha on the edge of the table and pushed her back with his body. Samantha braced herself with her elbows. She watched him. Ryan blinked at her bobbing breasts. With steady moves he put himself in trance. He had forgotten everything around him. There was nothing left in the world but this woman who had invited him. In her house, her heart and in herself. Ryan felt only the heat that threatened to burn him. His moves became faster and more intense. He heard Samantha's heavy breathing and felt her moves and her moaning under which her body quivered. For a moment, the world seemed to be stopped. Both enjoyed the happiness of the moment. Just slowly her heavy breath calmed down. Ryan pulled Samantha closer. She stroked her hands gently over his chest and smiled happily. Ryan's skin contracted under the touch. Samantha took his face in both hands and kissed him. Tender, like never before.

"Maybe we should use my bed. It's more comfortable", she whispered.

Ryan grinned.

"OK. It is still early in the evening."

Samantha picked up the clothes, took Ryan by the hand and pulled him into her room.

*****

Towards midnight, a truck approached on the gravel road. the grit crunched under the weight of the wheels.

Silently, like his own shadow, the young man scurried into the house. With a smile around his mouth he fell asleep.

After Ryan reported at breakfast what he had accomplished and learned yesterday, he took his stallion and went on his way to McLaughleen.

"I give you a one-week trial. Then we will see. Your food is deducted directly for your salary. Cash end of the week. First week two dollars an hour. Makes a hundred per week." McLaughleen was a real businessman. Cold as ice.

Ryan had not expected otherwise. He agreed with a handshake and on McLaughleen's face turned up a big grin. Ryan plunged himself into his work. For burning the calves must be sort out from the herd. Three cowboys and McLaughleen's son were already there. They did not talk to Ryan at first, but there was no problem at work. Every day, ten hours of hard back-breaking work Ryan got paid, but worked twelve hours. McLaughleen had never said anything, neither positive nor negative. Ryan did not ask. He waited until Friday evening the following week.

When McLaughleen finally handed two fifty dollar bills into his hand, Ryan scowled at him.

"What's about the first three days?"

"For me, the week always starts on Monday."

"I worked hard for eight days and all that very well!", Ryan demanded.

McLaughleen twisted his face, took a deep breath and pulled out another fifty-dollar bill.

"And now shut up, otherwise I'll take another one on Monday."

Ryan could barely contain his anger. Ten dollars less was a starvation wage. But he needed the job. Without a word he took the money and put it in his pocket. He climbed his black stallion, pressed the black cowboy hat deeper into his face and rushed away without a word of

greeting.
McLaughleen looked furious after him.
"Ungrateful people. The old ones are still tolerable, but the young breed is too rebellious."
McLaughleen's son, who had stepped beside his father, pushed his hat back with his forefinger but said nothing.

*****

Ryan handed the first pay to his father. He kept nothing for himself.
"For the moment, that's ok but not forever. The slog every day I don't mind. McLaughleen is a cutthroat. He knows that I'm a good, cheap worker for him. That's why he wants me to stay. Dad, at the end of the summer I will leave the Rez. There are enough good jobs in the Army and they are well paid."
The cat was out of the bag. Ryan took a deep breath. Just barely he defeated his irritation. Now he was waiting for what his father would say.
John Black Hawk's traits were solidified. He looked past his son as he said softly: "You sell yourself, son."
"Dad! Many of us served at the US Army. The veterans are honored for their courage and dedication also in our reservation. And you too."
Ryan shook his head with no understanding.
John didn't move. He was absorbed in thought.
"Yes, I know and I know what I'm talking about. I was there because it was an order to go to Vietnam. Still today I can hear the screams of my dying comrades. It wasn't an honourable fight", he silently replied.

"And I just know, Dad. It can't go on like this. I will not see how the horses have to leave our valley. I will not watch my family starve and I will not wait till Mother die because there is no money for the medicine that they will not give us here! This is our fight, Dad and I will fight for us and our horses. Maybe I will be honourable. I might break down. But if I don't do anything, then I lose my face to myself.!"

Ryan was irritated and he didn't try to hide it anymore.

"I have no better idea, Dad. Could you think of anything better? For sure, McLaughleen have to leave his Ranch. Red Eagle must accept the decision of the tribal council. Charles Windcoock will not be able to afford a cowboy, and those who get a job in the buffalo breeding project are already destined. You know as well as I do such jobs are relegated under the kinship, off the books."

Everybody remained silent.

Lucy had retreated to the kitchen. She dared not speak for her son or for the grandson. Robert and Andy waited on the porch and did not dare to enter the house. They had heard of the wordplay only the loud voice of their brother. They did not understand everything.

"Right now, it's very hard for me to support your decision", John said. He had been dejected for days.

"I have no vocational education, like Alex Crowman, husband of my older sister Carry. So I only can work somewhere as an unskilled worker for low pay. At the army i get a training and then a well-paid job as a specialist, technician maybe. I'm not stupid. I will learn. In addition, many of us have already gone this way."

John nodded slowly.

Ryan knew only too well that his father, with two school-aged sons, his old mother and his seriously ill wife, was left alone at the ranch. Ryan did not think the decision was easy. He knew he was needed here urgently. Finally he took a deep breath. The sharp pain in his guts tormented him. Helplessly he chewed his lower lip. The Eighteen-year-old Lakota felt like a wolf cornered. Only the will to survive gave him the strength to free himself from his predicament. He had no other choice and no other chance to save the ranch. Ryan wanted it, even if his departure from his family, horses, friends and home would be very difficult. But he did not want to give up. He never wanted to dream again with brandy and lousy marihuana in a better world. He had bad experiences. How many of his former gang had not survived, were in jail, or gone mad and killed themselves.

"Rely on me, father. I'll make it. The horses stay. The ranch will not go down. It's also my ranch, my home. One day I will return, have a wife and children. Breed horses as you and grandfather have done. This is my dream. I will send you the money I will earn."

John nodded again, as if he were far away with his thoughts.

"Never forget who you are when you're in the other world, son. I want to recognize you when you get home", John finally said softly.

"I will give my blood for it. I will dance, father. If I ask the spirits of my ancestors for help, then they will protect me in the other world. I will not come home faceless."

John looked at Ryan. His face seemed old and tired, but his eyes shimmered with a hint of hope.

"It smells good from the kitchen. We will have deer and I'm hungry as hell", John said. "Call your brothers for dinner."

Ryan calmed down.

He went out, leaned against the wall and lit a cigarette. He did not want to see or answer the questioning looks of his two brothers sitting there. Both went into the house. Deep inside, Ryan was upset. Now his decision was final. He wasn't completely sure doing the right thing. His mind fought against his feelings. It wasn't really his way and yet it had to be. His heart was pledged to the ranch and the horses. His mind had decided otherwise. The fact troubled his heart. The situation was so depressing. A strange fear sprouted in Ryan. He had never known that before. Maybe he would never come home again. He immediately suppressed this thought, but the queasy feeling remained. He had to talk about it with his friend Ojeda Two Moon. He would sympathize with him.

*****

Saturday afternoon, towards evening, Samantha Crying Crow approached with her father's Chevrolet. She located Ryan and Ojeda Two Moon beside the old Pontiac, who had been parked in front of the house. The hood was open. The wheels were almost invisible in the deep, dry grass. Samantha doubted the car, which once ended up on the junkyard, would drive again. Five years ago Ryan had traded him for a bottle of brandy and twenty dollars. She could remember that. Ryan had bragged in front of her and her brothers.
"Hey you two!"
"Hi Sam", both responded like out of one mouth.
"Did you get lost?", Ojeda Two Moon asked.

"No I have not. I wanted to visit someone and see if I could possibly help."

Ojeda Two Moons grin speak volumes. Ryan's head stuck between hood and engine and it seemed he screwed something. His clothes were dirty. He had bound his long hair with several rubbers. Finally, he looked up briefly and smiled.

"If you want to help Sam, get in the car and start the engine."

She did and the old Pontiac started to stir. He grumbled like an old bear who had awakened from hibernation. Satisfied, Ryan straitened up and slammed the hood. He held a screw-wrench in his hand and wiped his forehead with the back of his hand. His face was partially blackened. Samantha grinned at the sight.

"OK!", Ryan shouted to Samantha and the engine immediately stopped.

"Well, that does it, I guess", said Ojeda contentedly. "Thank you my friend!"

Ryan's joy was obvious. Finally his Pontiac worked again. Even Ryan had barely believed it.

"What do you think about the idea of a test drive?", Ryan asked hopefully.

He took off his shirt and wiped his hands on it. When he saw Samantha look, he said: "The shirt will still not be saved anyway. Jump in!"

Ryan jumped in at the driver seat, next to him. Samantha squeezes herself into the backseat. Ryan pushed the accelerator. The Pontiac began to pitch and moved slowly forward. Ryan grinned. Even at the risk the engine could break in every moment, he kicked the pedal right through. Raising plenty of dust, the car teared down the gravel road. The triumphal screams of the three young

people were swallowed up by the noise of the car.
"How's about McLaughleen?", Samantha asked.
"There is enough work but obviously he pulls me over the table. I will have to keep my feet still for some time. I need the job."
The old car acted like a hot-blooded racing car at his best time. The street went straight for miles. Ryan suddenly turned the steering wheel around. The back swerved and the car began to drift. Ryan uttered a cry that reminded of the old war call of the Lakota. Then he turned the car in the opposite direction, accelerated again and reached for the handbrake and pulled. The Pontiac swerved and turned around the front axle. Even before he stopped, the tires scraped on the asphalt and the car drove in the same direction he had come from.
Samantha laughed.
"You're crazy!", she yelled.
"That's called the perfect turn on the front axle. It works in the back too. Watch out!"
Ryan, who had already driven road races since he was fourteen years old, let himself be carried away for a short time. Samantha and held on tight. After Ryan had completed the maneuver, he continued his ride with a smile.
"The road is not a race track", he affirmed.
Ojeda Two Moon shook his head.
"Samantha is right. You're crazy."
Ryan grinned. "You just find it out yet?"
Ojeda Two Moon and Samantha giggled.
Ryan turned slowly onto the gravel road that led to the valley of the home ranch. said goodbye, saying he needed to help his father.
Samantha remained embarrassed and said nothing at

first.

"Did you miss me?", Ryan grinned smugly.

"Oh yes, Cowboy. We haven't seen each other for more than a week."

"Does your Dad know you're here?"

"Yes. He gave me his car."

Ryan smirked.

"What do you want help me with?", he asked.

"Everything. Most important thing, I'm close to you."

Ryan suddenly became serious.

"Let us not be under any illusions, Samantha. There is no future for us."

She looked at him sadly with her black eyes.

"You don't love me", she astounded quietly but amazed objectively.

"If I tell you so, it would be a lie. The truth is. After the Sundance I'll leave the Reservation. I join the US Army and I don't know for how long. One day I'll come back. No idea when that will be. So do not wait for me."

Everything Ryan expected now did not happen. Samantha remained calm and composed. She forced a smile and reached for his hand. Then she said: "Then we do not have much time. I want to be by your side until the day you leave."

Ryan took a deep breath. Hesitantly he closed the young woman in his arms and pressed her gently against him. It felt good and gave him strength. The lump in his throat, prevented him from speaking. But the intimate embrace of the young people needed no words.

The short, shared time ran through her fingers like desert sand. Ryan worked hard for McLaughleen, day by day, from sunset till late at night. He got a few bucks more.

At the weekends there was a lot to do on the Black Hawk Ranch. Ryan had to work hard, which finally exhausted himself.

After three weeks at the Hospital John brought his wife at home. Al Anny got out of the car she took a deep breath and it look like she found a new lease of life.

Late at the evening the black Stallion showed up on the hill. The Ryder wore a black hat and let the horse slowly go down into the valley. The animal had a long, hard work behind it. Ryan fed his Kolà, how he used to call him. He did not forget the soft, thankful words as he stroked his neck. After all the work was done he went into the house. Tired Ryan smiled at his Mother and welcomed her. Her a look of trepidation told him she knows about.

"You look tired young man and you'll be hungry."

Ryan nodded his head.

"Doesn't feed McLaughleen his cowboys?" she asked softly.

"Once per day."

Ryan pulled three bundled fifty dollar bills out of his pocket and laid them on the table.

"There will be three times more and that will have to be enough for the next six or seven weeks. Before October I will not be able to count on money, and maybe it will not be much anymore.

John sat on the table. On the background the TV was on quietly. Anny took the money and put it in a tin box in the kitchen cupboard. Ryan had followed her into the kitchen. He wanted to see if there was anything left to eat. Softly she said to her son, so that only he could hear it: "The price is high to keep the horses."

"There is no other way", he answered.

"I'll pray every day for you, Ryan and hope for your return.

Ryan nodded and took a piece of leftover roast out of the pan.

"Sit down while you eat. I warm it up for you."

"Thanks."

Ryan went back to the living room and sat down at the big wooden table. His brothers and his father were immersed in a movie and did not take any notice of him. Grandmother Lucy was sitting on the red-colored armchair, rummaging around in a small box. She looked up and smiled at Ryan. Hungry he ate the food and went to bed early.

Around three o'clock in the morning Ryan woke up and looked into a pair sapphire-gleaming eyes.

"When I came, you're already sleeping. Your grandmother let me in", Samantha whispered.

"You're crazy, Samantha. Not me."

Ryan smiled and put his arm around her.

"I want you to smile. If I dream of you later, I want to see you like this, sweetheart."

"Your father will curse me. Maybe he stands with his hunting rifle down at the front door."

"Are you scared?"

"Yes!"

Samantha laughed softly. "I protect you."

Ryan laughed.

"You are quite stubborn. And you are sure that nothing can happen?"

She grinned boldly.

"For sure."

*****

 Ojeda Two Moon had no idea that he would see Ryan for the last time on the Sundance. The family and Samantha had been silent about Ryan's plans. Three more busy weeks had passed. Because Ryan finishes the job at McLaughleen, everyone would soon know. On the last working day, after Ryan pocketed his compensation, he told McLaughleen that he wouldn't come back again. McLaughleen was so insane with rage.
"You damned, red rabble! You guys seem to come and go whenever you want! Were you brought up in a foreign culture? Not at all! Our government has not been able to educate you to be civilized!"
Ryan turned his horse and smiled unabashedly at McLaughleen.
"Red Eagle will send you another cowboy if he finds another fool like that again. I'll go to a place where they make me a civilized person. Maybe one day the chief will give you a job as a buffalo boy at the Lakota Ranch." Than he rode off.
McLaughleen snorted like a provoked bull and yelled after Ryan: "Damned bastard!"
Ryan did not seem to hear it anymore. And if it bounced off him.
That same evening he drove with his Pontiac to see Two Moon. He did not return until about midnight. They had a pretty long talk.
"Go", Ojeda Two Moon said. "You always will be my friend and you know where to find me if needed."

Although had lifted Ryan's burden, his inner disquiet continued to torment him. Ryan's father had barely talked to him. The closer the day came, the more silent Robert and Andy became.

Samantha gave Ryan his balance and kept his pride and smile.

*****

Red Eagle was angry and it wasn't easy to keep at bay himself. The buffalo ranch project made him headache and everyone in the council seemed to agree on it. Everyone was against him. Even Old Raven, who tried in vain to convince him and persuade him otherwise.

Before Leonhard Red Eagle went to his office at the beginning of the new week, he drunk up the courage. The brandy bottle had a special hideout. Not even his wife Lisa knew it. He always drank only as much as necessary. Nobody should notice. He described it as medicine, which he had to take regularly. Red Eagle knew he was being crushed between the tribal council and white renter McLaughleen. After all, once he had given his word. For years, McLaughleen brought him small gifts. Occasionally including a bottle of the best whiskey. With every passing day, the situation got worse and Red Eagle knew things had to be different. He also was frightened as the door of the office flung open and McLaughleen appeared in the doorway.

"Chief, you have not got your people under control!", he shouted at him.

McLaughleen did not seek control. Displeased, he

continued: "It's all over town! The buffalo ranch is a done deal and you think I'm a fool! That snooty guy, Ryan Hawk, said straight out: <maybe the chief will give you a job as a buffalo shepherd on the Lakota Ranch>."

Red Eagle pulled together his eyebrows, clenching his teeth and playing with his cheek muscles. Then he said: "Nothing is decided. The council meeting is in twelve days."

McLaughleen gasped and hissed at Red Eagle: "Make sure my lease is renewed! Finally, you benefit when my business is going well."

Without a word of greeting McLaughleen turned and left the office. The door slammed behind him. Red Eagle twisted his mouth and stared at the door.

From then on, he drank more of his medicine than was necessary to better withstand the pressure of the next twelve days. So he believed.

*****

One of the many sundance festivals that took place every summer in the reservations and in the Black Hills was due on the weekend. It had a special status among the Dakota, Lakota, Nakota and many of the neighboring tribes. This ancient ritual was the most intense way to connect with Wakan Tanka, the Great Mystery. The white America was terrified of this and other uncanny rituals they never understood. Therefore the white government had strictly forbidden the rituals by law to the indigenous people. But the native Americans were a part of Wakan Tanka, part of the Great Secret, the creation of all the creatures and elements, the nature that constantly surrounded them. They were sons and daughters of the earth. They wanted to live and this inevitably included their way of thinking, their rituals, their spirituality, from which they all drew strength for the future. They did everything not to forget anything. They were not allowed to forget who they really were. Forgetting that would have finally killed and turned them into white people. Now the punished, ridiculed and patronized people had found new pride. They still lived, then and now. But many things had changed.

Ryan wanted to be alone the evening before leaving for the sundown dance place. He was sitting on a prairie hill playing with a blade of grass, lost in thought. The black stallion stood near him and grazed. At Ryan's old, worn-out jeans, the stitches came off. The red shirt, which had become too wide, had no sleeves. The long hair shone in the evening sun. It reached far down Ryan's back. The wind played with it. The young man's brown skin shimmered like copper in the light of the setting sun. Ryan's gaze went into the distance, to some point on the horizon. He did not move. He thought he felt his skin taut over his protruding cheekbones. His whole body seemed tense as he followed his thoughts. Around his mouth, small dimples formed. At some point, Ryan heard the scream of a raptor. It pervaded his thoughts. Then it was quiet. Ryan began to nibble on the blade of grass. When the fireball hit the horizon, Ryan got up and looked around. When he was convinced that he was still here alone, Ryan raised his arms and turned his gaze to the setting sun. He stayed that way for a long time. He prayed. But only two words quietly left his mouth: "Omakiya yo!"

Slowly he lowered his arms again. Twilight dominated the hilly grassland. Then Ryan turned to his horse. He raised his head and snorted softly. The dark figure of the rider on the galloping horse soon blended with the starry night.

*****

The next day, Ryan set out determinedly with his family. The tipis poles lay firmly strapped on the truck bed and reached over the roof. Now and then the poles rattled against each other. The plane lay with the remaining luggage underneath. Everything the family needed for the next four or five days she had with her. It was a good feeling. It seemed they have left the burden behind them. The mood was exuberant and happy. Even Andy's laugh sounded carefree again. When the family had erected the white Tipi between the others, Ryan went his way. He met with and other friends. Together they raised the sacred tree in the middle of the dance place. Also in the evening Ryan stayed in the circle of his friends, who all wanted to take part in the dance.

That same evening, Ryan's sister Carry Crowman arrived with her family. She was four years older than Ryan and has been living in Rapid City since her wedding. It was customary that family and relatives, the Tiospaye, came to a festival where one or more family members were among the dancers. It was a joyful surprise for everyone. Carry immediately welcomed her mother and grandmother and embraced them. Her husband, Alex Crowman, welcomed his younger brother in law, Robert and

Andy. He looked in vain for Ryan, who was disappeared in the crowd.

Ryan showed up late at night and, after the short greeting, lay down in the family tent to sleep. For a long time he couldn't rest, tossed and turned all night. He had bad dreams and awoke without rest before sunrise. He got up at dawn and walked through the forest, down to the Little Stone Creek. It smelled strongly of ponderosa pine and spruce wood. The first birds chirped timidly into the new day. Ryan breathed some air deep into his lungs and refreshed himself by the cold water of the creek. After that he felt better. Happy children's voices echoed through the clear morning air as Ryan returned to the tipi. The light of the rising sun was already shimmering through the treetops. The children ran around among the tents. The smell of fresh coffee reached Ryan's nose. Anny had prepared the breakfast and cooked coffee on the open fire place. Ryan laughed when his four-year-old niece, Joan Crowman, took a piece of cake from the plate and slipped away with her friends behind the tent.

Ryan enjoyed the moment, as did many others. He had prepared for the sweatlodge. A sundancer prepared for the ritual by cleansing his body and soul, being one with himself, stepping with pure heart before Wakan Tanka, the great mystery. Only in this way a person could, according to the believes of the Lakota, show his gratitude from the bottom of his heart and hope that he would find the connection with the spirits. They should help him find the right path for the future and protect and lead him and his family. For that, the young man was ready to sacrifice his blood and flesh.

Ryan took a deep breath and got up.

Wearing only a boxer short and with a towel over his

shoulder, he went to the tent of Old Raven. Ryan would fast from now and in the next four days.

*****

Awe-inspiring aura was in the air and over the ground, as the dancers entered. A frame of young thin tree trunks, covered with pine branches, gave some shade. It would be a hot day today. Ryan stood next to his friend Ojeda Two Moon, side by side like last year. All eyes were on the dancers. Ryan did not see anyone, not even Samantha, who was facing him outside the circle. With all his strength and strong will, step by step, he danced himself in trance to finally overcome the doubt and fears. The drum beats echoed in his head and his heart beats against the chest. Ryan danced for his manner of living, that of his Tios-paye and that of his people. He was hoping for a vision that would show him the right way, approve his decision and give him protection. Ryan asked for help and pro-tection for his family, the ranch and for more respect for the people of his tribe. That's why he danced. The several weeks of back-breaking had hardened him.

The whistling of the eagle bone flutes he heard from far away. He, too, had her between his lips. The flutes called the eagle, the largest feathered brother. He was able to fly the closest to Tunkashila, Grandfather of all. He esta-blished the connection between the people and the universe.

On the evening of the first day of the sundance, Ryan lay exhausted on his air mattress. The heat of the day had demanded its tribute. He quenched his thirst with water. Ryan also slept restlessly in the following nights. Bad dreams tormented him. He dreamed his grandmother's dream. Wolves sneak around the house. They were many. Their yellow eyes glowed threateningly through the night. They bared their teeth. They hunted the horses. Ryan's silent screams did not stop them. He grabbed the broomstick and went after them. Frightened Ryan realized that he was suddenly alone on the ranch. Finally he woke up in a cold sweat. Before Ryan left with the dancers for the sweat lodge the next morning, he saw Samantha and smiled. He stopped for a minute.

"Do you want to watch?"

"I'm doing this. Since the beginning."

"In which tent do you sleep?"

"Back there. My whole family came along."

"There is no one of your family among the dancers."

"No", Samantha grinned and disappeared into the crowd in front of his eyes.

Neither on this nor the next day did they meet again.

*****

On the last day of the ritual, Chief Leonhard Red Eagle blocked Ryan's way.

"You talk too much", he hissed. "Be careful!"

"What do you mean by that?", Ryan asked.

"You talk about things to McLaughleen which have not yet been decided."

"Your breath, Red Eagle, smells of whiskey", Ryan said and puckered his mouth in disgust.

The Chief's eyes flashed sharply.

"Don't go butting your nose in where it doesn't belong!" Threatened Red Eagle and took a step toward Ryan.

Ryan took the ground. Some had become attentive and watched both.

"The sundance is our most sacred ritual. I will not enter the arbor to sacrifice my flesh, if you desecrate it with your whiskey smelling of a Wasicu", Ryan spoke hard.

The others were silent. The silence let them understand every word. Old Raven stepped next to the two men.

"I do not dance", Red Eagle answered sharply.

"You should do that when you are sober. Maybe you will find your way again", hissed Ryan softly.

"You of all people say that! Did not your father teach you respect?"

"Yes, he did. He also taught me to respect the brandy. So much respect that for more than two years I have not touched a single drop."

Red Eagle was foaming with rage.

Nobody had ever dared to talk to him like that. Before he could reply, Old Raven said softly: "Enough."

He signaled to Ryan to leave.

He pinched his lips and continued his walk to the others. The quiet circle dissolved in nothing.

Old Raven walked along with Red Eagle and talked to him. A short time later Leonhard Red Eagle got into his car and drove off.

Finally, Old Raven entered the holy circle as if nothing had happened. Like a year ago, Ryan did not flinch when the Holy Man pierced his chest. Ryan was now connected to the holy tree. His dance started. Following the rhythm of the drums and the beat of his heart, he went around the tree. The sun blinded him so that he saw nothing but countless circles flickering in front of him. His ears heard the drum beat. His thoughts what his heart felt.

I thank you for everything you gave me and for us and for sending my mother home. Now I ask for protection and help for my family, all relatives, all people of my tribe, for our horses and the valley, for our land, which is sacred to us.

Help me to help them all and that the way I will go is not in vain.

Forgive me for doing that, but I do it to live.

Omakiya yo!

Like in trance, Ryan heard the dancer's eagle bone flutes. Omakiya yo echoed his thoughts. Help me!

Omakiya yo shouted his soul as he threw back his emaciated body. The connection between the holy tree and his chest tensed without tearing his skin. The reflection of light in front of his eyes became wolves. Seven wolves creeping around the house bared their teeth threateningly. That wasn't a good sign. Fear shot through Ryan's body like a rush. Then he saw an old white-haired woman appear in their middle. Uncida! She smiled silently. Then she turned herself and disappeared in the fog. The wolves were gone too. It was quiet around him. The danger was banned. He was completely alone again. In front of Ryan's eyes bright light appeared but he couldn't see anything. Only the drum and the eagle flutes quietly reached into his consciousness.

Once again he threw back himself and fell backwards into the arms of the helpers. He hardly felt the pain, but thirst began to torment him. Two of his friends took him to the tent. The first thing he could see clearly before his eyes was Samantha's face.

She smiled and gave him a drink.

*****

One week later, the wounds were almost healed, Ryan saw the sun overlooking the valley for the last time. She still shone through the window. But far to the west, from the great Rocky Mountains, dark clouds were rising. Ryan closed the little black travel bag that was on his bed. He did not contain much more than a few personal items such as change of cloth, sports shoes and a bag for the laundry. They had told him that apart from a few personal things, he would not need much. The door opened quietly. Ryan turned around. Robert came in and closed the door.
"Hi Robert", Ryan said.
The fifteen-year-old stopped at the door and looked at the bag.
"I did not understand everything", Robert began.
"You said, to help us, you have to do it. The horses have stayed and we have food. My thoughts are confused and I do not know what to think."
Ryan nodded.
"One day you will understand, little brother."
"I want to say goodbye, big brother. I will miss you."
Robert smiled as he continued: "From now on I am the big brother and it will not be easy for me."
"Then better watch your hands in the future. The fence will have to hold for a while", smiled Ryan.
"I will. Pity you can't teach me to drive anymore."
"You're good at it!"

"I mean really drive", Robert grinned subtly.
"Maybe I will have a pass to go out", Ryan said.
"Yes, maybe."
They were silent for a moment.
"Toksah ake` wacin yanin ktelo", Robert said quietly and embraced his brother with all his heart.
Ryan had become role model to Robert. He was not only his brother, but his best friend too.
"Till the day we meet again", Ryan replied.
Then they separated.
Robert nodded.
Obviously, it was hard to say goodbye. He opened the door and together the brothers left the room and went downstairs.

When Ryan got up after dinner, he went straight to the bathroom. He had made a decision. Now the time had come. Until the next morning there were only a few hours left. Attentive he looked at his mirror image, as if he wanted to memorize it exactly. Finally he shook his head. Then he took the scissors and cut off his long hair.
"You'll have to get used to", he said to his reflection.
With some of his hair, he went out to his horse to say goodbye. He started weaving his hair into the mane. The stallion sensed that and let his head hang. Two eyes watched him so intensely that he felt the look on his back. Ryan turned his head slowly.
With tears in his eyes and strangled voice, Andy let go his desperate accusation, which tormented him, against his brother.
"You skip out of town on the problems and leave us alone. Once I was proud of my big brother! But now I don't even have one."
Before Ryan could speak, Andy ran away. Ryan looked at

him sadly.

He was still standing by the horse when a red Chevrolet appeared in front of the house. Samantha got out and came along.

"Hello Ryan", she said and crawled in under the fence.

"You did the first step on your way", she noted, pointing to his hair.

"That's the way it is. Good evening, Samantha."

A faint smile appeared on his face.

"I'm ready. Let's go for a while."

Ryan Black Hawk and Samantha Crying Crow walked slowly along the fence.

"When are you leaving?"

"Tomorrow morning, at sunrise."

"Do you want me to stay?"

Ryan stopped and grinned smugly at Samantha.

"If I look at you like that, I guess I have no other choice", he said.

She gave him a shove and laughed. "Hey!"

Then he started jokingly tweaking her. Samantha giggled and fled up the hill. Ryan ran after her. Although he was faster than she, he always gave her a head start. They ran up the hill and down again until Samantha was out of breath.

"I surrender!"

She laughed.

"That's right!"

Ryan took her by the hand and pulled her into the house, up the stairs and into his room. The traveling bag fell off the bed as he threw Samantha on it. The hours of the last, shared night, passed by unstoppably.

When he woke up, Samantha was still sleeping in his arms. Carefully, he pulled his arm away from her, picked up his clothes and reached for the bag. Before Ryan closed the door, he sent one last look to Samantha. She slept calmly and firmly. Ryan smiled and closed the door silently.

When he came out of the bathroom, the light was on in the kitchen. Anny looked around smiling and said softly: "I made coffee. Sit down and eat something."

Ryan sat down on the kitchen cupboard.

"Good morning, Mom. Did I make too much noise?"

"No. I have been waiting for you. I couldn't sleep."

Ryan took the coffee cup and drank carefully. The coffee was hot. Grandmother came in. Maybe she too had not slept that night. Her nightgown reached to the ankles of her feet. Lucy wore her dark green cardigan with the wooden buttons. She had not buttoned up the jacket but just wrapped herself and put her arms around her body as if she were freezing. Lucy approached Ryan and smiled confidently.

"The wolves have left", she said quietly, handing her grandson a small leather bag. Lucy nodded as their eyes met.

"They will not come back. Thanks, granny", Ryan finally said.

Grandmother Lucy's face appeared a beaming smile. The folds around her eyes looked like sunbeams. Her eyes seemed to shine. Then Lucy turned and left. Ryan looked after her. Then he started eating.

Anny wrapped herself in a blanket and accompanied her son out. Dawn overlaid the country. It was strangely silent. Only the wind blew in their faces. Anny stopped on the porch. Ryan put the bag next to his feet and took his mother in his arms.

"Toksa ake`wacin yanin ktelo, Ina", said Ryan softly.

Ryan felt her shake and he knew she couldn't talk. She clung to him as if she did not want to let him go.

"Until the day we meet again", Anny said bravely after a while.

She was strong and let her son go. Her eyes gleamed treacherously when she finally blinked at Ryan.

She looked after him as he got into his car. Her eyes followed the Pontiac until it was gone. She shivered.

When she stopped hearing the engine noise, Anny Black Hawk walked slowly into the house.

Capter 2
The other world

Gray clouds covered the sky and hid the sun. It rained on the runway of Ellsworth Air Force Base and turned it completely smooth. The moving jeeps whirled droplets of water into small streams of fog and pulled it behind them. The fighter jets of the US Air Force stood in a long row one alongside another. A strange calm overlayed the Air Force Base, northeast of Rapid City, on this first September morning. Hardly anyone worked out here. And if so, even that would happen in slow motion.

The young man who opened the door to the office building was carrying a black bag over his shoulder. After stepped in silently he closed the entrance door behind him. He looked around. He was alone. It was quiet. The corridor was short and narrow. Four wooden doors, two on each side. Between the doors, on the bare walls, stood a few chairs. As no daylight could penetrate, the neon tubes on the ceiling blinded the sensitive eyes. The air was musty. Ryan Black Hawk grimaced. Then he put his bag down.

With his hands he brushed some strands of hair out of the face. Then he knocked on the first office door. As no one answered, he leaned against the wall beside the door. As soon as he leaned against the wall and crossed his arms, someone came in from outside.

"Good morning", Ryan heard a strong, deep voice. He raised his eyes for a moment without moving. Then he answered the greeting of the big bearded man who came towards him. The guy was pretty well-fed and dressed in civilian clothes, had shoulder-length, curly hair and was a white man.

"No one inside?"

The stranger asked, pointing with his hand to the office door.

"No."

"That's great prospects, man! I wouldn't have thought that you may sleep as long as you want in the Army", laughed the fat. "I'm curious, how many are crazy enough to come here, as we do", the big boy laughed raucous. Ryan did not move. The bearded man actually reminded him of a grizzly bear on two legs.

A strange creature. At these thoughts he had to smile.

"You're Indian", the Grizzly realized, without getting an answer.

"Sioux?" he asked.

"Lakota." Ryan responded in a manner that would make the stranger understand he was not interested in a conversation.

That didn't seem to interest the grizzly.

"Goodman, Baxter Goodman", he introduced himself and held out his hand to the Lakota.

Ryan did not move. He did not answer either.

"Do you have a name?" Grizzly Baxter asked.

"Ye."

Ryan answered concise, and wrapped himself in silence again.

"Okay I understand. You're not really chatty."

Grizzly seemed a bit disappointed. He was silent for a while. Then five guys entered together and filled the room with their loud voices. Sayings and laughter resounded through the small room.

Ryan and Baxter, who were already waiting there, ignored this guys. A little later, the office door opened and a uniformed, yelling in loud command the first man in. Baxter grabbed one of the guys in the neck when he tried to push himself forward to get into the office first.

"Hey, the Lakota was first!" he grumbled.

"Piss off you jerk!" was the answer for Baxter.

Ryan looked up and noticed how grizzly pushed the guy against the wall. This was done with a stoic serenity that impressed Ryan.

"Do you have a problem? You wait until it's your turn", said Grizzly very calm.

The guy, barely smaller than Grizzly, blushed. He snorted furiously, but did not dare to contradict.

Ryan grabbed his bag and disappeared with the uniformed in the office.

Less than a quarter of an hour later Baxter Goodman followed. In another room, behind the office, where they first entered, the men were to wait until they were picked up. With a pile of paper in his hand, Grizzly sat down next to the Lakota. At first they sat there alone.

"We'll still have some fun with the fuckers", Baxter said.

Ryan glared at Baxter. His eyes sparkled dangerously.

"I don't need a Babysitter. I'm able to pay attention to myself."

That was spoken a lot for the Lakota. He didn't look at Grizzly anymore.

Baxter laughed in amusement.

'Hey, was there a spark of hidden humor?"

Ryan remained silent.

"Then, my friend, I want to hope for you that you will not be the only Lakota."

The brief conversation came to an end when the next guy came in with his papers. When everyone was together, they were picked up by another uniformed man. He called up the names in alphabetical order and ordered them to stay in a row. The number of the new arrivals had now risen to nine. Hawk came after Goodman. Ryan was listed in the papers under Hawk, Black, Ryan. Baxter turned and grinned as Ryan stepped right behind him. Ryan was half a head shorter than Grizzly and looked skinny compared to him. Both stood side by side on the laundry distribution terminal and signed the receipt. As they walked on with the pile of laundry on their arms, Baxter asked: "Why are you here?"

"My name is Hawk. You heard it. The Hawk must learn to fly", Ryan replied.

Baxter laughed with satisfaction.

"You actually have a sense of humory", he noted.

The way of the two led on to the doctor. Ryan left the room with a Band-Aid on his left arm. He threw the shirt over his shoulder and walked on to the dentist, like everyone else. The pile of papers he held in his hands had shrunk. The next station was the hairdresser. The first of the new contenders was already sitting in the chair and the hair dropped. Big, wide-bodied Grizzly was already leaning against the doorframe as Ryan stepped behind him. Baxter turned to Ryan and noticed how he grimaced. Unobtrusively, Baxter moved closer to his successor and touched his hand.

"Take it. So he doesn't cut you hairless", he whispered. discreetly.

Ryan let the paper disappear in his fist. Finally he got an acceptable haircut.

The next command was to take up quarters and be back at the big roll-call square in exactly twenty minutes.

Hawk and the Grizzly entered their quarters. Both paused when they saw the big room with the bunk beds, four on each side. It did not seem inviting. For Ryan, the room had something threatening about it and aroused his distrust. The Grizzly threw his bag on the lower bed. Ryan also preferred to stay on the lower side. Diagonally opposite to Grizzly a bed was still free. He shoved his bag in the cupboard. A pale, slender guy with freckles took over the place above him. A few simple steps, and Ryan's bed was ready. Then he changed his clothes. Ryan watched the grizzly. A smile flitted across his face as the fat man cuffed and squeezed his pants. His face was deep red and he was gasping for air. He closed the buttons with effort and need, let the pent-up air out of his cheeks and looked to Ryan.

He grinned.

"Thank you", he said to Baxter.

Baxter nodded and approached him.

"Are you going to tell me your name now?"

"Ryan Black Hawk."

"Do you want to be a pilot?"

Ryan shrugged. "I'm looking for a job."

"Me too. I'm a mechanic. I do not really want to go in the air. I'm afraid of heights", Baxter laughed.

It actually sounded like the hum of a bear.

"I fled from Olivia. She's a brick, but sometimes that's too much of a good thing."

Again Ryan had to grin.

"Not what you think. Olivia is my mother. We get along very well, but sometimes she simply crushes me. That's why I fled. At some point she must understand I'm able to clean my nose by myself."

"How old are you?", Ryan asked.

"Twenty-three."

"You look older."

"Thank you for the compliment, Ryan Black Hawk", mumbled the Grizzly. "Maybe has something to with my beard."
"Do you like it having hair on your face?"
"For sure! I'm born with this beard. Not everybody like you can walk around naked."
"You look like a Grizzly bear", Ryan smiled.
Baxter seemed to enjoy it. Laughing, the men went out.

*****

A short time later, all the men stood, in a semicircle, on the roll-call square, upright and stiff, under the banner with the stars and stripes.
Ryan had looked at the men. He had not yet recognized another native among them. He actually seemed to be the only one in the band right now. The instructors introduced themselves in their extremely friendly way. They made it clear to the candidates that they were a bunch of slobs and sissies. Then they promised to make men and soldiers out of them.

Like everyone else, Ryan ran with them, crawled through the dirt and jumped over obstacles. He completely lost sight of Grizzly. Late in the evening, when all the men were already lying on their bunks and no one had any mood for stupid things, Baxter Goodman's bed had remained empty. Ryan started worrying about the Grizzly. He was still awake when everyone else was asleep. It was after midnight when the Grizzly with wet hair sneaked up to his bed and let himself fall powerless on the mattress. He couldn't even cover himself anymore. Silently, Ryan sneaked up to him.

"What's up, Bear?"

"They taught me to dance half the night, because I got stuck on the track", he growled tiredly. "I am still a car mechanic and not a racehorse."

"How can I help you?" whispered Ryan.

But he only heard the steady breathing of a sleeping one.

The days of basic education were hard for everyone. Baxter grew beyond himself, losing at least twenty pounds in the first six weeks. The nights were damn cold and it had rained incessantly for the last four days. The track had turned into a disgusting mud pool and it made the instructors particularly happy to teach the wimps and milksops the mud fighting. Some of the men in the troop were battling with cough, hoarseness and sore noses.

Ryan became the special darling of his instructors. Since he carried out all commands perfectly and correctly and never revealed what he thought, he brought them to a boil. There seemed to be nothing to lure the Indsman out of reserve. Even the five big-mouthers Ryan and Baxter had met in front of the office on the first day had fallen silent, they let their frustrations go to the weaker. Apart from constant insults, they lurked individuals to beat them at regular intervals. The instructors did not take any notice of this. Nobody dared to interfere. Since the first day the guys made a wide berth to Baxter Goodman.

After ten weeks of basic training, a foreign captain appeared. He had the order to drag the Indian and brought Ryan to its limits. When the others left, Ryan had to run for hours through the pouring rain. Even at noon, he did not get a break, let alone eat something. Ryan was emaciated. His cheekbones protrude even more clearly and the traces of the drills were visible to him. As best in training, he was exposed to boundless envy. Especially the five guys from the first day stoked the envy. Ryan was no longer spared. At first he disregarded them with disregard, which riled the guys all the more. When they waylaid him, he did not come. That made them even more angry.

*****

By now it was November. It was always wet and cold. The limbs ached, and Ryan was glad to warm himself up inside. Ryan dropped himself tired on his bed. It seemed like he was alone for an hour. He closed his eyes.
"What's up, Damon", he asked quietly.
"They nearly beat my friend to death last night", whispered the young man with the freckles. He was hiding under Ryan's bed.
"I do not want to be the next one. I'm afraid."
"Go ahead", said Ryan.
"Watch out for Sydney Logan and his buddies. This time they are after you."
"What do the others say?"
"They're counting on you."
"Okay, Damon. Make sure you're not in your bed this night."
"What the hell are you doing?"

"Sleep. I'm tired." Ryan replied.
Damon quietly left the room.

*****

Baxter worked in the garage. He was happy because he did not have to spend hours crawling through the mud and there was a surprisingly large and colorful fleet at the Air Force. He was trained in automotive engineering. Baxter proved that he was unbeatable here. Even the instructors had realized that.
The bear jerked noticeably as Ryan suddenly appeared next to him. He spun around, startled.
"Do you have a rope for me"?, he asked softly.
"Man, my heart!"
Ryan looked around and pulled out a carabiner.
"This one too."
"What do you want with it?", Baxter asked surprised.
"I feel so lonely in bed at night", Ryan whispered.
His eyes wandered around attentively.
Baxter laughed. "I understand."
Baxter quickly found the right rope for his friend and gave it to him.
"Here you are! You can attach any truck to it. Three quarter inch, double braided."
"Could you bring it out inconspicuously?"
"You can rely on me. I'll put it on your bed."
Ryan shook his head.
"Underneath yours!"
Baxter grimaced in disbelief.
"Whatever", he mumbled.

Ryan had barely dared to sleep soundly since the first night in the crew quarter. His healthy mistrust warned him to be careful. Sydney Logan and his friends were a big-mouthed gang of thugs without brains and they were always in the majority. Ryan had still managed to stay one step ahead of them. That made the five guys even more angry than they already were. The gang was sure no one would argue for the Indsman. He had always kept out of the problems of others. That night, the guys had seen Ryan go into the room. But he had not come out. Everything remained calm until well into midnight. Those who were here, were fast asleep. Only Baxter was initiated and Damon had followed Ryan's advice. He was not here.

Baxter lay in his bed, pretending to be asleep. Ryan waited with his eyes wide open. He did not have to wait long to see the dark shapes entering the bedroom. Almost without a sound one of them scurried past him. Four more followed. The guys were good. He was wide awake and lurking like a puma, ready to jump. His hand grasped the hook to which the rope was knotted. The gang had stopped in front of his bed. Ryan saw a knife flash as someone pulled the blanket away. Ryan grinned when he heard the curses. Now everything happened very fast. Just then, when the guys realized that they had just attacked rolled-up blankets, Ryan hurled his projectiles at them. The whirring sound was followed by a loud groan.

Baxter jumped up from the bed with a cry of relief. His nerves had been close to tearing. The light from the neon lights suddenly flared. Ryan turned to the entrance, surprised. The light blazed, so he recognized Damon later. The eyes had quickly to get used to the light. Five guys lay like a Mikado on and in front of Ryan's bed.

"Good shot", Baxter acknowledged. "They will probably have an axe to the skull headache when they wake up."

Sydney Logan held a rolled rope in his hand, the end of which was tied to a sling.

"Just look at that", Baxter growled softly. "It seems to me that they wanted to hang someone. Damn macabre fun."

"That was not for fun", Ryan said just as softly.

Those who were here and had just slept peacefully had jumped out of the beds and formed a circle. Appreciative murmur spread. Ryan did not have time to lose. He cleverly tied the hands of the guys on her back. In a row he left her lying in front of his bed. Then he stood up and gave Baxter back the hook, which immediately made him disappear under the mattress. The men standing around, who were gradually awakening from their gawking stare, triumphed. Some cheered whistling. At last someone had forced this gang, whom everyone had feared, to their knees. No single man had been able to accommodate them. The men admired the Indian in their midst. They respected him. He not only had courage and spirit. Ryan had made them a team. Each of these men had the same goal. Everyone had provided important information to Ryan. And he had acted without talking. So with the respect maybe even the fear of the Indian grew. Nobody here wanted to have him as an opponent.

Suddenly the door was pushed open and the commander hurriedly stepped into the room. He stopped right in front of Ryan. Before he said anything, he let his gaze glide over Ryan and the five bound men.

He could not resist a grin.
"Who the hell did that?"
"Sir! Me, Hawk, Sir", Ryan reported correctly.
The commander gratefully puckered the corner of his mouth and nodded.
"Follow me, Hawk!"
Ryan executed the order.

*****

For five days, Baxter waited in vain for his friend's return. Ryan's bed remained untouched. But Baxter Goodman grinned every time he met the guys with their injuries on the grounds. After lunch, as usual, Baxter used the opportunity to serve himself on supplies stored in his closet. The art of cooking of the Air Force kitchen was not quite to his taste and he was never full.
"Hands up and turn around", suddenly, a voice ruled him hard. Baxter winced. With the sandwich between his teeth he raised his hands and turned around. He stared wide-eyed into the grinning face of Ryan Black Hawk. Baxter took the sandwich out of his mouth.
"You crazy guy", he said quietly and grinned also. Then he sat down on his bed.
"You were in jail", Baxter stated.
Ryan nodded.
"For every plaster head a day to think."
"These damned guys should have locked them up!", Baxter griped.
Ryan contemptuously twisted his mouth.
"But I haven't slept so well for a long time. I had a room for myself and there was enough food."
"You teach them a lesson. Now they are able to tell it to

their grandchildren. But they'll do their best to never know", Baxter laughed.

Ryan grinned.

"My captain is waiting for me. He has reserved the practice area for himself and me. He thinks I rested long enough."

"Well then have fun", Baxter pitied his friend.

"I always have", said Ryan calmly and left.

Baxter looked after the Lakota. He shook his head barely.

"I wouldn't want to change with you, my friend", he mumbled.

The captain, who called himself Gill and had come from another base, barely spoke. He drilled Ryan particularly hard from now on. He was probably of the opinion that he had to form a raw diamond into a jewel. Ryan did not know what happened to him. Hoping for a good job, he fought hard and did his best.

"The boy is damn tough. Like a cat. That might turn out to be something", Captain Gill said to Lieutenant Colonel Taylor, Air Force Base's highest ranking officer. Gill, as a personal trainer, had tested Ryan through his paces for the last two weeks. While Taylor played with the pen, listened attentively.

"That's why I recommended him. At Hawk all trainers have already cut their teeth on it. The Indsman is clever", Taylor finally replied.

"Does he want to fly?"

The Lieutenant Colonel shrugged his shoulders.

"There are only a few who sign up for ground personnel and even fewer who are eligible for special training. Hawk has the best conditions. He is currently doing technical training and he is one of the best. That's all I have to say. You should decide immediately, Lieutenant Colonel Taylor."

"Okay, then let him take a shower and come to my office, Captain Gill. We should talk to him."

The office was dim, so that the light was on all day. After all, it was late November. The 20`th, to be exact. The rain of the last days had turned into snow.

Taylor picked up the phone and gave orders for Hawk to appear in his office immediately. Few, clear words. Then he hung up the phone and leaned back in his chair. Gill went to the window and looked out.

Taylor was alone in his office. He sat at the desk absorbed in his work. When it knocked on the door, he raised his head.

"Come in!"

The door opened silently and the Lakota entered. He stopped in the room, greeted militarily correctly and waited. Taylor did not offer him a chair.

"Hawk, Ryan, eighteen, Lakota from the Pine Ridge Indian Reservation. Why did you come to the US Air Force?"

So the gray-haired Lieutenant Colonel began his questioning and leaned back.

"Sir! Because of the training, sir."

Taylor nodded.

"Of course. As a pilot?"

"If need be, that too, Lieutenant Colonel Taylor."

Taylor chuckled

"What else did you think of?"

"Sir! Drive a car, Sir."

Taylor grinned.

"And for this you join the Air Force?"

"Sir! Ground staff. There are cars here too, sir."

"You do not want to fly?"

"Sir! Only if there is no other job for me, Sir."

Taylor studied the Lakota very carefully. A smile crossed his face.

"It actually seem to me you're very clever, Hawk."

Ryan was silent. He hardly dared to breathe.

"Your basic training has already ended. Without exception, the instructors consider you tough and totally crazy. The captain will talk to you, Hawk", Taylor said.

Then he pressed a red button on the phone.

"Hawk is here", he said.

"That door", he said to Ryan.

"Sir, yes Sir", Ryan answered.

With a proper greeting, he said goodbye and went out.

He knocked on the connecting door and entered another office.

Ryan greeted in according to the regulations. He had no expression on his face at all. There sat the man who had made him his blood to water for the past two weeks.

What the hack, did that mean?

"Sit down, Hawk", the captain ordered.

Ryan sat down.

"So you prefer a job with the ground staff", Gill stated.

"Sir, if that's possible, yes sir."

"And if I order you to fly?" Gill asked.

"Sir, then I'll fly, Sir."

Gill studied the Lakota who sat in front of him very attentively. His eyes sparkled dangerously. Ryan avoided direct eye contact. The captain did not even blink an eye.

"Have you ever flown with a fighter jet?"

"Sir, no Sir."

"What are you afraid of, Hawk", Gill asked.

"Sir, the wolves, sir", Ryan answered promptly.

Gill raised his eyebrows. He obviously seemed surprised. He certainly had not expected that answer.

"Of wolves?" Gill asked astonished.

"Sir, yes sir."

Gill breathed audibly. He thought the Lakota was crazy but not mentally handicapped. Gill seemed to be considering. He knew that he couldn't question an Indian with impunity. Gill was not about to lose a word fight and decided to beat the Lakota with his own weapons.

"I will send you to a special force. You have the makings of surviving training. They are called the shadow wolves."

Gill leaned back in his office chair, waiting for the Lakota's reaction.

"Sir, yes Sir. Thanks Sir", Ryan answered without hesitation.

"Questions?"

"Sir, if I survive, will I get a job?"

Gill's lips twisted. He had to grin.

"Yes, Hawk. And if you survive the job, then you may even choose the next one."

"Aren't you afraid of wolves anymore?"

"Sir, as wolf among wolves? No, Sir."

"Do you have family, wife, children?" asked the captain.

"Sir, family yes. No wife and no children, Sir."

Gill took a deep breath.

"Okay then. Tomorrow you have a day off, Hawk. Get a bank account and clarify your personal matters. The day after tomorrow, six o'clock is departure."

"Sir, thanks. I will do everything, Sir."

"No doubt. You can leave."

Ryan greeted militarily correctly and left the office.

Another order for Ryan was to report to hangar three

afterwards. The Sergeant on duty had come up with a special task for Ryan. Ryan gave no emotion to his thoughts when he was ordered to scrub the remains of the birds from the roofs of the hangar. The sergeant could not resist a sadistic grin as he watched the Lakota.

*****

The weariness was written on the face of Carry Crowman. She had jumped out of the bed several times that night. Her little daughter Joan was shaken by a feverish infection. She screamed again and again. Exhausted, Carry had repeatedly fallen into a restless sleep. She could hardly put one foot before the other. She picked up the four-year-old and tried to reassure her. She took a short look to the watch. It was one o'clock in the morning. Carry was cold. She sang a song softly until the little one had calmed down again. Carry's man, Alex, slept next door. He tried it at least. He had a long, hard day at work. Carry hardly dared to go back to bed. She sat in the armchair and let her daughter sleep on her arm. Carry's eyes burned and the heavy lids closed slowly.

A softly knock on the front door made her startle. Carry thought she had dreamed and closed her eyes again. It knocked again.

Who is coming at this time? she thought.

Careful not to wake up Joan, she got up and went to the door. Someone tried to open it from the outside. Carry's heart was pounding to the head. A burglar would not knock. They also knew that there was nothing to be found among Indian families. The door was locked. The knob slowly turned back. She remained motionless at the door and listened. No steps, no voice, no breath was heard. Nothing but silence. When there was another soft knock, Carry held her breath. She took every ounce of courage.

"Yes, who's there?"

"It's me, Ryan."

Carry was relieved to hear the soft voice of her brother. Slowly she opened the door. She hardly trusted her tired eyes. A slim, black figure stood directly in front of her.

"Ryan?", she asked insecure.

"No worry, little sister. It's really me", he answered and entered.

He closed the door behind him. It was pretty dark in the living room. Only the weak light from the street lighting penetrated through the windows. Carry looked at Ryan as if he was just a dream. Their eyes had become accustomed to the darkness.

"Where do you come from, in the middle of the night?" she whispered in surprise.

"Special leave. Just one day", he answered quiet, not to wake up the child.

"Oh, Ryan." Carry was relieved. "We haven't seen each other for so long. I wanted...."

"Sch ..." he put his finger on his mouth and gently pulled her to the couch.

"How is my little Nice?" Ryan smiled and gently stroked her head.

"She has had a fever since last night and is already screaming half the night. I'm glad she finally fell asleep", Carry whispered.

"What does that mean?"

"She has an infection. She also coughs."
Ryan nodded and pulled his hand back.
"I want to tell you why I'm here. There is not much time, Carry. I'm going to the bank tomorrow. I need an account. Then I will come back and bring you the money for the ranch. I can't go back now. Not today."
"Alright, Ryan. How are you? You have changed."
"Only externally. I get a training and then a job."
"As a pilot?"
Ryan chuckled. "No, I stay on the ground."
"You look just as tired as I feel", Carry smiled. "You can sleep on the couch."
"With pleasure. Thank you Carry."
Ryan lay down on the couch while Carry sat down with Joan in the chair again.

    The following morning when Ryan drove his Pontiac to the bank, there was a sleet shower over Rapid City. The gray day started late and ended when dawn set in. The sleet shower had turned into snow. An icy wind blew through the streets. Ryan wore a padded Jacket of the Air Force. He had turned up his collar. He hurried to the front door. Carry was already waiting for him and opened immediately. Ryan gave her the envelope with the words: "I didn't leave the bank until the Air Force sent me the money. I will definitely not be back in the next six months. So I brought almost everything I had."
A smile appeared on Ryan's face as Joan sneaked into the living room. The marks of the restless night were clearly visible to her. She looked tired and pale. Ryan went into squat position.
"Hello little Jo. Are you feeling better?"
Joan hid behind her mom and carefully eyed Ryan. Carry laughed.

"Don't you know your uncle Ryan anymore?"
Joan shook her head.
"She is not entirely wrong. I hardly recognized you myself. Alex said 'strange man' to you this morning."
Joan studied Ryan for a long time. The smiling face finally seemed to be known to her.
"Leksi?" then she asked.
"Yes, Jo. Nileksi, your uncle", confirmed Ryan softly.
Slowly, the little girl approached him and let him take her on his arm. Her little hand tickled on the shaved neck and stroked through his short hair.
"She is feeling a little better. She hardly has a fever anymore."
"That's it", Ryan said as he sat down and put Joan on his leg. Then he took off his jacket and took out a colorful bag. There was a rustle when he opened it. Joan took a fruit jelly.
"They're good for your throat", Ryan smiled.
"I was at the pharmacy. They gave this to me for Joan", Ryan said, handing the bottle of cough syrup to his sister. "They said it's with honey. You should only give it to her in the evening before going to sleep."
Carry smiled.
"You are crazy. Thank you brother."
When Ryan had to leave three hours later, Alex came home. The twenty-five-year-old was built solid. His black eyes shone kindly. Carry's husband was happy to have met his brother-in-law. The men greeted each other and talked a few words before Ryan had to leave. Alex slapped Ryan's arm amicably and said: "Have a good flight and don't let it get you down."
Ryan smiled and nodded.
Then he disappeared into the darkness. The wind

whirled the snowflakes.

*****

Baxter had his own room after the end of his basic training. He was part of the team of mechanics and responsible for the car pool of the Air Force Base Rapid City. Baxter had achieved his goal. He slept soundly and contentedly. Two hours before midnight Ryan sneaked into his room. Ryan pressed his hand firmly on his bearded mouth and shook him awake. Stunned, the Grizzly's eyes blinked at him.
"Baxter, I just want to tell you I've been gone for half a year", Ryan said.
"And you have to tell me in the middle of the night? You scared me to death!", Baxter growled.
"It's only ten o'clock in the evening and you're already sleeping like a Grizzly in hibernation", laughed Ryan.
"When the day starts I won't be here anymore."
Baxter was suddenly wide awake.
"What! How so? Where?"
"Training for me. Where, they didn't tell me."
Baxter blew out the pent-up air.
"I hope to see you again."
"Maybe in six months, Mato."
"Mato?"
"Mita Kola Mato. My friend the bear", Ryan smiled.
Baxter chuckled.
"You also snore like a bear", Ryan laughed. "You should be more careful."
"I will keep that in mind. Let's hear something from you

and take care of yourself, my friend", Baxter said with a trace of concern.
"Hecetu", Ryan replied.
"Hece what?" Baxter shook his head. "Hey! You called me your friend for the first time!"
He was pleased and proud of it.
"That's the way it is. You've proved it more than once", Ryan said.
Then he said goodbye.
"Until the day we meet again", he said and left.
Baxter was still staring at the door in disbelief.

*****

Even before dawn the helicopter took off and disappeared in the dense snow flurry in a southwesterly direction. With Ryan five men got on board. All were obviously Indians. There was no talk. Hours later the helicopter landed in the desert. The sun was shining over the military base. The men who got out hardly had any luggage. They quickly followed their commander into one of the buildings. Icy wind whistled across the plain.
Ryan moved into his new quarter. He was amazed. It was a single room, sparsely but functional. In any case, it was more inviting than the large hall in Rapid City. The five other men were led on. Ryan looked around and threw the small, black travel bag into the narrow closet. As he looked out the window there was a knock on the door. He turned around instantly. The door opened and the strange lieutenant who had accompanied the men during the flight entered.

"I am Lieutenant Slater, you trainer. I have been ordered to take you to Major Cox. Follow me."

"Sir, yes Sir", Ryan replied stiffly.

Slater grimaced.

"I need to snap them out of this, fast."

The lieutenant turned and went ahead. Slater was the size and build of Ryan. His age was difficult to estimate. Maybe he was only a few years older than the Lakota. Slater wore a simple olive shirt, cargo pants, and a silver chain on the neck. No rank badge was seen. Ryan saw a tattoo on Slater's arm, partially hidden by the sleeve of the t-shirt. Ryan also noticed a tattoo on the neck. They were tiny letters and numbers. Maybe a code, Ryan guessed. Slater's hair was shaved very short at the beginning, while the rest showed something of a short hairstyle. Ryan had observed that everyone he had met before looked like this. Slater knocked on the door. Ryan followed him into the office.

"Major Cox", Slater nodded.

Ryan greeted the major in a militarily correct manner, as had been instructed, and stopped in front of the desk. The major also greeted and eyed the man standing in front of him. Slater also stopped.

"I am major Cox. Lieutenant Colonel Tayler sends you to this place, Hawk. You agree to the training."

"Sir, yes Sir."

"Your documents say that you want to be a driver", said Cox. "For us, driver training includes a lot more. We are not a racing team and it will not be a child's play. You will go through everything, point by point."

"Sir, yes Sir!"

The major paused.

Ryan didn't move.

The major was much younger than any senior officer he had met before. He wasn't wearing a uniform, just an olive cotton shirt with rolled up sleeves.

"Okay", he finally said and gave Ryan a portfolio of papers. "Read this and sign it. I can't spare you a check with our doctor, even if you only did it with the Air Force. Any questions?"

"Where am I?"

"In the desert of Nevada and our base is invisible. There is no connection to the outside world as long as you are in training here, Hawk. Let me just make that clear."

"Sir, understood Sir", Ryan replied.

"Lieutenant Slater is responsible for you. You already know each other. He will inform you of all the details. You can go."

Ryan immediately said goodbye in his built-in military regulations and left the room with Slater.

"The drill doesn't end here, Hawk, but we work here somewhat differently than at your Air Force Base in basic training. I also suspected that you don't even know what they're up to with you", Slater doubted as he walked down the hall with Ryan.

Ryan said nothing.

"I will tell you. Why didn't you ask Lieutenant Taylor? If you don't ask, you won't get an answer", grinned Slater.

"Sir, that's correct, but he did so mysteriously, sir."

"That sounds very Indian to me. You are Sioux?"

"Yes, sir. Lakota. Teton Ogallala."

"The army also has secrets, but only for people who have no reason to know. All right?"

"Sir, sure Sir."

Slater grinned and shook his head. Then he stopped and looked directly at Ryan.

"Taylor thought you were particularly gifted and crazy. That's why you're here. He wants to have a warrior who fears neither death nor devil. You will learn to be invisible. You will learn what you can do with a car and you will learn to think that you are always one step ahead of your enemies. They will fear you because none of your bullets miss their target. You will appear like a shadow out of nowhere and fulfill your command. You will hunt with the pack of shadow wolves and also alone. If you signed that up, there's no going back, Teton Ogallala."

Ryan had found himself staring at Slater as he spoke. He memorized the words that should determine his life. No, there was no going back. Ryan finally nodded. Slater went on with him. He led Ryan to a sports hall where a group of men trained in pairs. Head to head. Ryan watched closely.

"Military hand-to-hand combat with and without weapons", explained Slater. "Survival. Here you learn to use your body as a weapon. Attack and defense."

Ryan followed Slater into a swimming pool.

"Are you able to swim?"

"Not really, Sir", Ryan had to admit, watching the men darting through the water like arrows.

"Then it is high time that you learn it. Your fitness training is here every morning from 6 a.m. to 8 a.m." Then Slater led him to a shooting range.

"You learn to shoot in here, but also in the field and under different conditions and with different weapons." They didn't stay long. "You will always carry a pistol with you later, it makes sense if you know how to use it", Slater laughed.

"I'll show you your vehicle for practice later. I think you

will know how a car looks like. I'll take you to the doctor first", Slater decided.

Ryan also met the five other men who had arrived with him. Since they were not alone, the encounter was silent. Ryan immediately noticed that there were many Indian soldiers at the base. At all everything was different here than Ryan had ever known.

*****

The following days started at six in the morning and never ended until eight in the evening. The training continued at night at regular intervals. Ryan was in a team with several other Indians who came from different countries and belonged to different tribes. They all belonged to the elite and brought their experience and special abilities into training. The US Army particularly valued its ability to act silently and swiftly, which the warriors had always had and why they were feared. Hardly a white man could hold a candle to them. The men appeared like a shadow, suddenly, unexpectedly and deadly for their opponents. These skills also slumbered in Ryan. No military drill could push him as far as his own ambition. Neither Slater nor another instructor shouted their orders. They prevailed in a different way.

As a first lesson, Ryan had to learn to take his losses, in every way. Slater didn't show any consideration toward Ryan.

"If you feel the cold iron on your temple, you are dead before you have your hands up. Those who attack us are professionals, Hawk", he said. "Even as a driver you are always on the line of fire. And you will take you and the passengers and get out of there. I'll teach you how. Are you afraid of dying?"

Ryan answered without hesitation: "I am already."

Slater's eyes narrowed, but he didn't ask. Slater was an experienced professional through and through. Ryan was an attentive student. In theoretical lessons, he quickly grasped tactics. He learned about the vulnerable areas on his opponent's body and the diverse possibilities of self-defense and attack. Step by step he learned to fall in practice. He had done this many times from a horse to avoid serious injuries. When Ryan finally knew how to use his feet, arms and hands, the men were allowed to compete against each other. Although Ryan still had to take enough punches, he became increasingly faster in his actions and developed his own fighting style. Slater was pleased with him. At the same time Ryan's driver training was running. With some of his skills, he actually amazed his instructor. Nevertheless, Ryan learned a few valuable tricks from Slaters experience. Over time he had become more familiar to him. The training was based on this kind of trust and mutual respect. Ryan liked that and motivated him.

At the shooting range Ryan get another, older instructor. The state-of-the-art weapons that he got his hands on were in no way comparable to father's hunting rifle. Ryan was unable to hide his amazement. To hit the target with these rifles was easier. However, the targets went even further away from him. No problem as long they stood. Later when they moved, even quickly, it became more difficult. Especially with the pistol Ryan never had held in his hands. Shooting training was on the program every day and he scored more hits every day. The eyes were sharp and the hand was calm. It was only in the last third of the time that Slater took Ryan under his wing. He explained the principles of fighting the silent knife to Ryan before the two men went on to practice. Slater showed Ryan various techniques and finally let him do them. Ryan was obviously amazed when Slater said: "First you need to know how to handle the knife."

Ryan couldn't resist a smile. He really had some experience in handling a knife. Slater nodded recognizing when Ryan taught him the push from below. Skillful and quick from a safe position.

"OK. And now show me the push from above and then the change of handle."

Ryan tried, but Slater was faster and knocked the knife out of his hand. On the second try, Slater disarmed Ryan before he hit and went a few steps further. He put the blade to Ryan's throat. When he felt the cold metal on his skin, he surrendered to Slater. Slater laughed.

"You are dead. The principle is that the blade cuts your throat in a fraction of a second before you can make a loud noise."

Then Slater let go and gave the knife back to Ryan.

"OK. Show me again, but slower."

Slater did so and started again.

"The important thing is the technology and the quick reaction. You always have to expect that your opponent could be better. So never underestimate him, even if it seems harmless to you. That can be fatal. The rest is intuition, high school and to focusable."

Ryan nodded. He understood.

The daily trainings quickly improved him to a

professional in all disciplines. Slater called it 'the crash course'.

In the past six months, Ryan had actually learned his lessons, even swimming. He was in no way inferior to his teacher. A week before the deadline, at the end of June, Taylor contacted Major Cox to inquire about the current situation.

"Your Hawk is ready, Lieutenant Colonel Taylor. I have no concerns."

"I like to hear that, Major Cox. I urgently need the man back", Cox heard the voice at the other end.

The young major leaned back and played with his pen.

"In the next week he will have to prove himself. I won't let him go until he doesn't pass his exam. You will have to be patient for so long."

"I appreciate your work. That's why I sent him to you. He will pass the exam, I'm sure."

"We'll see", answered Cox. "I inform you immediately, Lieutenant Colonel Taylor", replied Cox and hung up.

Then he got up and looked out the window. He narrowed his eyes slightly. This Lakota would have to compete against him.

*****

On the second day of the following week, Ryan had to report to Slater after the morning swim training. Even though Ryan knew that everything depended on the next exam, he was extremely relaxed. He had trained, learned and strengthened himself mentally for six months. It was summer. Heat and dust dominated the

Nevada military training base and demanded from the young men everything.

Ryan had learned to trust, especially himself. He was ready for the exam that was the start of his new path.

"At your command, Sir!" Ryan nodded.

Then he climbed into the jeep with Slater. The men drove south across the large military compound. The practice area was located there. An observation vehicle appeared. Slater reported to Ryan that a major general, strange to him, wanted to follow the maneuver with binoculars. Ryan was supposed to make his way to the old buildings of a former military airport, where a limousine was parked. He should use them to escape. A unit of the base, trained shadow wolves, would prevent him from doing so. Ryan should not be seen during the entire operation, and he was given no weapons. Ryan confirmed to Slater that he understood. Then Slater exposed the Lakota in the site. Ryan ducked and ran to a dry stream bed, on the banks of which were some shrubs. There he found cover from the observational eyes.

Hours passed. The sun was approaching the zenith. The heat shimmered above the floor. Ryan honored his instructors. The strange general stood on the observation car. He used binoculars. His eyes searched the area very carefully. Every now and then he thought he saw movement. Hot wind blew his neck. When the general thought he had heard a click behind him, he turned around, startled. But only a swirling gust of wind blew fine grains of sand into his eyes. He swore softly as his eyes blurred in tears. For a long time he couldn't see anything.

Meanwhile, Ryan had crawled under the sparsely grown

bushes, discovered some shadow wolves and had used the course of the creek bed to remain undetected. For a short time he had even buried himself in a sand bed to be invisible. The hot air burned to the lungs and relentless thirst tormented Ryan. The grains of sand crunched in his mouth. Ryan made slow progress. There was no time limit, but before sunset he should be with the limousine in front of the office building of the base. Ryan could see them. His goal was within reach. There was hardly any cover to get there. Ryan could imagine that the shadow wolves who were supposed to catch him had the highest attention to this piece of land. Ryan considered. He waited patiently because he only wanted to attract one of his opponents and not the whole pack of wolves. Time and space were insignificant. The sun was at the zenith. There was hardly any shade. At some point Ryan felt the presence of a human body. He listened, but it was silent. Ryan felt the dangerous closeness. His inner voice warned him. He lay under a dry shrub, right next to a stone about two feet high, and buried his hand in the sand. Ryan had no intention of dodging. His heart was going fast, as were his breaths. Tiny pebbles crunched barely audibly under his boots. The man was standing right in front of him, pointing the gun at the Lakota. Ryan reacted quickly because no warning call from his opponent was allowed to betray him. His hand flew up and threw the sand into the man's eyes. At the same moment he tore him off his feet. The surprised man fell blindly to the ground while Ryan snatched the rifle from his hand. No shot should betray him. Ryan hit the man unconscious. Then he pulled his black balaclava over his head and slipped into the opponent's jacket. It all happened in just a few seconds.

Then the apparently lifeless body was left alone.

A short time later, Ryan reached his destination, the limousine. As expected, it was closed. Lying on the floor, Ryan let his gaze wander across the floor of the car and palpated it. He grinned, as he carefully took a tiny piece of metal. He thought of Slater's words about the major's preferences.

Ryan grinned.

The magnetic bomb was smaller than a matchbox and responded to shocks. The fourth man was Cox himself.

A second limousine pulled up and stopped right behind the one Ryan was with. He rolled over in front of the car and placed the small magnetic bomb on the floor. Even before the doors opened, Ryan rolled to the rear of the second car unnoticed. In a cold sweat he was gasping for air. Under no circumstances was he allowed to remove the balaclava. So Ryan was indistinguishable from the shadow wolves. Cox got out with one of his men. Ryan took a deep breath and held it for a moment. Ryan let the air out of his lungs very slowly. Cox would making himself a target for long. Both men went to the front car. Ryan grinned when the men couldn't find anyone. They actually seemed a little disappointed about it. Ryan had two opponents who wanted to prevent him from taking the car. He had to be quick.

Ryan aimed the training weapon he had captured at Cox's companion. He had to notice the dull pressure when the beam of red color hit him. In fact he cursed and immediately surrendered. That was the rule. Cox now knew exactly where the Lakota was. While the hit man lay on the floor and play dead, Cox immediately took cover.

Even Slater waited with excitement the outcome of the

event. The strange general searched the area with his binoculars. Nothing happened for a long time.
It was quiet.

*****

Cox carefully crawled along the floor. He used the limousine and the body of the man who pretended to be dead as cover. Seconds later, Cox winced when someone suddenly grabbed him from behind in a stranglehold. Cox felt painfully the hard knee in his back and at the same moment the cold metal of a knife blade on his throat.
"Game over! You are done Major General", he heard Hawk's soft voice on his ear.
The Lakota had emerged silently from nowhere and haven't hesitated for a sec-ond. Cox didn't stand a chance and surrendered.
"So far only a few have managed to do this. Maybe a handful", he growled.
"Okay Sir. See you later", said Ryan.
In three or four seconds, Ryan opened the door of the Limousine. Cox couldn't resist and turned on his back. He didn't want to miss the game.
Ryan started the engine and dashed off, a cloud of dust behind him. The whirled up desert dust sank slowly.
Cox waited in vain for the smoke from the magnetic bomb. He pulled the black balaclava off his head and stood up. He grimaced in appreciation as he looked behind the fleeing car. Despite his defeat, Cox maintained his stance. After all, he was proud of his

protégée because for him the success of Hawks was a confirmation of good work.

At the request of the foreign major general, Cox immediately ordered the Lakota over to him. Cox frankly showed Ryan his appreciation. The strange general major nodded approvingly and eyed the young Lakota in a manner as if he were a tailor who would have to adjust a suit on him.

Ryan grinned triumphantly. He had passed a difficult test, defeated professionals and was rightly delighted to be recognized.

The three men were standing by the parked limousines when Slater came up to them. The other observers were waiting in some distance. They used the break for a cigarette. Soft voices reached Ryan's ears. Finally Major Cox looked at the clock.

"Let's go back, Hawk. You take our guest, Major General Randall, to the base."

"All right, Sir."

Ryan opened the rear car door. Randall got in.

Ryan noticed that he was still watching him closely while Slater took place at the passenger seat.

Ryan started the engine and droved slowly. He looked in the rearview mirror and watched the car behind him. Major Cox himself was at the wheel. Ryan suppressed a grin. As soon as the limousine with Cox was rolled forward, a thick cloud of smoke rose and completely blocked the view.

Both limousines stopped immediately. Cox jumped out of the car and screamed angrily: "Damned red bastard!"

Ryan grinned broadly. Even Slater had to laugh.

"What up?", asked Randell.

"The car behind us just exploded, Sir", Slater replied

calmly, crossing his arms.
The general turned and looked out the rear window. Then he said: "How lucky to be in this car."

*****

The summer sun shone over the US Air Force Base Rapid City. In the midday hours the heat shimmered over the asphalt. Only a single jeep rolled over it slowly. The steel eagles stood abandoned in a long line. There was a deceptive calm as if you were having a siesta.
The young man who was polishing the headlights of a black Chrysler with a blue cloth was doing well. It was pleasantly shady in the vehicle hall. Sweat dripped from the forehead and nose. Now and then he wiped it with the handkerchief. Music sounded from a radio. The big, bearded man sang. Hardly anyone in the workshop shared Baxter Goodman's love of country music. But nobody dared to drop a comment about it. Baxter was now the undisputed boss in this workshop and responsible for all Air Force Base vehicles. The black Chrysler shone perfect. There was nothing more that Baxter should have polished. He stood up, crossed his arms and smiled in satisfaction. The one who got this car had every reason to be happy. This car was something special in every respect. Even Baxter had been amazed at things that he had never seen and that he didn't even know existed. Secretly he couldn't wait to instruct the future driver. His heart leapt with joy. But he had to wait at least three more days. Baxter checked his pants and shoes. All clean. He was satisfied and picked up the key.

The car had to go back to the garage. When Baxter was sitting in the driver's seat, he was enthusiastic again. He dreamed a little and spoke gently to the car as if it were a declaration of love. Finally he put the car in reverse and looked in the rearview mirror. There was one with one's legs apart behind him, in the middle of the exit.
"Another darn rubbernecker", Baxter growled.
He grimaced and waited for a moment. The man didn't think of going aside. Annoyed Baxter pressed the horn. Just a short push.
"Man!", he swore. "Are you blind and deaf?"
The guy didn't move.
Baxter couldn't know what rank the man had behind him. He decided to get out. The respect for the arena was too big, to risk to rub somebody the wrong way. He was glad he had been left alone since Ryan left. So Baxter got out, put on a charming smile, and went up to the man. The sunlight dazzled Baxter's eyes. The man had the sun in his back. He only recognized a dark shape. The man was wearing a basic uniform and had his cap tucked under his arm.
"Sir!", Baxter started.
It was only when the man came two steps closer that Baxter recognized him. The fat man's mouth remained open. He had been speechless for a long time and was looking for words. The man grinned amused.
Baxter cleared his throat.
"Do I have to call you Sergeant now?"
Then he blew up his cheeks and snorted.
"Man! Ryan! You wouldn't believe how happy I am."
"Hello Baxter Bear. How are you?"
"Well now, dazzling!"
He grabbed his friend with his paws and uninhibitedly

hugged him. Then he pushed him away to look at him.

"Damned! Do I have to salute a master sergeant now?"

Ryan grinned and nodded. Then he pointed his head toward the black car.

"Is it that?"

"Yes. Your jet without wings", laughed Baxter.

Ryan stepped closer to look at the car.

"And? What do you say?", asked Baxter expectantly.

"Looks good."

"Only good? This is...."

"I will tell you if it's more than good when I have driven it."

"OK. Tell me! How was it in the south? There are great rumors ahead of you. It is said that you threw them all out of the game and blew up the major with his buddies. So they probably wanted to get rid of you quickly and sent you back three days earlier", Baxter smiled.

"Cox refrained from further tests when I shredded his dummies on the shooting range the same day. He probably seeks revenge and he knew my weak spot exactly. With a combat helicopter, he let me fly to Canada at sunrise yesterday and threw me into the Hudson Bay. I grew up in dusty prairie. Baxter, I could never swim, but now I can and I survived."

Baxter shook his head.

"I don't know who is crazier. This cox or you?"

Ryan grinned.

"Give me the key to my new war pony", he said.

Baxter grinned too and handed him the key.

Ryan initially sat in the driver's seat and looked around. It smelled of leather, new plastic and chemistry. The cockpit truly resembled a modern jet.

"The gear lever is brighter so you can find it better, just

like the cockpit ledge", Baxter joked. "The baby has automatic transmission, four hundred and sixty horsepower, anti-lock and stabilization system. On-board computer with military GPS, headlights with which you can track the mice down to their holes. An air conditioning system that immediately filters the cigarette smoke out of the room air. You've already seen the tinted windows all around. The best is yet to come, my friend. They are bulletproof, just like the whole car down to the tires, almost anyway. The tires have always been the weak point. But with these you can get ahead, at least out of the line of fire. There is also a spare wheel for emergencies. You will hardly need that. Use this button to separate the back of the car in case someone is going on and on to your ears."

Baxter was completely in his element and glowing with zeal.

"There is a button in the back for what your ears should not hear or what your eyes should not see."

"Come on! Get in", Ryan said.

Baxter hesitated.

"Shouldn't you instruct me?", asked Ryan.

"Didn't I just do that?"

"No. I have absolutely no idea. I insist on practical instruction."

Baxter was obviously delighted when he climbed into the Chrysler with Ryan and slammed the passenger door.

Ryan started the engine and accelerated.

*****

Randell and Taylor stood at the window and saw the black sedan drive past.

"Yes, this is the guy from Nevada. I watched him on-site. Slater was very taken with him. He screwed General Cox."

Randell couldn't help but grin.

"With him and the car you are as safe as in the lap of the gods. So I had the right instinct to choose the crazy Indsman for it." Taylor cleared his throat. "Does Hawk know you're his commander?"

"Not yet", Randell replied.

"In exactly twenty-three minutes he has an appointment in your office."

Taylor looked at Randell in surprise.

"I know that your tenure starts here in just three days. Why this secretiveness?"

"I'm excited about his face when he sees me here."

Taylor shook his head blankly.

"Silly. Pardon me."

"I don't like to buy a pig in a poke. Why do you think I was in the training camp?"

"Because you trust nothing and nobody. Not even me", Taylor answered with a sharp undertone. "You will have to trust him."

Randell smiled in silence.

*****

Ryan was thrilled with his new car. The Chrysler was a comfortable bundle of energy.

"I've never driven anything like it. Not even in Nevada",

he enthused.

Baxter grinned triumphantly.

"All the frills in there. Now you know where our tax money stays. Maybe you should elope with the car and sell it", Baxter suggested amused.

"No, my friend. I prefer to drive it myself and they even pay me for it! The one I am supposed to drive with must have many enemies. He seems very careful and has thought of everything."

"Then the guy won a lottery with you and the car, I would say."

"A real war pony, Baxter. I will have a lot of fun with it."

"It's light years away from your Pontiac", laughed Baxter.

"Hm", Ryan did, got out and turned to go.

"Hey Ryan! That should be a joke", Baxter called after him.

He felt like he drop a brick, but he didn't know which one.

*****

The young master sergeant knocked on Taylor's office door on time. When asked to do so, Ryan came in, greeted and took the hat under his arm. Ryan looked at the man at the desk with no movement. He cleverly hid his astonishment that Major General Randell was sitting at Taylor's desk.

Randell, however, seemed a little disappointed.

"Sit down!", he ordered.

Ryan obeyed.

"Sergeant Hawk, you are now my personal driver and

you will be responsible for my safety in every way. Are you ready?"

"Sir, yes Sir."

"I mean, at any time and under all circumstances and are you ready to risk your own life?"

Randell spoke slowly, emphasizing each word.

Ryan's heart pounded quickly and hard on the chest, causing the reverberations to beat in his head. There was no time for self-doubt and withdrawal was impossible. The young sergeant looked directly at the major general. With his white hair, he looked older than he was. Randell's brown eyes were fixed on Ryan. He expected an answer. Randell's eyes were honest. The white beard, on the other hand, reminded Ryan of General Custer's picture. He would protect him under all circumstances and risk his own life for it.

"Sir, yes Sir", answered Ryan.

"Al right, Sergeant Hawk. Than we are a team."

Randell smiled in satisfaction.

"You are personally subordinate to me. I, Major General John J. Randell, and only me, are your sole commander. All orders are given by me without exception. No one else has to order you. Should you experience any difficulties, only refer to your command. There is no exception! Did you understand all of this?"

"Sir, yes Sir", answered Ryan.

Randell couldn't contain his grin.

"Our assignment starts on Monday at six o'clock in the morning. You have three days."

Randell paused.

"Until then you are on leave. Now go on, enjoy yourself. I can't promise you when it will be next."

"Sir! Thanks, Sir", Ryan replied.

He still felt Randell's staring eyes on him. Maybe the Major General was looking forward to an emotion, maybe joy or a smile? None of that. Ryan had learned to hide his feelings from strangers. Randell seemed a little irritated. Finally he said, motionless: "That was all. You're dismissed."
Ryan got up, took his hand to his head, and saluted correctly before leaving the office without another word. Randell's eyes followed him. He shook his head barely noticeably.

*****

Ryan went straight to his quarter and pulled his bag out of the cupboard. Minutes later his uniform disappeared into it. He was wearing his own clothes and sunglasses on his nose. He hung the black bag over his shoulders and played with the key of his Pontiac. With lengthy steps he left the site and walked along the paved road towards the parking lot. The old Pontiac had to wait a long time. As hardly to be expected, he replied to Ryan's attempt to start the engine with only a short "click". Ryan heard a "damn!" coming over his lips. The battery had no energy left for a spark. He had no choice but to ask Baxter for help. Ryan ran back to the workshop. Baxter wasn't alone, but he immediately raised his head when he saw the shadow at the gate. He stared at Ryan in surprise. In his eyes there was a question. Baxter went up to him.
"Hey, you look like a civilian. Did they kick you out?" Baxter asked softly so only Ryan could understand.

"No. Vacation. I want to go home. The Pontiac battery is dead. Will you give me a jump start?"

"Go. I'll follow you unobtrusively."

When Ryan reached his car, a black jeep came up to him. He stopped right in front of his car. Baxter jumped out with two jumper cables in his hand. Without a word he opened the hood of the Jeep and Ryan the hood of the Pontiac. While Baxter clamped the cables, without looking at his friend, he said: "The little one is grieved. He was alone too long. An invaluable collector's item."

Baxter kept talking because Ryan didn't say anything.

"You have to know every car has its soul. I talk to them and sometimes they answer me. The Commander and I get along very well", Baxter laughed with amusement. "Your Pontiac just doesn't understand why you abandoned him for so long. Tell him when you go home. Where are you actually at home?"

Ryan grinned.

"Is this your Commander?"

"Yes, and he's damn clingy. Try to start!"

The Pontiac started immediately.

Baxter removed the clips and packed his jumper cables. Then he slammed the hood.

Ryan stayed in his car and lowered the window.

"Just don't let him go out again! Have a good trip and nice vacation", said Baxter and looked directly at the Lakota.

"Pine Ridge Reservation. A Ranch. Near Potato Creek."

Baxter nodded, got into the Commander and cleared the way.

Ryan jumped on the gas.

Chapter 3
Endurance test

The sun was already setting towards the west. No breath of wind grazed the country. That was unusual. The sluggish silence looked almost scary. John Black Hawk crouched on the wooden bench in front of the house and stuffed his pipe. His gaze slid across the valley, over the creek and finally got stuck on the stallion. Only pulling on his pipe sometimes released him from his stiffness. The black horse tugged at the green and yellow stalks that grow on the dry property. It was hot and it hadn't rained for a long time.

Finally the stallion paused, raised his head and pricked his ears up. He kept looking in the direction of the dirt road. John also held the pipe without pulling on it. He also listened and looked in the same direction. The black horse whinnied and pranced excitedly along the fence. John suddenly felt his inner unrest with the sound of the coming car. The car stopped in front of the house. John couldn't believe his eyes. His ears and feelings hadn't deceived him. His heart suddenly pounded faster. He had waited for this moment for a long time. The worrying features on his face relaxed. John pulled on his pipe and watched the young man get out of the Pontiac. He seemed at the same time strange yet familiar to him. He too had changed in the past ten months. John's eyes follow Ryan as he came up the stairs to the porch.

Ryan stopped in front of him and smiled. Then he sent a wistful look to his black horse.

"Good evening, father."

"So there you are ", replied John, while he eyed his son, and pulled the pipe again.

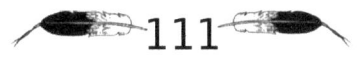

"Yes father. Here I am. Are you doing good?"
John nodded.
Ryan waited.
Father didn't seem to say anything else. Maybe he couldn't. John's eyes gleamed treacherously.
Ryan looked at his black horse and smiled. Finally he went inside.

Anny Black Hawk was in the kitchen, drying the dishes. She dropped the bowl when her son suddenly appeared.
"Ryan!"
Anny shouted stunned. Tears shot into her eyes. Then she hugged her son.
"How are you?", she whispered.
"Good Mom. And you?"
"Doc Even says well."
"And you?" Ryan smiled.
"Better. Did they give you spare time?"
"I'm on vacation until Monday at six o'clock in the morning. I will disappear on Sunday night."
When mother let go of him, Ryan pulled the envelope with the money out of his pocket and handed it to the mother. She nodded her thanks and put the money in the kitchen cupboard.
"If I can't come, I'll ask Carry to bring it to you. I will get more from next month."
"Thank you."
Anny smiled bravely. It looked sad.
"Where's Granny"
"She went to her husband's grave."
Ryan nodded, took off his shirt and went to the bathroom and came out a little later.
John was still sitting on the bench. He had tapped out his

pipe. Ryan joined him.

"How are you?", he asked.

John looked at Ryan. A smile appeared on his face. He looked quite satisfied. Countless wrinkles played around his eyes.

"Good. I am happy that you are here. And I'm happy that our horses are here too."

"Me too, father, me too."

"You look thin, son. Don't they give you anything to eat at the Air Force?"

"A little bit. Their hunting rifles are not as good as yours."

John laughed softly.

"Are you satisfied with your job there?"

"The training wasn't an easy ride. A rodeo. However, my job doesn't start until Monday."

"I'm not going to ask what you can't tell anyone anyway. But I want to tell you that you are my son. Whatever it was. You should know that I am proud of you."

Ryan swallowed.

Father's words stirred up his innermost. He had just gave back the face to his son. With shiny eyes, Ryan pressed his lips hard so that it hurt. Then Ryan nodded.

"Thank you father", he finally said softly. "My heart is with you, the family and the horses. No matter where I am in the other world, Lakota hemaca. I'm a Lakota. I`ll never be anything else."

John nodded.

"Look at the crazy black horse. We thought it was dead, but when he heard the Pontiac ...", John laughed softly. "The old stallion is acting like a bronco."

"Maybe I should go to the rodeo with him. I'll find out soon", Ryan grinned and got up.

John leaned against the porch railing and watched Ryan go.

Ryan went straight to his stallion to greet him. Kola jumped along the fence and neighed. Horse and rider exuberant and extensive greeted each other. A little later he had bridled the horse.
"Are you taking us with you, big brother?" shouted Robert.
Ryan turned in surprise. He had been so absorbed in his work that he hadn't heard his brothers come. Robert was sitting on a chestnut mare and Andy was next to him with his pinto mare.
"Why not?"
Ryan rejoiced and jumped on the black horse. He was prancing impatiently. Finally he dared the first jumps. Soon the three horses galloped across the dry ground. The brothers laughed happily. The horses were racing. The hooves thundered on the dry ground and whirled up dust. Suddenly Ryan stopped the horse and turned. Sometimes he hunted one, sometimes the other brother, for pleasure. They skillfully avoided each other. The horses enjoyed their game. Finally, Robert and Andy teamed up and tried to force Ryan to give up. Ryan jokingly dropped from the horse and lay on his back. He laughed.
"I surrender!"
The two younger brothers jumped off their horses. They immediately began to graze while Robert and Andy settled in with their older brother.
"The horses have stayed. It's good. How are you?", asked Ryan.
"Good. I can drive with my father's pickup truck and I

can handle it well", Robert answered proudly.
"If you want, you can drive the Pontiac while I'm here."
Robert was obviously happy.
Because Andy was silent. Ryan turned to him.
"Nishunkala, your little brother, grew up. Is he still so clingy?"
"Yes", answered Andy.
Then he had to smile.
"He'll stay with you, little brother", Ryan assured.
"With the money you sold yourself?", Andy asked skeptically.
"No Andy. From now on I have a real job and the money I get for it I will have to earn hard. One day I want to come home and run the ranch."
Andy was silent. He seemed to be considering.
Ryan got up and went to his black horse. Kola lifted his head, snorted contentedly and let himself be petted.
"What do you have to do for them to give you so many dollars?", Andy finally asked.
Ryan grinned at him.
"Drive a car."
"At the Air Force?", Andy asked incredulously.
"Can't they do that themselves?", Robert asked in astonishment.
"Doesn't look like. They definitely need a Lakota", Ryan laughed.
Robert and Andy were laughing too. Exuberant and happy, like they used to do many times before. Space and time were lost in it. It is a good sign for the future. The wolves would not dare return to fetch the horses.

*****

The following day Ryan worked the whole morning at the ranch. There was a lot to fix. House and shed showed clear traces of the limited possibilities of the recent past. In the afternoon, Ryan handed the Pontiac's key to Robert.

"Hoka hey! Here we go!", Ryan said. "Show me what you're made of!"

Robert's joy was unmistakable. Ryan climbed into the car on the passenger side. Robert jumped on the gas. Robert had actually become a good driver. Ryan watched him closely, but didn't say a word at first.

"What do you think?", Robert finally asked.

"Good! What am I going to teach you?"

"The perfect forehand twist, for example", grinned Robert.

Ryan laughed.

"That can't be that hard, brother. One of the easiest exercises. You accelerate. Pull the handbrake with your right hand while pulling the steering wheel with the other. You have to have nerves and the feeling for it, like riding a horse. If the processes do not work harmoniously, you overturn or slow down."

Robert looked challenging at Ryan.

"Do you want to say goodbye to your Pontiac?"

"Why? I have no intention of separating from him. Just do what I tell you."

"Okay", said Robert and hit the accelerator.

He followed Ryan's instructions exactly and also showed the necessary strength of nerve. The car turned and stopped in the opposite direction. Ryan nodded approvingly. After Robert had turned the Pontiac several times, Ryan showed his brother the rotation around the rear axle out of the reverse gear and the full turn. Robert

cried out in triumph and laughed proudly. The brothers did not return until evening. They both laughed as they went up the porch stairs. Ryan pulled out the cigarette box and held it out to Robert.
"Do you want one?"
"Thanks", he said, pulling out one.
Ryan lit it.
"I feel like you've never been away, brother. I wish you could stay."
Ryan pulled his cigarette in silence and slowly blew smoke through the narrow crack of his lips. Then he asked: "What happened to Sam?"
"I saw her at the post office four weeks ago. She's working there."
"Did she ask?"
"No."
"Did she find someone?"
"Don't know", Robert shrugged.
Ryan took a deep pull from the cigarette.
"What about our neighboring Ranch? Is McLaughleen still leaseholder?"
"No, he isn`t. He actually had to leave at the end of the year. Charles Windcoock is our neighbor. He breeds cattle. The buffalo is difficult and will take some time."
"Bad times for Red Eagle", Ryan grimaced.
"Since McLaughleen left, he seems to be feeling better, even though he is chewing on his defeat."
Ryan caught himself mocking the corner of his mouth. Maybe a hint of gloating.
"McLaughleen's good whiskey will be missing", Ryan said finally.
"I do not know what you can find on such stuff. It tastes awful", said Robert.

Ryan looked at Robert in surprise.

"Did you drink whiskey?"

"Tried. That was enough for me."

Ryan smiled a little predominant.

"Then you let yourself turn on the cheap booze. A really good Whiskey is not to be scoffed at."

Robert shook his head.

"Did you drink good Whiskey when you ...", Robert broke off.

"Yes, I tried that. Until I no longer knew my limits. The stuff is addictive and I finally poured everything into myself. I was afraid to get sober again. It's over. I haven't touched a drop for more than three years."

"I know. Now you despise the people who drink."

"I despised myself, Robert. I did so many crazy things when I was drunk and I might have gone the same way as Scott. Everyone has to find out for themselves. I was a bad role model for you and Andy."

"We never despised you. Maybe father. I was worried about you. But you were the best racer alongside Scott and respected in the clique. They listened to your words and people spoke of you."

Ryan took one last puff of the cigarette and stubbed it out. "If you want to listen to my words, brother, don't touch it."

Robert nodded.

"Don't you come in?", he asked, when Ryan played with the car key.

"Later. I have something to do."

*****

Samantha had already closed at the post office when an old, white-haired woman asked to write a letter for her. Samantha smiled gently and put her bag down again.
"That's all right. Sit down Inila."
The woman nodded her thanks and sat down.
"I'm able to write." She said. "But it's a letter to the Bureau of Indian Affairs."
"I'll help you", Samantha said gently.
She took a sheet of paper and the pen.
That evening Samantha left the post office an hour later than usual. When she turned to the street her limbs came to a halt. As if petrified she stopped. The blood suddenly shot hot through her body. Samantha's eyes stuck to the figure that was leaning against a Pontiac and smoking directly opposite the entrance. The figure wore a black cowboy hat and smiled at her. Samantha was unable to take the next step. Ryan stamped out the cigarette and came over to her.
"Hello, Samantha."
"Hello", Samantha replied softly.
Her voice hardly obeyed her.
"Can I take you anywhere?"
"Do you want to tear open old wounds?", she whispered.
"Sometimes it's easier than hush up."
"There is no future for the two of us, Ryan. Those were your words."
Samantha's rigid disappeared and went past him. She thought she could feel his eyes on her back. Her heart rushed and the blood was pulsating in the carotid artery. Out of the corner of her eye, Samantha watched Ryan get into the car and drive away. She felt like crying. Like a Robot she walked along the street. Less than five

minutes later a car stopped next to her.
"Hello Samantha! What are you still doing here?"
"I`m going home."
"Get in, or do you want to walk home?"
"Thanks Winona", Samantha replied absently and got into her friend's car.
"Did he run into you? They say he's back here."
"Who?" Samantha asked in surprise.
"Ryan Black Hawk, your heartbreaker. Does he want you back?"
"Stop that Winona! It's over. He's with the Air Force."
"Then you must have met his spirit the way you look", Winona smiled.
Samantha lowered the mirror of the sun visor and looked inside. Then she shrugged. Winona laughed and Samantha finally did too. They changed the subject. The sun sent its warm rays diagonally to earth. The moving shadows grew longer as the car parked at the entrance to Samantha Crying Crow's parents' house. Winona said goodbye and drove away.
Samantha walked briskly along the path to the house. As she was about to open the door, she heard a low voice behind her.
"Is the door still sticking?"
Samantha winced, turned and looked directly into his eyes. Heat suddenly shot through her body like an electric shock and took her breath away.
"You are crazy!", she hissed at Ryan.
"Do you have another man by your side?"
Ryan asked very directly.
Samantha swallowed, dodged his eyes, and hardly shook her head.
Ryan stopped asking. He tilted his head towards her and

Samantha felt his hands pull her body closer to his. Without will she let it happen. When her lips burned on hers, she felt dizzy. Finally she wrapped her arms around him, the man she loved, and held him tight. Breathing heavily, Ryan pulled away from her mouth and looked around. Without further ado he took the young woman in his arms and carried her to his car.

"They will have seen us", Samantha feared quietly.

Ryan didn't answer and drove on undeterred. Less than ten minutes later he turned off the street. He parked the Pontiac at the foot of a steep slope. With a strange smile and a strange shine in his eyes, he took Samantha back to his arms. He bypassed the steep slope. The path led up, past pine trees, buffalo berries and white stones. The wind blew into their faces and played with Samantha's hair. Her weight didn't seem to matter at all. She didn't dare to say one out loud. In a hollow on the plateau, Ryan put her down gently. It smelled of fresh earth and pine needles. Ryan threw his shirt on the floor before settling down. Wordlessly they merged in their embrace and an infinite kiss that left no doubt. When Ryan started to undress Samantha, she trembled.

"I'm afraid."

"I protect you. Nothing can happen", Ryan whispered to her.

"And you are sure?"

He laughed softly. "Certainly."

"And if I have a baby?"

"Then I'll marry you both", Ryan said firmly.

Samantha sighed.

Ryan smiled.

Samantha couldn't escape him. She didn't want it. It was too late for that. She trusted him. He stroked her bare

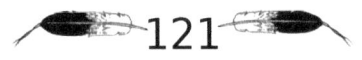

skin. She contracted under his touch. Ryan touched her breast. Samantha's slender legs wrapped around his waist. He breathed faster. When Samantha finally felt him inside, she closed her eyes. The heat of her bodies grew in rhythm with her movements. Both panted. At first slowly, then faster, the waves crashed through their bodies until they finally exploded like the surf of the ocean on the cliffs. Roaring and wild. Panting, they surrendered to their deep feelings. Only slowly did the blurry images begin to clear before Samantha's eyes.

The serious face of the man she loved so much appeared right in front of her. He eyed her as if he wanted to memorize every inch of her naked body. Then a smile appeared on Ryan's face. Beads of sweat had formed on his forehead. With the setting sun, the shadows of dawn came up. The horizon turned blood red as if it were on fire too. The sun finally dipped behind the ridge of hills like a fireball and took the colors of the day with it. The beginning of the night brought hardly any refreshment. The two human figures lay closely entwined on the hill, under the protection of the pine trees, and gazed silently up at the starry sky.

*****

He only came home with the sunrise. Ryan's last day of vacation came. Churned up inside, he crept into his bed and fell asleep exhausted. His last thought had been Samantha. He got up tired and powerless after a few hours. Ryan didn't let anything show. Nobody asked. Grandmother Lucy smiled meaningfully and mysteriously at him. Her grandson avoided this smile. Finally he tacitly packed his bag with the few things he would hardly need. That evening, Ryan tossed his small black travel bag into the trunk, which seemed almost lost. Robert appeared behind him as he slammed the trunk lid.

"Can we do another trip before you leave?"

Ryan grinned and threw the key to him.

"It is yours."

Robert stared stunned at his brother.

"Are you serious?", he asked skeptically.

"What I say I mean. He'll be standing around in the parking lot for far too long and blame me if I can't take care of him. With you he is in better hands. You bring me to Air Force Base and take him back."

Robert's eyes lit up when he was still shaking his head in disbelief.

"Okay, Ryan. Hecetu", he replied.

"But how do you want to get back home?"

"No worry. When the time comes I will be home."

Ryan laughed.

*****

About an hour before midnight, the Pontiac drove to the Air Force Base car park in Rapid City. Ryan himself drove the last stretch, perhaps to say goodbye to the car. Then the brothers got out. That evening there was exceptionally busy flight operations. Robert stopped and watched the jets taking off one behind the other. Ryan leaned against the Pontiac and pulled a cigarette out of a box. The deafening noise temporarily swallowed each of their words so that they were silent.

While Ryan was smoking and also watching the plane, he noticed a black Jeep Commander pulling up. He stopped right behind the Pontiac.

Ryan grinned.

Baxter got out and greeted the two young men.

"Hi there! What are you doing here so early?", Baxter asked.

"Withdrawal symptoms", Ryan replied. "And you?"

"I fled", Baxter growled.

"Olivia Goodman had invited her church chorister aunties. That is hard limit. I scrubbed myself up." Then he laughed.

Ryan offered him a cigarette. Baxter took one.

"Did you bring us reinforcements?", asked the Grizzly.

Robert eyed the stranger unobtrusively.

"This is my brother, Robert Black Hawk, Indian Cowboy and new owner of the Pontiac. He knows how to use it better than me in the coming time", said Ryan.

"Glad to meet you, my friend's brother. I'm Baxter Goodman, a mechanic, twenty-four, single, homeless and currently asylum-seeker with the Air Force."

Robert smiled.

"You're just as much a chatterbox as your big brother. He wanted to strangle me after the first half hour."

Baxter giggled and pulled the cigarette twice in a row.

"Well. If the Pontiac is causing you any problems, I can help you. Just call me."

The big bearded man spoke directly to Robert and gave him a business card with his cell phone number.

Robert nodded.

"Thank you."

The peculiar strange man seemed to mean it honestly.

With a grin, Ryan stubbed out his cigarette and took his bag out of the car.

"Toksa mishunkala."

"Aho, bro", replied Robert and looked his brother in the eye as he thanked him: "pilamaya yelo."

"Tokashni, hecetu yelo", Ryan replied, which meant something like: *Okay, no cause*.

Baxter watched the two skeptically and shook his head like a freshly bathed dog.

"Yelo what?"

"I'll explain that to you later", Ryan reassured him.

"Bye Robert. I wish you a junk and wrinkle-free flight home!" Baxter called to the young man and raised his hand in greeting.

Grinning, Robert climbed into the Pontiac and rejoined the greeting. The white man at the side of his big brother seemed extremely strange to him.

Ryan watched the Pontiac until it was no longer visible. Then he went in with Baxter.

*****

The fresh morning air gently stroked the brown skin and revitalized the senses. Ryan took a deep breath as he waited in front of the main building in the black limousine. He had got out and was walking up and down a few steps. They had given him a new uniform and a stack of new shirts. Ryan, however, could not make friends with the tie. He kept turning his head to the side or trying to loosen it with his fingers. The feeling that this throttled his throat remained. Ryan took a few deep breaths. The light of the sun was reflected on the paint. Ryan was wearing aviator glasses. He immediately took a stance and gave the correct military salute. Randell greeted back.

"Well, let's get started now, Master Sergeant", he said, getting into the limousine.

He took his briefcase with him to the back seat. Ryan slammed the door from the outside and got in too. He waited in silence. Randell was already rummaging around in a pile of papers.

"Go ahead", he commanded his driver after a few minutes.

"Sir. Where Sir?"

"Denver, Colorado."

Ryan started the engine.

Why didn't Randell fly? he wondered.

He wouldn't ask him.

For hours Ryan drove silently south across Nebraska. Randell's trip to a friend in Big Springs made it dusk when the big city of Denver appeared before them.

"Park the car in the hotel's underground car park and come to the reception immediately", the order was.

Randell got out and was accompanied to the hotel by a bell boy. He carried the suitcase himself. Ryan found what he thought was a suitable place in the spacious underground car park. He stopped briefly at the elevator next to the stairs. Ryan chose the stairs. In the foyer, he finally reported to his boss, Major General Randell. Meanwhile the Major had the keys for two rooms. He gave one of these to his driver with the words: "The rooms are right next to each other and are connected by a door. Let's go."

Randell went on talking.

"Should it be necessary for any reason, I call you. Otherwise we'll see each other tomorrow after breakfast. Exactly thirteen after eight you drive up the car."

"Sir. Yes, Sir", Ryan confirmed.

Then the two men climbed into the elevator.

The door closed automatically. With an ample stride, Randell finally headed for his room on the eleventh floor. He seemed to know his way around well.

"Oh Hawk. I almost forgot. Come in for a moment", Randell said, inserting the card into the lock. It sounded like a request, not an order. Ryan followed him into the spacious and comfortably furnished room.

Randell put the mysterious case on the table and opened it. He took out a small black box.

"Have a look at this. Do you know anything like that?"

"A mobile phone Sir. Yes."

"OK. Always carry it with you. It is our most important connection. My number is already saved. It belongs to you." Randell cleared his throat and tried to look in Ryan's eyes.

"I don't trust anything or anyone. My experience has taught me enough. I will have to trust them. Don't disappoint me."

Ryan nodded when he replied: "Sir. You can count on it, Sir."

He pocketed the phone.

"Do you allow me to go, Sir?"

"Yes of course. If you want to eat something, let it count on the bill."

"Thanks Sir."

With these words Ryan turned and left the room. The adjoining room was smaller, but no less comfortable.

Ryan looked around. Even a new toothbrush lay on the console above the sink. He freed himself from the annoying tie and the uniform jacket. He got a chilled water bottle from the bar and half drank it in one go. Then he threw himself on the broad bed with the new phone in hand. He had quickly studied the functions and settings and set up everything according to his wishes. In second place, right after Randell's phone number, he had saved Baxter's number. After all, he was in the service of the US Air Force too, so Ryan had no concerns. He called him.

"Hello my friend!"

Ryan heard Baxter's surprised voice. "How are you?"

"Good. The Chief gave me a new cell phone so I'm permanently accessible", Ryan laughed.

"So? So he keeps you on a long leash. Beautiful. I'm glad to hear from you!", said Baxter amused. "Are you sitting in the Chrysler and be bored?"

"No. I am currently lying on a large, soft bed in a very classy and comfortable hotel room. I even have a bar with ice-cold drinks."

"I must have done something damn wrong", Baxter growled.

Ryan grinned.

"Okay, see you next time, Mato.

"Yes, Yes. See you soon. Have fun."

Ryan placed the cell phone next to him and reached for the remote control from the television. Then he grabbed an apple out of the fruit bowl and took a bite with relish.

*****

Ryan waited three hours the other day in the limousine in front of a glassed-in convention center. Already he had read the newspapers he had taken out of the hotel in the morning. His order was to wait here and stop with the car. He got out and went around the car once. Then he lit a cigarette and leaned against the door. Ryan had barely done three pulls, Randell came with a stranger about the same age. Ryan immediately stubbed out the cigarette and opened the back doors. The two men got in without a word.

"To Buckley Air Force Base", the stranger ordered.
Ryan looked in the rearview mirror.
"Sir?", asked he.
"Well, go ahead. Time is running."
The stranger looked a little nervous.
A smile appeared on Randell's face, if not a mocking one. He crossed his arms.
"Without a command from Major General Randell, the car will not move from here."
The stranger became restless.
"All right Randell. Would kindly give your driver the order to take us to the base."
"Us? You, Conell", Randell emphasized and laughed.
"Okay, Sergeant Hawk, bring us back to the base. The airplain should start in thirty minutes and a delay would be a medium-sized catastrophe. Can you handle it?"
"If you particularly wish sir, I can do it."
"More than that, Hawk. It depends a lot on it. Okay then. Get out from the engine as much as possible."
Ryan smirked and stepped on the gas without hesitation. The Chrysler turned out to be a good racing car and Ryan was in his element. Now he was finally allowed to show what he was capable of. The limousine meandered

through city traffic. Meanwhile, Ryan knew exactly how to get to the base. The car literally pressed itself into the curve on the way to the city motorway. Conell had suddenly become very silent. His hand clung to the handle above the door to avoid being flung to Major General Randell. Ryan saw the many cars in front of him that seized all lanes and swam in the flow of traffic. He quickly dodged the hard shoulder. He was usually free. Ryan rushed ahead with the Chrysler at top speed. The military base was already visible in the distance and also an airplane that was approaching the landing.

In front of the black limousine, other cars suddenly appeared with flashing warning lights and blocked the hard shoulder. Ryan kept moving towards the abandoned car at undiminished speed. Ryan looked briefly in the rearview mirror. Conell, pale in terror, his eyes opened wide. Ryan noticed very well that he gasped in panic and tightened his grip on the handle that he cracked. Ryan grinned. Randell, on the other hand, looked more relaxed on the outside, but his face also became increasingly pale.

The closer he got to the breakdown vehicle, Ryan's tension and the adrenaline in the blood increased. He saw the people fleeing to the side and immediately pulled to the left. The car behind him was forced to make an emergency stop. The tires squeaked. Ryan also braked hard to avoid ramming the car in front. Seconds later he was on the free shoulder again. The car stood against the traffic. Ryan braked. As soon as the car stopped, he put the car into reverse and accelerated. As Ryan glanced over his shoulder, he noticed that Conell was obviously not doing well. When the apparently last drop of blood left his face, he only gave a groan.

Followed immediately by a terrified scream that Conell probably could no longer influence. The Chrysler turned around the rear axle in the desired direction. With a squeak of tires, the car struggled to move forward and finally flicked forward like a jet taking off.

Twenty minutes later Ryan stopped the limousine at the destination. The two passengers in the back were silent. While Conell remained motionless, Randell wiped sweat off his forehead with his handker Chief.

"Sir. Would you like to get out here or should I drive up to the taxiway?"

"It's all right Hawk. We're getting out of here", Randell said and swallowed again.

Ryan opened the doors. The two superiors no longer seemed to be in such a hurry because they got out of the limousine hesitantly and slowly.

"Wait here, Hawk", ordered Randell and walked away with Conell.

The briefcase Randell was guarding like a sanctuary was on the back seat. Ryan grinned as he looked at the two generals. He got out, leaned against the car, and lit a cigarette. When Major General Randell returned a little later, his face looked healthy again. Ryan stood by the right rear door to open it for him.

"No, Hawk. Not necessary. I prefer to sit in the passenger seat."

Randell opened the door himself. He took a deep breath before getting in.

When Ryan was ready to drive away, Randell said: "We're going back to the hotel. I have an appointment tonight. So we have a lot of time for the way back."

Ryan had understood. Slowly he let the car roll.

"Yes, Sir."

Ryan focused his view at the street, but he watched Randell out of the corner of his eye.

"Are you a resident of the Pine Ridge Reservation?", he asked.

"Yes, Sir."

"Do you have a family?"

"Yes, Sir."

"What were you doing before the Air Force, Hawk?"

"Horse breeder and cowboy, Sir."

"Cowboy?"

"Yes, Sir."

"I was told that you were a race car driver?"

"Outside the business, Sir."

"They're pretty good for that, Hawk. Damn good."

Ryan said nothing. He didn't like being asked.

"Do you like music?"

"Yes, Sir."

Randell started a CD and listened. The delicate sounds of a flute alternated with gentle piano variations and finally ended in a firework of the orchestra. Randell waited in vain for a reaction from his driver. Ryan noticed Randell's gaze, which gave him a very direct look. He was still silent and looked out of the windshield.

"You don't like to talk, Hawk?"

"That depends on the situation, Sir. But usually not."

Randell nodded and took a deep breath.

"Look, Hawk. We both, you and me, will spend a lot of time together in the future. America is big and wide. Inevitably, we cannot avoid talking to each other in the long run. Do you have any questions?"

A smile actually played around Ryan's mouth.

"Yes, Sir. Just one."

"And that would be?"

"Have you ever flown at the Air Force, Sir?"
"Yes, I am. Passionate, just like you by car. I was obsessed with it and I was pretty good. Damn good. After eighteen years, an idiot of a military doctor liquidated me. No more start approval for Randell. For health reasons. From then on I was tied to the desk. Although my military career was steep, I was dissatisfied. I never got on a plane that I cannot influence myself and I will never do that."
"I understand, Sir."
Ryan was obviously grinning.
"Would you let someone else drive you, Hawk?"
"I have that. If it is inevitable, yes Sir."
A smile appeared on Randall's face.
"Were you at all apprehensive earlier, Sir?", asked Ryan.
Randell's smile turned into a broad grin.
"Do you want to know if I was scared? I have often been to the limit in my life and have looked the grim reaper in the eye more than once. I can handle that. But I was really impressed by your driving talents. I think I'm on the best way to trust you. Although you are still very young at the age of nineteen, I have no impression that I'm dealing with a greenhorn."
"Sir. I've been driving since I was ten years old."
"Well done!" Randell nodded approvingly.
"I want you to accompany me to an official reception tonight. An anniversary celebration. After the formal part, I want to disappear inconspicuously. You are guiding me out of there", Randell said after a while. It was an order.
"Is there anything I should know, Sir?"
"We are not necessarily friends."
Ryan nodded.

After about half an hour the black Chrysler drove to the hotel. Ryan let the Chief get out at the entrance and parked the limousine in the garage.

*****

In the evening Ryan followed his Chief, as he called him, to the said reception. Despite the air conditioning, Ryan found the air in the hallway too stuffy. The shirt collar was scratching and the tie seemed to be closing his throat. He had loosened it more than once. Ryan was not feeling well. Although his throat was dry, he declined the glasses with various alcoholic beverages. No drop of alcohol, he had sworn to himself. Ryan positioned himself inconspicuously away from the hustle and bustle, watching everything and everyone, and especially Randell. When the host finished his speech, the crowd moved.

People made each other known, talked about the usual trivialities and clinked glasses with one another. Randell glanced at Ryan and nodded. The sign of departure.

A lady wearing a black cocktail dress and high heels got in Ryan's way with two glasses of champagne. Perfume smelled on his nose.

"Good evening", she smiled. "May I offer you a glass of champagne?"

"No thanks ma'am."

"You don't know what you miss. It tingles gently on the tongue."

"Then drink for me. Please excuse me."

Then Ryan passed her without paying any attention to

her.

"Oh that's very unfortunate. I don't even know your name", Ryan heard her voice as he left. A little later Ryan came to Randell and stopped behind him.

"Go in front of me, Sir. I'll stay right behind you", he said so quietly that only Randell could understand him.

"Oh, you want to leave already?"

A strange Major General stood in the way of Randell. He was a few years younger than him. He wore the same uniform and was about half a head taller. The friendliness of the voice made Ryan suspicious.

"Yes. Urgent business. You know that."

"Who is the gentleman behind you? Your shadow?"

The stranger smiled a little haughtily.

"He's my chauffeur, Major General Tanner", Randell replied, completely unimpressed.

"Well, well", he grinned.

"I'm sorry", Randell said, pushing past Tanner. Surrounded by crowds, Ryan literally pushed his Chief to the elevators. A few minutes later they were in the underground car park.

"I hate these underground garages. They're scary to me", said Randell.

Ryan paused and put a finger to his mouth. Then he pushed Randell behind a large pillar.

"Is there anything I should know?", hissed Ryan and looked Randell straight in the eye for the first time.

"I have a mission", Randell replied quietly.

"Me too. Next to the Chrysler is a Hummer. Underneath you disappear until the start approval."

Randell nodded without contradiction and did what his Bodyguard demanded.

Ryan climbed into the Chrysler. Finally, he could free

himself from the hated tie. Then he threw jacket and shirt on the back seat. Someone seemed to be waiting for the black Chrysler to start. But he didn't and that had to worry that somebody in the long run. Two men finally came to the limousine. While one opened the driver's door, the other guy was about to open the right rear door. When the guy had his hand on the door handle, he winced as if a surge had passed through him. He did not dare to move because the blade of a knife pressed directly against his throat. From the corner of his eye the guy recognized the muzzle of a pistol aimed at his accomplices.

"Hands up! Drop your weapon!"

A voice ordered sharply behind him.

The guy at the driver's door stared at Ryan, who was using the other man as a shield. Then he actually did what Ryan asked for. He held the pistol by the barrel in his raised hand.

"Throw it to me!", Ryan requested.

The addressed laughed dirty and hurled the weapon past Ryan, far behind him. She didn't hit the ground. Someone must have caught it!

With the man in front of him, Ryan turned fast and hurled him to the third shape. Two quick shots rang out. The hurled man fell groaning to the floor. Before the next shot rang out, Ryan lay flat on the floor. The bullet whistled over his head and bounced off the black limousine. Ryan didn't hesitate, took aim and pulled the trigger. The bullet hit its target. The shooter fell to the ground. The third man who had stood at the driver's door had disappeared.

Lying on the floor, Ryan saw Randell pausing under the Hummer. Ryan gestured for him to stay there. Seconds passed. Nothing happened. Ryan was on his feet looking for the third man. But it was actually no longer in the underground car park. Now it was time to be quick before the missing man returned with reinforcements.

"Sir. Everything okay?", asked Ryan.

"Yes", Randell replied.

"Get in the car", Ryan ordered as he crawled under the Chrysler. Slowly and with great caution, he pulled out a small, gray piece of metal that was no bigger than a matchbox.

"A monkey on their back?", asked Randell.

"The same small magnetic bomb as in the training camp. Just this one is live", Ryan replied. "No cables, no igniters and difficult to find. They wanted to be on the safe side."

"Pin them to the fuse box there. It is made of metal and does not move. I immediately inform the bomb squad. They are here in about five minutes. We disappear. I don't want to answer any questions", ordered Randell and immediately sat in the car.

The Chrysler slowly drove up the driveway. He plunged north into the night.

Ryan sensed that he had to drive through the night. He hadn't spoken a word in hours. He hadn't missed Randell's discomfort. He didn't speak either. Ryan didn't dare to close the partition. Not even when the Chief was on the phone. Ryan inevitably listened to the conversation. The name Tanner was heard several times.

Ryan had noticed that Randell didn't know the three guys in the underground garage. He suspected that they had worked on commission. As Randell hung up, there was an embarrassed silence between the two men as they crossed the undulating plains of Nebraska.

Randell asked at some point: "Aren't you tired, Hawk?"

"No, Sir."
"Do You Have Questions?"
"No, Sir."
This ended the conversation on the way to the Air Force Base in Rapid City.

*****

When Ryan woke up, he had slept for four hours. The sun had long passed the zenith. Ryan showered extensively, got coffee and had breakfast alone. He hadn't eaten in nearly twenty-four hours. Then he went in search of Baxter. There was no one left in the workshop. His legs involuntarily carried him to his company car. The garage door was open and country music sounded from the radio. That could only be Goodman. Ryan leaned against the doorpost, crossed his arms and grinned. Baxter slid on his knees in front of the Chrysler and polished on the passenger door. Brushes, pastes, paint pens and a pile of white cotton towels had gathered around him.

"The first order, my little one, and you are already disfigured", he growled. "But trust me. Good uncle Baxter can fix that again." Baxter shook her head.
"Are you talking about me?"
Baxter winced and looked up, startled.
"From who else? He doesn't have the scratches from me", Baxter growled reproachfully.
"Not from me either", Baxter.
"Now wouldn't be nice if you shoot our own baby!"
Ryan had to laugh.

"That sounds like we're married."

"We're already eating and sleeping together", grinned Baxter.

"Then shave before you think of kissing me", Ryan said.

Baxter grabbed one of his cleaning rags and threw it at Ryan. Laughing, he caught it.

"What are we going to do this evening? I have a pass and actually wanted to be gone long ago", said Baxter.

"Me too, but only on a long leash. I can't go far."

"OK. Here is a cozy pub nearby. Let's go and have a few beers."

Ryan nodded in agreement.

Portly Baxter cleared up his stuff and sent a scrutinizing look over the black car. He smiled contentedly and closed the gate with the words: "Good night little one. Sweet Dreams."

On the way to the parking lot the two talked without interruption. When Ryan was standing at the Commander's passenger door, Baxter threw the keys to him.

"Are you serious?"

"No", Baxter growled. "I just want to prove to the guys that I have a chauffeur."

Ryan laughed and sat in the driver's seat.

"Why a Commander?"

"It feels good to tell a commander where to go. Ha ha ha." Baxter laughed amused. "It was love at first sight. Quite simply."

"Then you're already taken", Ryan said. "You can keep your beard."

"Don't turn me on, little one", Baxter growled.

Ryan laughed. "Forget it!"

The bar that Baxter had chosen shone like a decorated

Christmas tree. Music sounded muffled across the parking lot. Dust and heat from the day were in the air. The Commander stopped in the row of parked cars. The two young men got out laughing and disappeared through the door. Smoky air hit them. It was full. All tables were occupied. Baxter pulled Ryan to the bar.

"Hello Baxter Goodman!", greeted the blond curly lady with the conspicuously powdered face and bright red lips visibly pleased.

"Hello Diane. You look dazzling! How are you?"

"Splendid", she laughed.

"Beer for you and your friend?"

"You guessed it. Nice and cold, yes."

"A coke for me", Ryan demanded.

"It's all right", she replied gently.

"Hey, what's up? Are you sick?"

"Why?"

"Because you order sweet booze."

"I like sweet booze."

"Let at least pour in a good whiskey. Then maybe you can drink the stuff."

Ryan shook his head firmly.

"Not when I'm standby."

"Long leash", summarized Baxter.

Diane brought the requested. "Cheers you two."

"Cheers", said Baxter, raising his beer glass.

He drank it in one gulp. A stranger came to him and tapped on his shoulder.

"Hi Bax. You owe me a revanche. How does it look like? Baxter looked at him.

"Hello Jimmy Boy! You haven't given up yet?", grinned Baxter.

"No!"

"OK. What's your stake?"

"A bottle of the finest whiskey, Bax. And your one?"

"I'll keep up", Baxter nodded.

Ryan drank his Coke while watching Jimmy Boy. He was smaller and slimmer than Baxter. He seemed very convinced of what he was doing, whatever it was. He was wearing blue jeans and a plaid shirt. His hair was short and straight. Jimmy squeezed himself between Baxter and Ryan to the bar. Provocative he put his right arm on the bar.

"Come on. High five."

Baxter did that.

Diane laughed, shaking h er head. "You hot heads!"

"Give the signal, Diane!", Baxter demanded.

"OK. Ready - and - go!"

Baxter grinned when he seemed to be pressing effortlessly against his challenger's arm. He grimaced, which turned increasingly red. The men had noticed, gathered around the two and cheered on them.

"Hey, Jimmy Boy. Don't wet your pants!", one shouted.

General laughter spread.

"Come on! Show him!", shouted an another one.

"Do you want to bet?", Baxter asked.

"Get him and give us the Whiskey. Saves us a lot of effort."

Everyone laughed again.

"Why me?", Baxter asked.

"Because Jimmy Boy has to give you the bottle and you can't take it to the base."

The guys enjoyed themselves and they knew that they would definitely win.

"Is getting boring with you", Baxter growled and finally put Jimmy's arm on the counter.

"Before your skull bursts, Buddy", he said.
Propitiating then Baxter patted him on the shoulder.
"You get better every time", Jimmy Boy.
"Do you really think?"
"Of course!"
Ryan smiled.
"Well Ryan, do you want to give it a try?", Baxter asked.
Jimmy turned to the Indian.
"Ah, he belongs to you", he said.
"Yes. My friend Ryan."
"Are you in the Air Force too?"
"Yes, I am", Ryan replied.
"Let's try?", asked Jimmy Ryan.
"Do you want to spend another bottle of whiskey?"
"Or you, we'll see."
Ryan and Jimmy took up positions and Baxter gave the signal. In a fraction of a second, Jimmy's arm slammed onto the wood of the counter.
"Hey, that was a rip-off!"
One of the men protested from the crowd.
"How did you do this?", Jimmy asked, clearly puzzled. Jimmy was also not squeamish and had a good muscle mass.
"Should I show you again?", asked Ryan.
"And don't try to screw us again!"
"I haven't cheated. I was just faster than Jimmy", Ryan said.
Further back someone started to jumping up and down. As he patted his lips with the palm of his hand, strange sounds were made. Baxter didn't hesitate and grabbed the drunk guy by the collar.
"For you Whiskey is deleted today!"
He snorted angrily. Baxter pulled him to the door and

bunged him out.

"A bottle of the best, Diane! On Jimmy's account. The second bottle is on me", Baxter shouted.

Diane smiled and placed two bottles of whiskey and many glasses on the counter. Nobody asked. Good things made the men laugh again. When Baxter offered Ryan a filled glass, he declined.

"Ahh!" Baxter said curt and drank both glasses.

"It is really good! No booze. You don't know what you're missing, man."

"I know it, Baxter."

Jimmy stuck to Ryan.

"Come on Ryan. You wanted to show me how you did it."

Ryan nodded and raised his arm.

Jimmy struck tense and visibly excited.

"And – go!", Baxter shouted.

Jimmy's arm slammed down again in a fraction of a second. Again he looked at Ryan questioningly.

"You showed me again. Yes, but how does that work? It was far too fast", he said, puzzled.

"That's the way it is. Your reaction is too late. While you think I acted."

Jimmy nodded approvingly and ordered a bottle of whiskey from Diane, which immediately found its way to the pack.

"I prefer to stop, otherwise I'll go even poor. Do you drink a Whiskey with me? We make peace."

"Give me a cola. I'm on duty and still have to drive. I am allergic to whiskey."

Jimmy laughed out loud.

"That's what they're doing right now."

Diane gave Ryan a coke.

"Thanks", he said.

The next bottle of whiskey was decapitated. The handful of guys around Baxter chatted on and on. When one started to crack jokes, they laughed louder and louder. Ryan laughed too. The Whiskey had loosened its tongues, made the men silly and breathed childish spirit into them. Baxter was barely noticeable. He always talked a lot and had this wonderful gift for making others laugh. Jimmy leaned against the counter with glassy eyes. His tongue refused to obey him when he spoke to Ryan: "another Coke, hick, for my new friend here", he shouted at Diane. Jimmy, hick, buy a round today. So I drink you under the, hick, table, with the booze."

Grinning, Ryan opened the next Coke.

Hours later, well after midnight, the noise had subsided. The alcohol that had loosened the tongues made them heavy and soothed the men. They struggled with tiredness.

Jimmy would probably have fallen if he hadn't leaned against the counter. Some of the guys had left in the meantime. Two crouched on their chairs, using the table as a pillow. Baxter flirted with Diane. Before dawn, three people strolled across the parking lot to the jeep. Baxter and Ryan dragged Jimmy Boy with and put him in the back seat.

"Boy, pull in your bones, otherwise I won't be able to close the door", growled Baxter and pushed against it. Then he climbed awkwardly into the passenger seat of his jeep. When the door closed, he ducked his head.

"Not so loud! My skull hums like a hornet swarm."

Ryan grinned.

"Already?" He started the jeep.

"Where does your friend live?"

"Jimmy boy? I do not know."
"You can't be serious?"
"Wait my friend. I have to think. It was just as dark last time."
Ryan waited.
"I got it!" Baxter announced after a while.
Jimmy grunted contentedly.
"Drive carefully, Ryan. Jimmy Boy is not good with the curves."
Ryan shook his head and accelerated. At some point the jeep bumped through the potholes of a dirt road. Jimmy groaned and raised his head. Ryan had to stop. Baxter hurriedly pulled Jimmy out of the jeep and held him when he vomited on the side of the road.
"Shame about the beautiful Whiskey, Jimmy, Jimmy Boy."
Baxter put his arm around Jimmy's shoulder and snapped his wrist. With the other hand he grabbed his belt.
"Here we go! A few more steps, then you did it. Ryan! We prefer to walk."
The commander rolled after the two swaying figures and illuminated the path. It was actually not far to the house. Then Ryan brought Baxter and himself back to Air Force Base. Even though Baxter kept talking and laughing, he still knew exactly what he was doing. However, when he dropped limply onto his bed, he cursed loudly.
"Heck! The thing turns like a carousel."
Seconds later he snored.
Ryan grinned shut the door.

*****

Baxter stood up and awake in the workshop just in time for the start of duty.

"Where do you want to go so early?", he asked Ryan, who showed up at the gate in his jogging suit.

"Fitness training. Since no Commander drilled me hard, I have to be careful that nothing grinds with me."

Baxter laughed.

"Have fun my friend."

"See you."

Ryan turned and ran.

Baxter shook his head.

"Nutcase."

"I heard it!", Ryan shouted back.

In the afternoon, Sergeant Hawk's orders came. He immediately appeared in his uniform with a small bag over his shoulder. He drove the black Chrysler out of the garage. Ryan stopped in front of the workshop to say goodbye to Baxter.

"Where?"

"Top secret. I don't know yet."

"Call me."

"I will. Toksa Mato."

"Toksa Ryan."

Ryan stood in front of the door with the limousine when Randell came. The Chief made a point of being on time. After the brief, formal greeting, Randell got into the back of the car. Waiting, Ryan sat behind the wheel.

"We will be on the road longer this time. Our path takes us to Tucson, Arizona."

"Sir. Yes, Sir", Ryan confirmed and started the engine.

He adjusted the rearview mirror so that he could watch the major general. Randell opened his mysterious case and studied the documents. His facial features appeared very tense. Something seemed to work hard in him. He was so absorbed in his documents that he jumped when Ryan spoke to him.

"Sir."

Randell looked up. "Yes?"

"The way to Arizona is far. You should talk to me. This cannot be avoided inevitably."

"The matter is strictly confidential. If everything goes well, that's my last job."

"And if things go wrong, too", Ryan replied. "You know very well that i am not just your driver. Otherwise you could have taken someone else. And you expect me to do exactly what they sent me for training. I think your strictly confidential matter is at least as hot as an anniversary celebration in Denver."

"Hawk, you're getting too curious. That's not your style."

"If you don't ask, you won't get an answer, Sir. As long as I am at your side and obey your orders, it also concerns me. Only then I can fulfill my order well."

Randell took a deep breath and seemed to be considering.

"Pull over, Hawk", he ordered.

Randell gets out of the car. With his suitcase, he took a seat in the passenger seat.

"Okay. You're driving, I'm talking."

Ryan smiled triumphantly.

"Alright", Randell started. "I've been following a Major General Tanner for two years now. We saw him at the anniversary celebration in Denver. The man who got in my way when we wanted to go. Tanner sells US Air Force weapon technology secret information to people who pay him huge sums of money. For three months now finally we have had reliable evidence in our hands to

take him to the military court."
Randell paused.
"Tanner has now found out that they are on his track", Ryan stated, "... and he sent the men in the underground car park."
Randell nodded. "Yes."
"But Tanner doesn't work alone. There are more men like those in the underground car park."
"For sure. He can afford it. paid killers", Ryan noted.
"Yes. He has no friends."
"Who do you work for, Major General Randell?"
Randell grinned openly at Ryan.
"For the U.S. Air Force."
"Which department, Sir?"
"Internal."
Ryan nodded.
Around eight o'clock in the evening, the two men reached a motel south of the green river, state of Utah.
Randell ordered to stop. They wanted to stay here for the night. It seemed inconspicuous to him and he was also hungry. Ryan and Randell moved into two adjoining rooms. Despite their simplicity, they looked inviting. Randell ordered Ryan to change. A little later, in civilian clothes, they entered the steakhouse on the opposite side of the street.
The next morning, they met in the lobby for breakfast. There was hardly any talk. When the men climbed into the Chrysler, Randell chose the passenger seat again. During the ride he started talking about his plans. Mouthan Air Force Base in Tucson was the target. Ryan listened carefully.
"I trust you, Ryan. You saved my life", Randell concluded.
"Yes, Sir", Ryan nodded.

Around noon they crossed the Arizona border. Ryan turned to a gas station. While he was fueling the car, the Chief was in the store. He wanted to be back in about thirty minutes, he had said.

Ryan pulled over so the Chief couldn't miss him, leaned against the car, and waited.

"Hi buddy. Do you have a light?", asked a strange voice. A strong guy dressed in jeans, a red cotton shirt and a leather vest stood next to him. Ryan nodded and gave him the lighter.

"Thanks buddy. I am called jumper."

"Ryan."

The stranger stopped next to Ryan, lit the cigarette and took a few puffs.

"It seems you don't feel quite comfortable in your clothes. Look like a dandy in your uniform."

Ryan grinned openly.

"Right. The collar scratches and the tie cuts off the air."

"I hate these things too", laughed the stranger.

"There are only a few idiots who jet across the states, except for us truck drivers."

Ryan laughed and nodded toward a red truck.

"Is this your truck?"

"Hm hm. All my pride. Whether from the high north in the east or from the deep south to the west, it is best to roll with Jumpers truck."

Jumper's eyes shone eagerly. He was silent between two puffs of his cigarette and looked at the man in the uniform unobtrusively, at least that's what he thought.

"Sorry, my radio", he said.

He hurriedly kicked out the cigarette and ran to his truck in a few steps.

Ryan heard him speak into the micro. Jumper spoke loud

and clear. His style and stature reminded him very much of Baxter Goodman. Ryan grinned at his thoughts. A few minutes later the trucker came back to Ryan.

"A great invention. So I'm always up to date."

Jumper pulled out his cigarette packet and offered one to Ryan. He refused.

"May I have a fire again? I already left the darn thing in the truck."

Without answering, Ryan lighted the cigarette.

"Thanks buddy. Five miles south is a road block if you want to get there. It may take longer. One of us involuntarily distributed his load on the highway." He laughed.

"My friend Bunny. I want to see if I can help him. The cops are giving him hell."

Jumper took a deep breath and shook his head.

"It was nice to meet you, Ryan. If you ever need a fire, please let me know. You probably have no radio in your elegant carriage?"

"Another frequency. MCPS."

"Look, if you get bored on the way or you need help. Jumper shoved a handbill into Ryan's hand.

"I am out there alone far too often. Then it's good to know that trucker stick together, because nobody else does anything for you."

Ryan nodded.

"Thanks jumper. I will keep that in mind. Only my truck is a little smaller than yours."

"Don't worry about it. Maybe he's still growing."

Jumper winked, amused.

"Bye buddy. See you sometime, somewhere", and went away. When he drove his truck from the parking lot, he raised his arm in greeting. His horn sounded powerful, like that of an ocean liner. At the same time Chief Randell appeared.

"We drive a bit further and then look for accommodation. I don't want to be at the base this evening. Tanner is there. We'll surprise him tomorrow morning", he said.

Ryan nodded and got in the car too.

The morning when Major General Randell showed up at Mouthan Air Force Base in Tucson, Tanner looked restless. Especially when Randell was sitting in his office before Tanner entered. A lieutenant from the base stood in a perfectly rigid position in front of Tanner's desk, silently. He obviously felt uncomfortable in Randell's presence. A few minutes later the office door opened without anyone knocking. Tanner struggled to maintain his composure and greeted Randell kindly. He smiled when he said good morning to Tanner.

"What brings you here?", Tanner asked.

"Sit down, Major General Tanner."

Tanner was consumed by rage. He sat down.

"I had a strange call the day before yesterday. Maybe you can help me, Tanner."

Tanner cocked his head and looked at Randell, whose hair shimmered silver and who was about fifteen years older.

"I'll do what I can. What kind of call?"

"Well, the call was anonymous. It was the voice of a woman who claimed an assassination attempt is planned."

Tanner's eyebrows rose in astonishment. In thoughts he went through his affairs. Nothing was impossible.

"Nothing is impossible", he replied stupidly.

"I thought so", Randell said.

"And why are you bothering to come here personally?" Tanner doubted. "What an honor."

"Well, my main concerns are the Air Force's reputation. There will be a mud fight, rummaging deep in the dirt."

Randell's words had an effect. Tanner shot the blood in the head so that he blushed. He swallowed audibly.

"Are you afraid to die?", Randell asked unaffected.

Tanner didn't answer.

"Do you have an idea of who tries to eliminate you and, above all, why?"

Tanner also failed to respond to Randell.

"I don't know what to make of it. Maybe the whole thing is just a fake." Randell cleared his throat. "I think you should check your friends, business partners, or your contacts as much as possible before the truth comes out, Tanner. Because the day she does that, you may be dead."

Tanner sucked the air audibly into his lungs and said nothing.

"That's why I'm here", Randell closed his rather one-sided conversation and got up. As he tucked the papers on the table under his arm, Tanner stood up.

"What do you have there?" he asked.

"A few cobblestones for the path to truth."

"From my office? Without my knowledge?", snorted Tanner.

"From an Air Force Base office", Randell smiled and left Tanner's office.

He glowered after him. Tanner ran his hands over his eyes as if trying to wipe away a bad dream.

*****

"The old man sniffs around too much. This time nothing should go wrong!" Tanner growled softly.
"His driver was with him in Denver and he's here too. The guy is more than he claims. Randell was got the jitters and got a professional", answered the lieutenant, who was rooted to Tanner's desk.
Tanner's ice-gray eyes seemed to be trying to pierce the lieutenant.
"That shouldn't be a problem for you, Peterson", he hissed. "You are also professional, or am I wrong?"
"No sir. I have to separate him from Randell."
"The guy is your thing. I take care of Randell."
Tanner went to the window and looked out. He had clasped his hands on his back.
"Cursed crap", he hissed.
"Get out of here!", Tanner ordered brusquely.
Peterson went out without a greeting. Tanner heard the office door click into the lock behind him.

*****

It wasn't until evening that Randell returned to Tanner's office. This time in Tanner's presence. Ryan remained at the door at Randell's command. He waited there motionless like a statue. Even for his ears it was impossible to understand the words that were exchanged between Randell and Tanner.

Two Staff Sergeants came down the hall. They carried a stack of papers and files, which obviously had to be quite heavy. They stopped at the side door. They seemed to completely ignore the post in front of Tanner's office, they were so intensely engrossed in their conversation. Ryan understood every word.

"Since Randell's arrival, the old man has turned every roll of toilet paper the Major General had in his hands. He took apart Tanner's office and monitors every fart."

"And I have to check the whole bunch of Tanners phone calls", the other groaned. ".... and to write a list of all conversations of the past twelve months."

The one who had spoken first whistled softly through his teeth.

"Man, he must be damn deep in the dirt. I don't want to be in his skin."

The door finally slammed from the inside. Then it was quiet.

Ryan let his gaze wander across the corridor. Minutes later the glass door opened and a Lieutenant entered the hall. Ryan dropped his eyes. It almost looked like the guard was sleeping in front of the door. But the lieutenant stopped right in front of Ryan, so he was forced to salute. The lieutenant returned the greeting.

"Your car, the black Chrysler Limousine South Dakota, is in the way, Sergeant. Move the car to another place."

"No Sir."

"No?"

"No."

"That's an order!"

"By whom, Sir?"

"From me, Lieutenant Peterson."

Ryan just twisted his mouth. He did not move from his unbending attitude and ignored the command.

"What? You refuse to execute this command?", asked the tall blonde lieutenant angrily.

A second lieutenant suddenly appeared and they both stopped in front of Ryan. As a rank lower, Ryan had the duty to greet this one too. He did it correctly.

"Sergeant Hawk! drive your car away immediately. That's an order", Peterson repeated gruffly.

"Sir, no Sir."

"This is a refusal to obey an order!"

"No Sir."

"Who the hell made you a sergeant?"

"The Air Force on behalf of the United States, Sir."

"Damn then they forgot to teach you obediently, Sergeant. Come on!"

"No Sir."

Lieutenant Peterson grew louder.

"I command it!"

"I'm not authorized to take orders from anyone, Sir. I am solely under the command of Major General Randell."

The strange lieutenant who had stood up next to Peterson laughed. then he nodded to Peterson. he also nodded and drew his service weapon.

"Take the sergeant into custody, Webster. He opposes the senior officers."

Webster took a step towards Ryan. Before he put the foot on a second time, Ryan pulled him backwards and pressed the knife to his throat. The man did not dare to bat an eye. He gasped.

"Does your origin push through now, Indsman?" hissed Peterson.

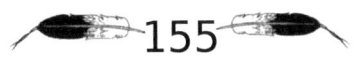

"The US Army made a civilized person out of me, but if you even think of twitching your finger on the trigger, my knife will be faster."

"Who are you, Hawk?"

Webster, whom Ryan had had in his grip, began to sweat down the temples. Ryan smiled barely. He didn't think about answering.

"You're not just Randell's driver", Peterson snappily stated. "Drivers wait in the car or polish it. Drivers your age are not Master Sergeant. You follow Randell like his shadow. You are someone other than you pretend to be, Indsman. You are Randell's watchdog."

Ryan showed no reaction.

Seconds later the office door opened. While Randell cleverly hid his amazement and looked calmly at the situation, Tanner gave the order: "Lieutenant Peterson. Put the weapon away immediately and follow me to my office, Webster too."

With that, Tanner turned and left. Peterson and Webster followed him.

*****

Randell didn't ask. With a gesture he indicated Ryan to follow him. He had the rear door of his car opened and got in. While Ryan started and drove off, Randell started to report.

"I finally got him in the trap. Tanner just delivered me the last piece in the puzzle. I have enough solid evidence to take him to the military court. I immediately write my report and make a call to Washington."

Although Randell maintained his stance in every respect, his triumph was unmistakable.

"What happened in front of the office door?"

"These lieutenants ordered me to drive our official car away from the entrance."

Randell laughed softly.

Amused, he said: "At least you could have done that to them."

"Sir, they needed an excuse to lure me away from you."

"Hm."

Randell nodded and frowned.

"Tanner knows that he has nothing left to lose."

"He'll bustle his killers to hunt us down."

"Yes. The dance is not over yet", Randell replied and picked up the phone.

Ryan looked at his Chief in surprise. Even though Ryan was wearing his aviator glasses, he lowered the sun visor. The sun was deep in the west and blinded his eyes. Randell had the Laptop on his knees and was delving into his report.

"Sir", Ryan finally spoke to him. "We have a burdock at six o'clock."

Randell looked up and turned his head to the rear window.

"He has been following us at this distance for four minutes. He could have caught up with us long ago", Ryan noted.

"Keep the speed and direction, Hawk."

"At your command, Sir", Ryan smiled.

"The evidence is in the case?" asked Ryan.

Randell continued to type without reacting. About ten minutes later he sent his detailed report directly to the military court. Then Randell closed the Laptop.

"Yes, everything in the case. How does it look like?"
"Unchanged Sir."
Randell thought for a moment and started grinning. "Turn off the highway to Casa Grande and continue north. I'll tell them where we stop."
"All right, Sir", Ryan confirmed.
The car behind the Chrysler also turned. In a posh suburban neighborhood, about forty miles south of Phoenix, Arizona, Randell finally ordered to stop. Ryan stopped the Chrysler in front of a Spanish colonial mansion. The white house was surrounded by well-tended gardens.
"Take our things with you, Ryan", said Randell and got out.
He carried the briefcase himself. He hurried to the entrance. The way there was paved with light granite. Ryan did what the Chief said. He followed Randell. On the way to the entrance he looked around. At the moment there was no sign of the car that had followed them. When Ryan closed the door behind him, he was in a large lobby. The windows reached to the floor and had pink curtains. The floor was lined with oriental carpets that swallowed every step. To the right and left of the reception, which also seemed to be a bar at the same time, stairs with white banister led up to the top floor. Randell had already sat on a bar stool and was talking to a well-dressed lady. Ryan greeted, but stop by the window. He put the bags down and watched the street constantly. A voice came to his ear as Ryan followed his thoughts.
"Good evening. My name is Lilly and what's your name?"
"Ryan", he replied without turning his head.
Auburn curls appeared close to his face. Bangles jingled

softly against each other. When Ryan noticed that she was raising her arm to touch him, he turned and avoided that touch.

"What's up? You don't like me?", she asked disappointed.

"I'm on duty", he avoided.

"Men in uniform are simply irresistible."

Lilly smiled and put her arm around his waist.

"There is a U.S. Air Force Major General, my Chief, Lilly."

"I know him. He is very nice, but he rarely comes and when he does, he only asks about Josy."

Ryan seemed irritated. He basically avoided questioning Randell's orders. Involuntarily he looked over at him. The Chief was still deep in conversation with the lady, who was probably called Josy. He sipped on a glass of champagne.

"Well, it will take a while with the two of them. Don't you want to come up with me? It's more comfortable there. I like you. Your boss is generous and I will spoil you generously. You look kind of starved."

Ryan laughed softly and glanced at the street.

"You do it for money?", he finally asks and exaggeratedly surprised.

"Yes. After all, you have to live from something. So what's up now?"

"Not without his permission", he replied.

"Oh. You are an obedient soldier. Pardon me, I don't know your ranks. With me you are primarily a man."

Lilly, trying so hard to get Ryan's attention, stroked his neck and one of her gentle touches along the neck to his lips. Ryan was getting hot. Lilly was right. He was starved.

"Come on! You want it too. I feel it."

"No one knows what I want and what I do. But I want to tell you I wouldn't do it for money."
Lilly cuddled against Ryan and whispered in his ear.
"I would do it to you even without money."
Ryan laughed softly.
Randell came up to them.
"Sir."
"We will continue our return in civilian clothes. Josy gives us her car. Nobody here will remember us."
Ryan nodded, reached for the bags, and followed Randell.
Just a few minutes later they left the luxurious brothel in a white Cadillac. Randell sat on the passenger side and grinned contentedly.
„We misled them. Tanner will burst when his watchdogs tell him where we are. Let's go to the South City Hotel. I had booked two rooms under a different name and I'm hungry for murder. Don't you too?"
"Yes, Sir."
"Would you have done it?"
"What Sir?"
"Well, you know what I mean." Randell grinned broadly.
"Not without your order", Ryan grinned too.
Randell laughed with amusement and kept chatting. Ryan learned that Josy was his youngest sister. When he took off his uniform, he was only a man who could have been Ryan's father, maybe even a grandfather.
Randell let Ryan get closer this evening than ever before. When Ryan expressed concerns that Josy was apparently in danger with their girls, Randell nodded.
"Josy is a smooth customer. She'll stop the guys for a while or call the police. If that doesn't work, the girls know exactly how to swindle anyone for a quid."

He grinned triumphantly.
Ryan's skepticism remained.

Josy looked up from her work when the door opened. When she saw the two uniformed guys, an icy hot shower went through her. There they were. Ryan and Randell had just left and still in town. Josy forced a professionally friendly smile.
"Good evening. Can I invite you for a drink as a welcome?"
"No thanks. We are on duty. Do you know these two men?"
The tall blonde showed her two photos.
"We never give information about our customers."
"About this already. They are wanted."
"I'm afraid I can't help you, Sir."
"For sure you can!"
Peterson snorted and leaned over the counter.
"I'm really, really sorry. I don't know these men", Josy finally said.
"Don't lie to me! Their company car is still outside the house. I myself saw they go in here exactly thirty-two minutes ago and haven't left the house yet. I give you a second chance. I can also turn your classy shed upside down."
"Why should I lie?"
"Because maybe he paid you for it?"
"Many guys have already paid me for everything, honey", answered Josy confidently.
"Me too", Peterson grinned diabolically. "Search the two, Web!", he ordered the young man who had come with him.
"You don't have the right to do it! Our guests enjoy

absolute anonymity here!"

"I am not in the least interested."

"I have to ask you to leave my house", demanded Josy.

"Not until we caught these two men", Peterson hissed.

"If you don't want it any other way ...", said Josy calmly, feeling for the emergency button under the counter.

As soon as Josy had said the words, Peterson jumped over the counter and pushed her back against the stairs.

"Then I'll have to make sure that you won't stop us, honey."

In no time he grabbed her and pushed her under one of the stairs. Josy fought against her fear. She gasped for breath as the angry man pushed her onto a chair. She did not dare to protest, not to shout, or even to resist. Her brother had warned her not to do anything about these men.

Only seconds later Josy found herself tied to the chair. With the broad tape over her mouth she thought she was suffocating. Josy stared wide-eyed at the curtain the guy was pulling behind him. It grew dim and silent around them.

Anger was no longer an expression when Tanner yelled into the phone: "What!?"

He snorted like an aggressive bull as he paced back and forth in his bedroom. He lacked the words.

"What am I paying you for, professional idiots! Find them! I want the suitcase! Immediately!"

Then Tanner slammed the phone against the door frame.

"A noble brothel ! I can't believe it! He must fucking need it, this randy old goat", he spoke to himself in rage.

Steps approached the door.

"Honey? What's the matter?"
Mrs. Tanner went to her husband and put her arms around his shoulders soothingly.
"Trouble?"
He nodded.
"If you don't take care of everything yourself ...", he said softly.

*****

It was felt a long time later when Josy heard noises. The door opened and closed. Someone came up with quiet steps.
"Hello?"
Finally asked a male voice timidly.
Josy made herself felt, even if she couldn't bring out a reasonable word. The pink curtain moved. Someone carefully pushed him aside. A familiar, spherical face appeared. Josy breathed a sigh of relief.
A middle-aged officer stared at Josy in horror. Then he immediately removed the tape from Josy's mouth. Involuntarily the tears came to her eyes.
"What happened?", the officer whispered.
Josy made: "Pst. Call the reinforcement, officer. There are killers in the house."
The fat little officer cut the shackles. Josy nodded gratefully and massaged her joints.
The officer was crouched on the ground when he made radio contact with the headquarters. He quietly reported his code and location. Before he could continue talking, someone snatched the device from his hand.

"Everything all right", said a tall man, who suddenly appeared out of nowhere next to him and switched off the device.

He was completely dressed in black. His mirrored sunglasses did not allow eye contact.

"I would rather not do that", he said in an icy voice.

Two younger men stood next to him.

Beads of sweat appeared on the officer's forehead. With wide eyes he stared at him and swallowed hard. The two men grabbed his arms and pulled him onto his legs.

"Get him out!", Tanner ordered.

He didn't need any witnesses. Tanner was ready to walk over corpses. He had nothing to lose. He did not hesitate to press the barrel of his pistol against Josy's temple.

"Where are they?", he asked dangerously quietly.

"Who?"

"Two of my men. Their car is outside."

"Everyone can park the car here.

"They went through that door and they didn't come out through that door. So it is very likely that they are or were here. My men say that they are not in the house. You helped them escape!"

"Why should two Air Force men run away from their own people?"

Tanner grimaced.

Roughly he reached into Josy's curly hair and jerked her head back.

"My patience is running out! Don't think I have any scruples to blow your head off whore."

Josy was scared. Fear of death.

"I gave them my Cadillac. They are on their way to Rapid City Air Force Base."

"There you go."
Tanner pulled her hair again and grinned.
"If I had time, the three of us would have an incredible amount of fun with you. Maybe another time. If you want to live you never saw us. Otherwise we'll be back. I swear to you."
Josy nodded.
Finally, Tanner let her go and put the weapon away. He gave a sign to his men, whereupon they left the house. Tanner cut the phone wire before disappearing.

*****

Randell and Ryan had now finished dinner in the hotel restaurant.
"They'll be looking for us", Ryan said softly when they were on their way to their rooms.
"They won't find us", Randell replied.
"They will come."
"They will not find us. We stay here under different names."
"They will have forced the women to speak."
Randell stopped, took a deep breath and looked at Ryan doubtfully. For the first time he questioned Randell's decision. He stepped closer to him.
"Josy is my sister", he whispered and finally grinned.
"Tanner has nothing left to lose. He won't sleep that night", Ryan whispered seriously.
„We will continue driving that night. Before he finds us here, we're gone, Ryan."
Ryan did not share his Chief's opinion, but did not dare

speak again. He nodded and followed. Randell said goodbye to him outside the door.

"The night is getting short. Four hours of sleep must be enough. Sleep well, Ryan."

Ryan hadn't interrogated. Randell had been calling him by his first name since some time, as long as they were alone.

"Good night Sir. You too", he replied.

Randell closed the door behind him. Ryan carried the briefcase with him. He stopped thoughtfully at the door. He listened. Then he went to his room next door. A few minutes later he left it again. He handed over his travel bag at the reception, signed and received a small key for it. He stuck it deep in his pocket. Then he strolled across the illuminated parking lot to check on the Cadillac. A black rover parked directly opposite. Ryan liked the SUV. *Better than a white Cadillac,* he thought and grinned. The white Cadillac was far too striking and easy to find. Ryan was wearing black clothes and stopped in the shadow of the hotel's driveway. From here he could watch the parking lot without being noticed. The fresh air felt good and no tie constricted him. He sat on the floor, leaned comfortably against the wall and lit a cigarette. Ryan cleverly covered the telltale glow with his hand. It had long been his habit to hold his cigarette down like a pen. Ryan was absolutely sure he couldn't sleep that night. Restlessness dug deep within him, confused the balance and cautioned him. He looked at his wristwatch. It was an hour and thirty minutes before midnight. If he had to, he would wait here all night, because only when Tanner found the Cadillac would he look for Randell. Ryan knew that Tanner would not give up until he could destroy the evidence. Not only the briefcase, but also Randell himself. Whoever had nothing left to lose was dangerous.

*****

Major General Randell startled from sleep and stared into a pair of sparkling eyes. The head of the man who was above him was covered by a black balaclava. But Tanner's voice was unmistakable.
"Where the hell is the file?"
Randell's eyes and mouth widened in disbelief. The light from the streetlights came in stripes through the slats on the window and over his face. Tanner shook him roughly.
"Answer me!", he hissed impatiently.
"In the suitcase."
"She is not!"
Randell carefully pulled himself up on the pillow to sit up. He was breathing faster and his heart was pounding.
"Where is the file? I count to three."
Randell saw the muzzle of a pistol pointed at himself and realized that it was equipped with a silencer.
"I put it in the case, Tanner!"
"One."
"It must be in there!"
"Two."
"Check it out. It's in the briefcase. If you kill me, it won't help you much."
Tanner actually looked nervous. He almost seemed to lose his nerve when he angrily tipped the contents of the suitcase onto Randell's bed.

Hotel magazines and advertising sheets ended up on the bed.

"Are you kidding me!", Tanner shouted.

Randell laughed spontaneously.

"You think you're very clever. Did you hide the papers in the brothel?"

Randell laughed amused, despite his controversial situation and drove Tanner insane.

"Well. Another one was probably faster than you, Tanner", said Randell ironically when he calmed down a bit.

"I actually don't know where my papers are."

"For sure you know", hissed Tanner.

Angrily he snapped Randell and pressed the pistol to his forehead.

"You are a dead man. Is it worth it?"

Randell glanced at the gun and swallowed. Yes, he was scared.

A black shadow suddenly appeared from the dark behind Tanner. Like a lightning bolt, a hand ran against Tanner's neck. He slumped silently on the bed. Ryan picked up the gun.

Randell breathed a sigh of relief. When he wiped the sweat from his forehead, he asked: "Where have you been so long?"

"I got held up, Sir"

Then Ryan pulled the unconscious body off the bed and tied him to the bedpost.

"Excuse me Sir when I remove your bed company. I didn't know your tendency so far", grinned Ryan.

Randell shook her head.

"And I hope you never tell anyone about my tendencies!", Randell laughed at Ryan's joke.

"Sir, you can turn on the light."
Randell did so and blinked.
"I almost died! When did you clear out my briefcase, sly dog?"
"When you were in the shower, Sir."
"And where is the file now?"
"In the hotel safe."
Randell grinned contentedly.
"You allow me to go. Two old friends are waiting for me in the Cadillac. Lieutenant Peterson and Webster."
"You want to leave me here alone with Tanner?", asked Randell.
"He will not dare to move. The thin wire around his neck would immediately cut his throat."
Randell nodded.
"Okay. I call the base."

The military police came before sunrise. They brought the three men out of the hotel immediately and without any hassle. All guests still seemed to be asleep. Randell and Ryan went for breakfast. The restaurant smelled of coffee, eggs, toast and bacon. They were alone here and chose a table near the TV so as not to miss the news. Ryan thought about the sensation that the white Cadillac and her civilian clothes would cause when they arrived at the base. He had to grin.
"Why are you grinning like that?", asked the Chief.
"I was thinking of our arrival at the base, Sir."
Randell laughed softly.
"You will bring the Cadillac back to my sister. And you will spend the night there before starting your way back. I'm waiting for you here in the hotel. That's an order.

Little Lilly was disappointed when we left in such a hurry."

"At your command, Sir", Ryan smiled.

"You saved my old messed up life for the second time, Hawk. You deserved a reward", Randell said.

"I was just doing my job, Sir", Ryan replied.

"I expected nothing else", said the Chief.

Chapter 4
Inuk, the white bear

For two and a half years, like every morning, Ryan has been doing his rounds. He was alone and always he took the same route over a distance of six miles. Now he knew every blade of grass, every stone and every sound that accompanied him. The mist made the air heavy and smoke came from his mouth. It was the last November morning of this year and the night had given way to dawn. Frosty temperatures and icy wind bites in cheeks and nose. Ryan felt the cold deep into his lungs, but his body was warm. Ryan was already on his way back, because in an hour he was supposed to pick up Major General Randell in front of the main building. The last time, because the chief had been transferred to Air Force Base Orlando, Florida, until he retired. Randell should spend this time at the desk without exception. Ryan quickened the pace as if he could run away from his thoughts. Clouds of mist weaved around the planes standing on the ground. Like dark shadow spirits, their outlines appeared and disappeared again. Scattered voices weakened his ears.

Unreal and strange, these voices reached the base workshop. The croak of a few quarrelsome crows interfered. The big, bearded man yawned several times while he was cleaning a black limousine with a vacuum cleaner. The device drowned out the music. When Baxter turned off the vac, his new technical lieutenant was behind him.

"Slept badly, Goodman?"

Baxter spun around quickly.

"Good morning", Baxter greeted disrespectfully and

eyed the young greenhorn named Rice. Baxter did not like this guy and sometimes forgot, that he was employed by the military. Baxter Goodman had done his job. In order to get his master's degree as a mechanic, he had become first technical sergeant. They looked up at him. That made Baxter a little proud, because he was in charge in the workshop. Nobody was allowed to chase him through the area with field pack for miles.

Baxter, unimpressed, finally continued with his work.

"Have you already submitted the order?"

"No", Baxter growled.

"Well, I'll do it now and you'll take care of the Wrangler's gas pump. With the Chrysler, the oil must be changed immediately. It must be ready for use in an hour. Can you still do it?"

Baxter was in a rage and narrowed his eyes.

"The Wrangler's gas pump is gone and the new one has been ordered for three days. I changed the Chrysler oil yesterday, before basic cleaning. The vehicle leaves in 30 minutes.

"Beautiful. Why is the gas pump not there yet?"

Baxter rolled his eyes.

"A certain Lieutenant Rice must have put it on the list with invisible ink", Baxter answered pointedly.

"Goodman, you are responsible, that everything is in place and ready on time."

Baxter went to the open gate, sucked the thick, heavy air deep into his lungs and looked up at the sky.

"If you don't send me help soon, I'll wring Rice's neck and cancel your friendship!", he murmured.

At the very moment Ryan appeared at the gate.

"Thank you! Mind if I come jogging a bit with you?" Baxter growled.

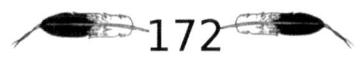

Ryan stopped and moved over to him.

"Are you sick?", he asked worriedly.

"Trouble's brewing! I need oxygen otherwise I feel sick."

"I'm on my way to the shower. Feel free, Baxter. The track is clear", Ryan grinned.

"Beware of this man. His eyes are silent when his tongue speaks. They are dead", Ryan whispered to his friend.

"What? Don't drive me crazy! What are you talking about gibberish? He's just a ... I prefer not to say it."

Baxter was angry and just waved it off.

"See you soon, Baxter", Ryan said and walking on.

Baxter watched him go until his shape disappeared into the fog.

"Hey Goodman!", Rice shouted. "Where did you hide the lists? Order seems strange to you. You can't find anything. What are you doing here all day?"

Baxter gasped.

"Sleep. What else", he grumbled.

Then Baxter opened a drawer below the workbench and brought out a thick block of paper. He smiled very friendly when he pressed it into Rice's hand.

"Here you go, gentleman. And make sure that the copy is perfectly legible, Rice."

"Lieutenant Rice! Even if you are now a civilian worker in the Air Force. I'm a lieutenant!"

Rice seemed to attach great importance.

"All right, Lieutenant Rice", Baxter repeated correctly. He didn't think Rice could drag him across the arena. He wasn't sure what Rice was doing. Therefore, Baxter urged caution.

The US Air Force had recognized Baxter Goodman's skills and had come to appreciate them. He had been made chief mechanic, master, and finally technical sergeant. At

his own request, Baxter was a civilian employee for life. He was proud of what he had achieved. No one had to tell him what to do. The superiors treated him with respect. Exactly four weeks ago they put a freshman technical lieutenant under his nose. Although Baxter was of the mind, this greenhorn had no idea and was of no use. At first he thought it's wiser to refrain from making any statements about it. Only Ryan knew about Baxter's displeasure.

Baxter reported to Rice to refuel the vehicle.

"Okay, but hurry up, Goodman! The Chrysler will be picked up at any moment."

Baxter slammed the door and pretended not to hear it and started the engine. Smiling he steered the car over to the quarters. The gas tank was already full, but the test drive now seemed essential. Baxter got out, leaned against the Chrysler, lit a cigarette and took in the cold morning air. That was good, even if the air wasn't the best. Baxter didn't have to wait long for his friend. Ryan threw his bag in the trunk and sat in the passenger seat.

"Can we swap? I'm driving Randell to Florida and meanwhile you're cleaning up the workshop", the bearded grunted.

Ryan grinned.

"You wouldn't find anything anymore."

"I'm already doing that."

Baxter grimaced. "Are you driving me to the workshop? Is quite far and I am not well on foot."

Ryan laughed. "Can you afford a chauffeur, my friend?"

"I'm the boss", grinned Baxter.

Ryan laughed again.

"Then make room for the chauffeur."

Ryan dropped Baxter off right in front of the workshop

gate.
At that moment, Rice came hurriedly through the gate with the lists in hand. He was about to say something, but closed his mouth again immediately. His face looked as if he had just bitten into a lemon.
Baxter couldn't stop his mocking grin.
"Thank you my friend. That feels good! The guy will ask himself for the rest of the day why I drive up with the major general's limousine and his chauffeur. I wish you a junk and wrinkle-free flight."
"He seems to have a problem with it", said Ryan.
"Toksa Mato."
Baxter laughed. For him it was refreshing satisfaction. Ryan drove away. He was expected on time.

*****

Randell took a seat in the passenger seat while Ryan packed the suitcases into the car. Then they left the premises.
"I'm sorry that our time is over. In Florida they'll put me in the museum and maybe dust off now and then", started Randell.
A smile played around Ryan's corner of his mouth.
"You have a good but damn hard job, Ryan. You're worth every dollar the Air Force pays you. I don't know anyone better than you."
Then Randell laughed. ".... even if you never flew."
Ryan smiled.
"We were both on the road for two years and eight months. When was the last time you were at home with

your family?"

"Two years and eight months ago, Sir."

Randell shook his head blankly.

"I gave you vacation."

Ryan nodded to confirm.

"My sister lives in Rapid City."

"What will you do when your Air Force time runs out one day, Ryan?"

"I go back to the reservation when I have enough money so that we can live on the ranch. I want to breed, train and sell horses. I want to teach some people to ride and maybe one day, give tourists a place to stay. That is my vision, my dream, my life."

"How much is 'enough money'?"

Ryan shrugged.

"When the day comes I will know."

"Does this tell you your Manitou?"

Ryan shook his head.

"With us Lakota it means Wakan Tanka, Great Spirit."

"I had two sons", Randell started to tell.

"One died in a car accident, the other crashed almost two years later with a Jayhawk training aircraft. On that day I stopped believing. When my wife died of cancer three years ago, I cursed the one I no longer believed in. Back in the underground garage when you saved my shitty corked life, I thanked him again for the first time. You are now twenty-two years old and you could be my grandson. May he protect you, whatever his name is."

Ryan nodded.

The road ahead was long and led through several states. Randell had drawn the subject to more amusing memories of his earlier days. He laughed often and Ryan grinned every now and then. Ryan then stayed at the Air

Force base in Florida for three days. At that time Randell was keen to show him some, in his opinion, sights worth seeing in this unknown south. Ryan was most fascinated by the ocean. When he had to make his way back in the morning of the fourth day, the chief did not miss the opportunity to say goodbye to him personally.

Randell said warmly and with a brave smile: "I wholeheartedly wish you that your vision, your dream of the tourist ranch, will one day come true. I firmly believe in it. If anyone can do it, it's you. You're smart and clever. Stay as you are, my son."

No. Ryan hadn't interrogated. He noticed that for the Chief it was difficult to speak. His eyes gleamed treacherously as he winked confidently at Ryan. Then Randell reached for him and pressed him briefly and firmly against himself.

"Thanks", Ryan replied, touched. "Sir, all the best to you too. Don't let it get you down, Chief."

Then Ryan took a stance and saluted in accordance with the regulations. Major General Randell did the same. Ryan gritted his teeth hard as he got into the car and started. In the rearview mirror he saw the motionless figure of the chief who was watching him go. She became tiny and finally disappeared from the mirror and from Ryan's life.

*****

There was silence over the valley crossed by the stream, the water of which led to the White River. The icy northwesterly wind had turned the drizzle into a gentle drift of snow. The flakes were still tiny and lay timidly, like powdered sugar, over the country. The dawn of the gray late autumn day gave way to darkness early. Through the thick snowflakes, sunlight no longer penetrated to earth. The atmosphere swallowed the engine noise of a jeep that came along the dirt road. The stones crunched under his heavy tires. A few horses were dozing, huddled tightly together in the paddock. The jeep stopped right in front of the porch stairs of the house. Two men got out. Both wore black, padded US Air Force jackets. A tall, bearded man opened the trunk and took out two large bags. The other a small black travel bag and a backpack that he hung over his shoulder. Then the tailgate slammed. Together the two men went up the stairs. The light was on in the house.

"Maybe I should go straight to Olivia", Baxter doubted.

"You stay! You're my guest", said Ryan firmly.

Baxter didn't dare to contradict. He was not afraid to meet Ryan's family, but a queasy feeling had spread through his guts. On the way, Ryan had told him in a few sentences from his family and the ranch. It wasn't much Baxter knew about the life of the Lakota in Pine Ridge Reservation. Actually nothing. The only thing that stuck in his mind was that he should just be who he was. For Baxter it was surprising that the tobacco was sacred to the Lakota and indispensable as a gift. When he took a very large pack of the best pipe tobacco while shopping at Walmart, he couldn't really interpret Ryan's grin. He was unsettled.

Ryan knocked and opened the door.

The people sitting in the living room looked at the two men. Freezing cold blew through the door. Ryan leaned against it and closed it behind his friend.

"Good evening", he greeted and put down his bag and backpack. Robert got up from the chair and came up to Ryan.

"Is it really you or am I dreaming?"

Ryan put his hand on Robert's shoulder.

"It's me. But are you my little brother?"

Robert laughed.

"Your younger brother."

Ryan took off the jacket.

"I brought a guest with me. Baxter Goodman, my friend. Tomorrow he wants to go to Rapid City to see his mother."

Baxter was still rooted by the door, feeling the eyes on him. He cleared his throat before croaking.

"Good evening."

"Good evening, Baxter Goodman", said John, staring at him amused. "Come and sit down!"

Baxter came out of his stasis and went to the table on which he put the bags. The one of them fell over. Apples and oranges rolled loosely across the table. Robert jumped to the other side to stop them while. Baxter threw himself over the table and started putting everything back in the bag. He let slip: "crap, damn it!"

John and Robert grinned.

Ryan hugged his mother and finally grandmother Lucy warmly. Then Anny brought a basket for the fruits.

"Thank you", she said to Baxter.

"There is more in the bags. We bought bread, steaks, and frozen vegetables", said Ryan.

"That makes a good dinner for all of us", Anny enthused. "Bring it straight to the kitchen, Ryan."

Ryan did that. Then he sat down at the table with his father and gave him a whole pack of cigarettes. John smiled happily at his son and nodded. Baxter took a seat next to Robert.

"How is the Pontiac?", Baxter asked the young man he had already met.

"Everything okay. He runs."

Baxter grinned sheepishly and scratched the back of his head. Then he slapped his forehead with the flat of his hand.

"Man, I almost forgot the most important thing."

He pulled his backpack towards him and rummaged around in it. Finally, he pulled out the big bag of tobacco. Robert watched his every move in silence. The tall, bearded man got up, went around the table and stood up right in front of John. Baxter cleared his throat again before saying: "Sir, well, that, ehm ... the tobacco here is for you. A gift."

As he stammered the words, he peered suspiciously at the cigarette packet that Ryan had given his father. He almost thought he was fallen into his friends trap. John Black Hawk smiled and thanked him politely.

"Do you also smoke a pipe?", Baxter asked to clear his doubts.

"Yes of course. The tobacco will be enough until you come home again."

Then John laughed, which again unsettled Baxter. Ryan wrapped himself, smiling, in silence and watched his friend's goings-on. He was now heading for grandmother Lucy to greet her. She smiled gently and greeted in the Lakota language. Robert told Ryan things Baxter didn't understand. So he decided to go to the kitchen. It was separated from the living room by a wooden wall. There was no door.

"Mrs. Hawk, may I help you anything?"

Anny looked at the tall stranger leaning against the wooden post. Then she smiled.

"The dinner will be ready soon. You will be hungry."

"It's written all over my face?"

Anny giggled and turned the steaks.

"I would be happy if you call me Baxter, ma'am. I'm not much older than your son, even if it looks different. Just over my dead body I separate myself from my beard. Even Olivia has given up on it. She is my mother. I will visit her tomorrow. She has been waiting for it for a long time. She lives alone north of Rapid, but she keeps everybody busy. A whirlwind."

Baxter laughed softly.

Anny liked Baxter's entertainment.

"Do you like tea, Baxter?"

"Hop flower tea the finest." He laughed. "Yes, ma'am, there is nothing like a hot tea in this awful weather. That's good for chilblains and pharyngitis.

Anny was giggling again.

"So you're in the Army too?", she finally asked.

"US Air Force, yes. Ryan and me, we're both with the ground staff. Since a short time I'm a civil servant. Ryan, on the other hand, made him a Master Sergeant two years ago. Some believe that a non-commissioned officer should not drive people. For a week now he's been Chief Master Sergeant. Even I would have to stand to attention if he wanted to."

Baxter laughed amused.

Anny looked at Baxter in astonishment because Ryan never talked about things like that.

"I'm a mechanic. I can disassemble a car in a short time and assemble it again. With an airplane, however, I would need a handicraft sheet, otherwise it would

probably also become a car. One with jet propulsion."
Anny kept grinning.
Then she put the plates on the kitchen cupboard and placed the cutlery. Without losing a word, Baxter picked it up and carried it out. It clanked when he put them on the table and distributed them. Baxter was very hungry and the smell of roast meat that had been in his nose all the time tortured him. He became increasingly restless. Again he sneaked into Anny's kitchen. Anny gave him a friendly nod.
"The food is ready."
Baxter took the large, heavy meat pan and carried it to the table. *Too heavy for a petite woman like Anny Black Hawk*, he thought. When everyone had finally gathered around the table, John spoke a few words in Lakota that Baxter did not understand. Yet he listened carefully. It sounded strange in his ears and yet these strange words captivated him. They penetrated more deeply than he had ever believed. The other world no longer seemed to exist in this timeless instant. The voice of John Black Hawk and his words reassured Baxter, though he still didn't know what his friend's father said.
When the prayer ended, Baxter cleared his throat, muttered a quick, unintelligible *thank you*, and reached for the cutlery. Baxter's eyes shone with desire. Anny gave him a large, juicy piece of the roast. He enjoyed it. After what he got from the Air Force and what he did himself, it was a holiday dinner. The food that Anny had prepared tasted completely different from what he had known before. But it was very good. He smiled happily when he noticed that Anny was watching him constantly.
"That was truly delicious, Mrs. Black Hawk", gushed

Baxter. "The best thing I've ever eaten in my life", he praised exuberantly and gesticulating.

When Anny got up after a while, Baxter jumped up immediately, stacked the clattering plates into a leaning tower and disappeared into the kitchen.

John grinned amused. "Wakan Tanka is puzzling. He sent you a Wasicun as a friend, but it breathed a Heyoka into his mind", he whispered to Ryan.

Ryan grinned.

"Yes, Baxter is obsessed with a rascal ghost. He has a special gift for making people laugh. That's good medicine."

The hardness that had reminded Ryan of his father had left his face. Ryan hadn't expected anything. The easier it was for his heart to be welcome again. Ryan had noticed the glow in his father's eyes when he entered. John didn't ask questions.

Ryan, whom nobody had asked about his life in the other world, remained silent.

Baxter came to clear the rest of the table.

"I'll do it", he called. "Since I founded a single household, I have been almost the perfect house man. I can even cook", he announced proudly.

"Microwave and canned food", Ryan confirmed.

"On free weekends, I let Olivia invite me or call the party service. Then there is pizza and Feng Shui."

„Since when Feng Shui is eatable?", Ryan asked in astonishment.

Baxter just laughed and disappeared into the kitchen with dishes and a pan. Anny flinched when it rattled loudly.

"For Christ sake!", Baxter swore.

Ryan, Robert and John laughed.

"Nothing broken!", Baxter called, staring at Anny in horror when she suddenly stood in front of him. She didn't laugh at his misfortune. She also said nothing. Anny put down the rest of the dishes and just seemed to ignore it.

"Sorry", Baxter said sheepishly and thinking about what Olivia would have said.

Now Anny smiled when she saw the big, bearded man kneeling on the kitchen floor in front of her as he picked up forks, knives and spoons. Anny wiped the floor with a damp rag and said: "Waste. All right."

Baxter sneaked out of the kitchen unobtrusively before doing more damage. When he sat back on his chair at the big table, John was stuffing his pipe.

Baxter watched each of his movements in silent. He had no idea that John had noticed it and was looking at him unobtrusively.

"Do you smoke, Baxter Goodman?", he finally asked.

"Yes, Mr. Black Hawk. Usually only cigarettes, ... so far ... anyway ...", he stammered.

John nodded to Ryan.

He tore open a box of cigarettes and offered one to Baxter. Then he took one for himself and pushed the box across the table to his younger brother. Baxter took a first deep drag and felt his inner calm, which seemed to bring him back on track. His doubts and insecurity towards these people subsided from him. A feeling of harmonic self-confidence remained. That gave him the belief that he was what he is, and it's right.

*****

The next morning Ryan and Baxter stood at the paddock watching the horses. An icy wind swept over the prairie hills and valleys. Tiny ice crystals glittered in the air. Ryan had turned up the fur collar of his denim jacket and pulled his hat deep into his face. The valley shimmered white. Snowflakes migrated southward. The rays of the sun only timidly penetrated through cloud holes and spread a strange, unreal light.

"It's damn quiet here", Baxter said. "I didn't know there was anything like that."

"Yes. You brought the noise to this country and destroyed the sound of silence."

"What?", Baxter asked.

Ryan grinned.

"Do we want to ride?"

"Are you crazy? I have never sat on anything like that", replied Baxter indignantly and pointed with his hand at the piebald stallion.

"A good choice. The young stallion is very spirited. He would have had fun on an excursion."

"Who does it belong to?"

"Us."

"And who of you is crazy enough to sit on him?"

"Andy, my youngest brother. He is fifteen and still goes to school."

"I didn't see him last night or this morning. Doesn't he live here?"

"Sometimes, in winter, he stays with his friend in Kyle for the week. Classes often go until late in the afternoon, when it is already dark. Sometimes the school bus can no longer get through and he has to walk along the gravel path. That's a good four miles."

Baxter was amazed.

"In Pierre, where we lived at the time, the streets were mostly cleared and something was always driving. No chance for an additional school free. Not even the heating wanted to fail."

"You are alone with Olivia. I noticed that much. What about your family?"

"My father just left us. I have no siblings. I had a friend. He and his father often took me to the dragster or car race and everything that had to do with horsepower. Unless this one of course."

He laughed softly and pointed to the paddock.

"When we moved, I had several friends, but not a real one. Olivia wanted me in the children's choir. I like to sing and I might have a good voice, but the hum of the motors was the better music in my ears. It had a stronger appeal to me. I learned in a car workshop, after school. It was too boring and I dreamed of the racing teams. But I didn't manage to leave Olivia alone. You know the rest."

"The US Air Force always relies on powerful technology and speed. Maybe just barely past a racing team", Ryan said.

Baxter grinned.

"Well, but at least I have a lot of experience. Until recently, I even really enjoyed it and it could have been the job of my life. One day I'm going to kill this Rice."

Baxter grimaced.

Ryan smiled and shook his head.

After a while Baxter went on: "Your family will be happy when I leave. I think, I not only have your cutlery and crockery, but also messed up the whole order."

"How do you come up with such thoughts, my friend?"

"Well ... they talk very little and your father's smile

insecure me, frankly. I would like to know what he thinks about me."

"A strange white man will never read a Lakota's mind if he doesn't want to."

"And you? Can you read his thoughts?"

"I can bring my stallion to clear, fresh water. But I can't force him to drink. I'll have to be patient until he does it himself. You have to learn to accept things as they are. He does it too."

Ryan saw in Baxter's face exactly how hard he was trying to understand. It took some time before Baxter finally nodded.

"Hmmm", he growled. "Okay then. I have to leave. Olivia is waiting for me. Christmas is just around the corner and at this time she is always in high spirits down to sentimental. I was hoping she would find someone who would take her for what she was. But so far, every applicant has fled." Baxter laughed softly. "Next time you are our guest. I'm looking forward to. How do you always say? Toksa?"

"Yes. Toksa Mato. Goodbye bear."

"Mato, that's me. And what do I have to say? Toksa ..."

"Toksa Cetan Sapa", Ryan helped. "But Kolà is okay too."

"Cola? Pepsi or ..."

Ryan smacked Baxter's arm before he could continue talking and laughed.

"Kolà means friend."

"I can barely remember that. Toksa Cetan Sapa. Thank you for being your friend."

Ryan nodded and stuck his thumb in the back pockets of his jeans. He watched Baxter go to the house.

Baxter jumped up the porch stairs, knocked briefly and

opened the door.

"Merry Christmas and toksa all together!", he called into the room.

But only grandmother Lucy sat on the old sofa and embroidered. Smiling she looked up and politely replied: "Toksa ake wacinyankin ktelo."

These were the first words Baxter heard from her mouth. He waved and closed the door. Then he shook his head like a freshly bathed dog.

"Ryan just told me half, oh, not even half", he murmured and got into his Jeep Commander.

When he turned, he pressed the horn twice.

Robert stepped up next to Ryan and grinned. He did not say anything. When the commander left the valley, Ryan asked: "Can I borrow the Pontiac?"

"If you want to see Sam, she's no longer here."

"Hm", Ryan did.

"She is now married to an Apache and has gone to New Mexico with him."

"That's okay. I didn't want to see her either."

"You can have the Pontiac. Will you stay here longer this time?"

"One week."

"That's good. Do we have a ride? Andy's piebald is impatient. Kolà too."

"Yes, why not. I see that there are some new wooden posts."

"The beginning has been made, brother. Now I'm a real professional in wire drawing."

"Good. Come on, let's go before I freeze. I've been standing in one place for too long", Ryan said.

"You are not used to anything good!"

"We will see!"

Shortly afterwards the two brothers sat on the horses and disappeared over the hill that surrounded the valley. The path led them to the upper creek, on the bend of which stood an old, gnarled tree. Not far from there was a small wooden hut, from whose chimney a thin column of smoke rose. Two ponies scraped their hooves for the sparse blades of grass on the bank. They raised their heads as the two riders approached. Then they resumed their search for something to eat. Kola snorted contentedly. When the brothers arrived at the house, the door opened. An old man appeared. His grey hair was penetrated with white strands. He was wearing a leather vest, the fringes of which reached up to his knees. Old Raven smiled.

Ryan and Robert jumped off the horses and greeted him. The old man preferred the language of his people when he returned the greeting from the young men.

"Welcome. I knew that your path would lead to me. That's why I made tea. Come to my fire and warm up."

They let go the horses that joined the ponies and followed the Wicasa Wakan in his hut. There was only one room. On the wall was a stable corner bench, two chairs and a wooden table. The men sat down. Old Raven placed three large cups on the table.

"I made fresh herbal tea."

He took the kettle from the cast iron oven and poured the tea into the cups. Then he sat down at the table.

"It was a long time since we last saw each other, he said."

Ryan gripped the cup with both hands and nodded.

"It's good to be here."

Old Raven smiled in satisfaction.

"Hila, your sister, has already left?", asked Robert.

"Yes, I'm leaving soon. It is time."
Then the old man laughed hoarsely and stuffed his pipe. "What am I in the icy winter without my car, my gas heating and my TV. Done. I would freeze to death out here alone and the loneliness would torture me. This is the cycle as long as I'm able to remember."
Robert grinned.
Old Raven lit the pipe.
"The sun, the moon and our mother earth are round and always describe, a circle on their way. Without beginning, without end. We also move in circles, while dancing, our tipis are round and the fireplaces. Wakan Tanka has taught us that true power, all power, is hidden in it. Everything is reflected in the circle and he sent us our medicine wheel, in which each of us finds his place. Our life was in harmony with everything that was given to us."
Old Raven paused to slowly take a long pull out of the pipe.
Ryan smiled and looked around the log cabin conspicuously. But he did not speak his thoughts. Old Raven caught his eye and understood the question in it.
"Many, many years ago, a white man wanted to tell my grandfather that the future was in square, solid houses and so he built it. It withstood many storms and offered protection. But he couldn't find the middle of his life anymore. His inner balance began to falter. He called the ghosts in vain, but they no longer wanted to speak to him. Maybe they just couldn't hear him anymore. The songs that grandfather sang and his prayers sounded muffled and the thick walls seemed to swallow his voice. Even though he knew that it was strictly forbidden, he secretly took out the poles and the old buffalo skin

tarpaulins and set up the tipi with his wife. When he slept with her in the tent the following night, he had a vision. A mysterious fog had wrapped around the tipi and a proud warrior emerged from the fog in front of him. He had a beautiful young woman at his side. And he recognized his grandfather and grandmother in them. The young woman was silent and smiled. The warrior said to him that they wanted to accompany him into the future to see what had become of your children and grandchildren. The spirits of our ancestors live in the tipi of Old Raven. Our fathers left it to us to teach our children and leave it to them."

Then it was quiet.

Old Raven pulled a few times, slowly and deeply, on his pipe. Robert and Ryan looked into their teacups as if they could read into.

Finally, the old man knocked out his pipe and said: "Your tea is cold. I'm going to pour you more."

He did so, poured his cup again too and sat down.

"Do you think Red Eagle has found its center again?", Ryan asked softly.

"What do you think?"

"He will never forget that I couldn't be silent."

"As long as you cannot control the storm in your own heart, the waves will not settle."

Ryan said nothing. He knew it only too well.

"You have started a long journey, my grandson, and Tunkasila will accompany you. Follow your way. It will lead you back to who you really are."

Ryan pressed his lips together and nodded. For a few hours he felt like he was in the middle of his life before reality was to throw him out of balance again. But now he felt strong enough to face her again.

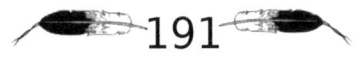

Old Raven brewed another jug of herbal tea and chatted about this and that. There was a lot of news. The time seemed endless, but the sun in the west leaned towards the horizon.
Together the three men left to be at home before dark. The tent of the ancestors had long been stowed away for winter. Left to the protection of the log house, which was lonely at the bend in Makoce Wakan, the holy land.

*****

In a cold sweat, Ryan threw himself around in bed. There they were again, the wolves. A whole pack around him. They bared their teeth, wrinkled their noses and growled menacingly. In the light of the full moon, her eyes shone like glowing coals. Ryan was completely alone in a snow-covered forest clade. He wanted to escape and thought of climbing a tree, but his feet seemed to have grown on the ground. Ryan couldn't move anymore. He frantically pulled the pistol that hung from his belt. He aimed it at the beasts and fired, but the trigger clicked empty. Ryan felt a chill shiver through his body. His pistol was always loaded. Not today. He carefully felt for his knife. It was in the usual place. Relieved he pulled it. Not a second early because the wolves attacked. They started to mangle him. They tugged on his legs, bit his arms, but he fought back with all his strength and fear. Ryan let out a loud scream that hurt his ears. But the wolves were not intimidated by this. Blood dripped into the snow. His blood. Ryan thought at that moment that he was going to die.

Finally, he leaped up from the bed and stared wide-eyed into the dark.

It was quiet.

Ryan switched on the lamp above the bed and gasped. He was given a room to himself. It was small. There was a bed, a cupboard, a table and two chairs. When Ryan knew where he was, he jumped out of bed and went to the bedroom. It was just before midnight. So he hadn't slept for a long time. Ryan turned the shower on and stood under the cold water. The skin contracted. He took several deep breaths and stroked his head with both hands. He was here alone. After ten minutes he reached for the towel and scrubbed his skin dry so that it turned red. Then Ryan went back to his room. His eyes caught on the little dream catcher that grandmother had made for him. On the day of his departure, she had pressed it into his hand. Now he was hanging on the post of his bed.

"You no longer have any effect in the other world. You should help me", he said softly.

Ryan's mouth twisted into a faint smile. Then he lay down on his bed, crossed his arms behind his head and stared at the ceiling. A few minutes later, Ryan turned off the lights. Nevertheless, he did not find his way back to sleep for a long time, and that was on the first night after his vacation. It was after midnight and December the 27th. Ryan had to rest and report in great shape to Taylor's office at seven in the morning. He knew he was getting a new Chief today. Ryan didn't think that might be why he couldn't sleep.

What will await me? he wondered.

Such thoughts were previously unknown to him. He shook his head as if to shake off his thoughts.

What's wrong with me?
Bad dreams.
A bad sign?
It's just a job, damn it.

That was his job and Ryan vowed not to disappoint the new one, Randell's successor. He risked a look at the clock. It was thirty minutes past two in the morning. At some point he finally fell asleep. The restlessness fell asleep and the fear of this dream. The dream actually haunted him and he returned to the same place in the forest where the wolves shredded his flesh. It burned like fire. Ryan was now looking in vain for his knife. Something whirred past his shoulder. One of the wolves howled and let go of him. Something buzzed through the air again. Two arrows had pierced them. The other wolves fled into the forest. Ryan looked around, but nobody showed up. It was very quiet. Again he couldn't move. An old, gray-haired man appeared between the trees. He had a bow in his hand, nodded to Ryan and smiled with satisfaction.

"Mitunkasila!", whispered Ryan.

Ryan's grandfather had gone to the spirits world ten years ago. At that time Ryan was twelve. It was very difficult for him to say goodbye. He could still remember grandfather's face, his voice and his words. Now grandfather had come into his dream to protect him.

The old man lit a fire.

"Tunkasila", Ryan spoke to him.

Grandfather looked at him and smiled confidently. Then grandfather's shape blurred.

Ryan tried to get up. His feet carried him to the place where grandfather had lit the fire. There was no footprint in the snow. The dead wolves were gone. Only the drops of blood remained in the snow. Ryan shivered. He was alone and wondered which way to go. But he didn't find an answer. Ryan was still thinking about it when he was already awake. It was only a quarter past three.

*****

The alarm clock teared Ryan out from the deep sleep. As heavy as lead he got up and made his way to the shower. This time he wasn't alone. A couple of naked men throw a bar of soap through the area and laughed like cocky boys. Ryan tried not to show his leaden tiredness, although he wanted to hit his skull against the wall to put his thoughts in order.
"Didn't sleep well, Hawk?", someone shouted to him.
"Yes", he replied shortly
"It's no fun alone", another one shouted and laughed.
"Or he jumped up too much once and now needs his rest", said the one who spoke first.
The men laughed with amusement.
Ryan did not respond to the sayings and turned on the water.

When Ryan was standing in front of the desk in Taylor's office an hour later, he felt wide awake and made no sign of anything.
Across from Taylor was a dark-haired major general. He was much younger than Randell and eyed the Lakota with strangely skepticism.
"That's him, Chief. Master Sergeant Hawk, the specialist

in all explosive cases", started Taylor.

Then he looked at Ryan.

"This is Major General Fox, your new boss. From now on you are under his command."

Ryan nodded.

"Sir, yes Sir!"

"He is still very young and seems to me to be rather inexperienced. Taylor, do you think he's suitable for this job?" , Fox doubted.

"Hawk is the best man for the mission the Air Force can give you!", Taylor emphasized.

Once again Ryan felt the skeptical looks that studied every inch of his body. Ryan looked uneasily at an imaginary point on the wall and locked his thoughts behind a motionless mask. Nobody noticed that he was watching fox. His stubble hair stood up. He didn't have a beard. The face was angular and the nose flat, as is often the case with boxers. His age was difficult to estimate. *Maybe twice my age*, Ryan thought.

"Well. At least what we have heard about it... It must have made some people sick about his driving style. But driving fast is no longer a special art nowadays and a turn around on the spot I can do that too", Fox interrupted Ryan's thoughts.

"If you insist, I'll send you another driver", Taylor said.

He could hardly hide his displeasure. He took a deep breath. Fox actually dared to doubt Taylor's decision.

"Not necessary, Taylor. I will try with him. Is he loyal?"

Ryan remained rigid. The men talked about him as if he didn't exist.

"You can rely on it."

"He's Indian", Fox noted.

"Do you have a problem with it?", Taylor asked indignantly.

"The Indsman don't have a bad reputation with the US Army. On the contrary. They can officially show that they are good warriors and that as a US citizen. Well, that's how times change. Has he ever flown?"

Taylor's voice got snappy when he answered Fox: "Ask him yourself."

Ryan was silent when he noticed the questioning look on him. Fox was obviously waiting for an answer. When he realized that he didn't feel addressed, he finally asked Ryan directly.

"What is it? Have you ever flown, Hawk?"

"Yes, Sir, in a transport helicopter", Ryan replied.

Fox grinned smugly.

"You will prepare for the fact that we will fly to the individual bases and get you a car on site. Our first assignment is in Alaska. The plane starts in exactly two hours. Any questions?"

"Sir. No Sir."

"You are dismissed."

Ryan greeted correctly and left the office.

Taylor pressed his lips together as if to say something or force himself to remain silent.

"He doesn't speak too much. I like that", Fox said contentedly.

*****

Ryan threw himself on his bed, but his restlessness drove him up again. He couldn't have closed his eyes now. When he had packed his few things, he threw his small black bag over his shoulder and left the accommodation in direction of the workshop. Wind blew icy on his face and around his ears. The smell of snow was in the air.

When Ryan entered the workshop, he took off his aviator glasses and looked around for Baxter. Two strange men wearing overalls were immersed in their work and had neither heard nor seen him coming. Baxter, on the other hand, was sitting on the workbench, holding a magazine and reading. A coffee mug was at hand next to him. Ryan grinned, crept up to him, and punched the paper. Baxter winced, dropped the newspaper, jumped up and greeted with all his mouth after all the rules of art.

"Sir! Good morning Sir!"

When he had overcome his fright, he laughed and added: "The black Mustang is ready for use and paws with its hooves, Chief Master Sergeant."

Ryan laughed.

"Is the hangover not in the house?"

The two young men had now also noticed that a senior had entered the workshop. They stood stiffly next to a car and greeted correctly.

Ryan replied.

"Carry on!", Baxter ordered.

"He has the mange", whispered Baxter to his friend. "Rice reported sick yesterday. The poorest has a cold."

"That's great for you."

"For me he can stay snuffed forever. But tell me what's wrong with you? Are you ill too? Looks like you haven't slept all night."

"I don't have."

"What's going on?"

"I had bad dreams. Something's up."
"Don't make yourself hot about it, my friend. Sometimes I dream the biggest shit together.
Ryan nodded and said nothing.
"Do you have to drive now?"
"No. To fly."
"And the black one?"
"Remain in your care for now, Baxter."
"You're allowed to tell me where you go?"
Ryan's mouth twisted into a smile.
"Nobody forbade me. Alaska", he said softly.
"Man!", Baxter grunted and added quietly: "just dress warmly so that you don't get a cold too."
Ryan shook his head.
"At sixty degrees below zero a virus cannot survive."
"Of course! The Alaska killer virus", Baxter said.
"Alaska killer viruses?"
"Yes. The one with the thermal socks. They are as stubborn as lice."
Ryan had to laugh.
Then he said goodbye to Baxter indefinitely and left the workshop.

*****

A short time later, Ryan was sitting in an Air Force transport machine and looked out of the window. When the plane flew out of the clouds, untouched, endless forests, white mountains and mirror-clear lakes appeared beneath it. Ten the pictures disappeared again in the clouds. It got dark around one o'clock in the afternoon. When the plane landed at a military base in Alaska about thirty minutes later, it was dark. The snow all around lit up in the dim light of the lighting.

A man wearing a white Overall received the incoming men. The hood protected his head and part of his face from the cold. He and Fox seemed to know each other. They greeted each other confidentially and went ahead. Ryan followed without being asked. It was quiet on this comparatively small base. There was only one runway. The Air Force Base was home to a helicopter squadron near Anchorage. Two long buildings with vaulted roofs stood side by side. They looked like huge snow piles. There was dense forest all around the base.

Fox hadn't spoken to Ryan during the flight, or now, when he was following the men to one of the buildings with antennas and satellites.

Ryan listened when he heard wolves howling from far away. An icy shower involuntarily crept over his back. Then the door closed behind him. The room he entered appeared to be a canteen. It was pleasantly warm and smelled of coffee. The yellow light from the lamps spread warmth and comfort, so snow, cold and darkness could be quickly forgotten. Ryan followed Fox across the room. The stranger who was leading Fox had stripped off his hood and opened a door at the end of the canteen. The ones who arrived had been watched tacitly. Ryan closed the door behind him. The three men walked down a dimly lit aisle.

"Welcome to my humble realm, Slim. You haven't been here in a long time", the stranger said to Fox.

"Right. I only have my orders."

The stranger turned to Fox and grinned.

"Besides, you freeze your balls off up here", growled

Fox.

Through the next door, the three men entered a room that corresponded to a mixture of office, technical operations center and warehouse. The stranger finally took off his Overall while offering Fox a seat.

Ryan stopped.

"Speak! Where is the Farmingdale currently?"

"Exactly twelve miles northeast from here towards Tower Rock."

"And that's why you request us? Because of meagre twelve miles of road?"

"Didn't they inform you, Slim? I thought you knew everything very well?"

"I know it! But I think it's over the top. You just have to talk to them properly", said Slim and grinned deliberately. The stranger glanced at Ryan and looked at him disdainfully from top to bottom. The other two men who were in the room went about their work without taking the slightest note. They seemed to work like robots.

"Oh that's why you brought an Indian with you, Slim Fox. Clever!"

"This is Chief Master Sergeant Hawk, driver at Rapid City Air Force Base, South Dakota, and currently under my command", Fox said, turning slowly.

Ryan greeted the stranger, whose rank he still couldn't make out. He stared at him, whistled softly through his teeth and returned the greeting shortly.

"Lieutenant Forner", he introduced himself.

"Do you have vehicles ready for us?"

Forner nodded.

"Snowmobiles. There is no other way to get through the wilderness here, at least not until the road is ready. Or

do you prefer to have a helicopter?"

"No. Is too much turmoil for me at the moment. We try the gentle tour first. I don't want to scare my friends right away. We take two snowmobiles. Hawk? Do you know anything about that?"

"Sir. No Sir."

Forner took a deep breath.

"It's like a Quad. It only has runners under it so it wouldn't sink into the deep snow", he explained.

"Sir. I know what a snowmobile is. I just haven't had a chance to drive one. I'll drive it as soon as someone instructs me, Sir."

Forner instructed one of the men in the room to take Hawk to a certain Lone Wolf, who should familiarize him with the vehicle immediately. Ryan followed the man.

"Quite snooty, the Indsman", Forner noted. "I do not trust him."

"He was personally recommended to me by Taylor and what I have learned about him speaks for him. He's considered damn tough, clever and crazy. And who, if not an Indsman, should be better suited to the job", Fox grinned smugly.

"And if he comes round?", Forner doubted.

Fox grimaced and shook his head.

"He won't dare. He has a family to look after."

The man hired by Forner brought Ryan down and introduced him to the technician. Ryan remained alone with the man named Lone Wolf in an underground vehicle hall. He was amazed at what could be found here, deep under the earth. In addition to the snowmobiles, there were tracked vehicles, snow removal equipment, wheel loaders, trucks and two

Humvees with monumental tires. Lone Wolf's black eyes blinked amused at Ryan. The old man's wrinkled face seemed to be made of brown leather. The Indian wore his white-gray hair short. Without further ado he started to explain everything to Ryan.

"It's like riding a horse. If you have a feeling for it, you will have no problems with it. Register in the clothing issue and get dressed. You won't get far here with your padded Air Force blouson. You will freeze to death. Fox and Forner don't care how you drive around out there. They would send you naked to Tower Rock yourself. They think we are tough."

He looked at Ryan strongly. Their looks met. Ryan nodded. He had understood.

"Are you from South Dakota. Are you Dakota?"

"Yes. Lakota. And you? Inuit?"

"That's right, my friend."

Ryan followed the advice of the old, lonely wolf and took all the equipment to his quarters.

Fox ordered to head to Tower Rock the following morning. He wanted to talk to the people. Ryan spent the time waiting for sleep wondering why he should accompany Fox to these people. Fox could and wanted to drive a snowmobile himself, so he didn't need a driver. Nor did he seem to be a fearful person who did not dare to cover such a distance on his own. Fox might have expected to back him up in conversation with these people. Ryan didn't know who these people were. But his instinct told him, it had to be Inuit. There were too many inconsistencies. Fox hadn't felt it necessary to inform Ryan of the situation. The job, or whatever came up to him, would be difficult, and Ryan had a bad feeling about it, despite not asking Fox what that meant.

The day in the far north dawned and sent a gleaming twilight on the snow-covered earth. This dawn gave way to a weak daylight only around noon. The two snowmobiles made the only noise in the silence. Fox drove ahead. He knew the ways around here. Ryan followed. Fox seemed to want to challenge him. He raced like a madman through the forest, in a slalom around the trees and jumped over the bumps. Ryan kept up and stayed a short distance behind him. He even enjoyed driving the snowmobile. The impassable route led steeply downhill from a plateau. Fox didn't brake. Ryan wondered if Fox really just wanted to play the hero to prove what he was capable of, or something else. Suddenly Ryan heard a whir in the air and looked up. At that very moment something tore him off his vehicle with an extremely rough jerk. Ryan landed in the snow.

When he jumped on his feet to free himself from the noose, a white shadow knocked him over again. Ryan struggled. Two men wallowed in the fight like two pumas. Another five white figures take up position around the fighting ones.

Six wolves in the snow!

Then Ryan felt a hard, painful punch on his lower jaw. With a soft moan he gave up his resistance. The man who knelt on him raised his knife.

"You traitor!", he hissed angrily at him.

When he tried to run Ryan with one's knife the fight started again. The noose around Ryan's torso had loosened. He took the knife from his opponent's hand, jumped up and pulled the loop completely away. The men around them did not budge. Ryan stopped with the knife in his hand and looked at his opponent who was standing opposite him.

"The next time you want to catch a Lakota, you have to be faster."

"Next time I would have killed you right away!"

The man in the snowsuit had to be an Inuit, just like the other five, and maybe as old as Ryan.

"And what have you been waiting for this time?"

The Inuit contemptuously grimaced and spat out in front of Ryan.

"Tell me, how did I deserve your hatred?"

"Because you're on the wrong side, traitor."

Then he gave a sign to his men, whereupon they grabbed Ryan and tied his hands on his back. Ryan let it happen.

"You go with us!"

One brought the Air Force snowmobile. Ryan had to sit up in the back. The one who fought with Ryan had to be the leader of the gang. He took over the snowmobile. The other men followed with their mobiles. The path continued towards Tower Rock, where Ryan wanted to go anyway. Slim Fox was completely gone. Everyone could see his clearly left marks. When they drove past an orphan road construction site a little later, Ryan rhymed a lot. These people, who belonged to his people, the indigenous people, did not agree with this street. It was clear. Ryan could also guess why. But was that the only reason? The Inuit used the fixed edge strip with the snowmobiles. The road went straight for miles, straight to Tower Rock.

At the foot of the rock mountain, which stretched vertically upwards, there was a village made up of several huts and a large long house. In front of the house the men stopped. Before anyone could touch Ryan, he dismounted. He was angry with himself. Fox had disappeared and Ryan didn't know where, and he had failed the first day.

The young Inuit pointed him to move forward into the large wooden house. People stood crowded and talked quietly to each other. The Inuit pushed through and pulled Ryan behind him to the opposite side. Two men sat there, side by side. An old man with white shoulder length hair and a major general of the US Army.

Slim Fox.

The Inuit stopped in front of the old one.

"You wanted to talk to one of them, White Bear. This is one of them. Not a white one. Just a traitor", said the young Inuit with contempt. "But I see you've already got yourself one."

The men around laughed.

Slim Fox too. He looked at his captive and bound sergeant. Ryan gritted his teeth and tried to curb his anger. His breath was shallow and quick. For the second time in his life he had lost his face to himself. He had failed. Fox was not the only one to enjoy his defeat. The Inuit mocked him. Ryan stretched his body, flexed all his muscles and kept his head held high. At that moment, as Fox had analyzed, he felt like a warrior. Black Hawk had learned to endure defeat.

"Where were you, Sergeant Hawk? I was really worried", Fox finally said. "It seems to me that there was actually someone faster than you?"

Ryan noticed the mockery of these words and avoided looking at anyone. He didn't answer.

The old man with the white hair had his gaze on Ryan. He seemed to be considering.

"My grandson, Wolf Shield, is supposed to take the

shackles off our relative. We want to talk to each other and make our decisions as free men", he said.

The young Inuit obeyed.

"Who are you?", asked the old man.

"I am Ryan Black Hawk, Lakota Nation, and Chief Master Sergeant of the U.S. Air Force."

White Bear nodded and pointed at two vacant chairs.

"Sit down!", he ordered.

So Ryan was sitting next to Wolf Shield. He avoided even looking at him. Wolf Shield also looked exclusively at the old man who was his grandfather. White Bear started talking.

"We approved the construction of this road, but under different conditions and requirements. The Farmingdale Road Company does not adhere to the given construction plans. They reject our protests. Why, General Fox?"

"The current route from Tower Rock to our base is the shortest, the least expensive and therefore the most environmentally friendly way", explained Fox.

"But this decision is up to us!", replied White Bear.

"No. At the client", Fox contradicted.

"The course of the route was agreed in writing with the US Air Force, your military base, and sealed by mutual agreement. We were even promised compensation. A subsequent change without our knowledge and without our consent is not permitted. This country is our country!"

"We are here on American soil. Alaska is American territory. It's ours", Fox said mildly, smiling.

"The government has given us this piece of land on Tower Rock that has belonged to us from time immemorial. On top of that, it is designated as a nature reserve and we have sole fishing rights."

"Then clarify this with the person who signed the contract. The US Army has no influence on this, and the small Air Force base here on the world's ass certainly doesn't. I just want to tell you, White Bear, that it would be wiser not to block the work of the Farmingdale Road Company any further. There's only a paltry twelve miles! We shouldn't make life difficult for each other. When they have finished their work, you will never see them again. The road also brings advantages for you and your infrastructure. You are already in a good position with the commercial agreement at our base. So keep your people in line. You are a wise and influential man, White Bear."

White Bear nodded.

"We'll talk to the chief of the company. He has to come and explain why he doesn't stick to the blueprints. Maybe there is a very important reason. Then we have to find a solution and keep the damage as low as possible. Until that day the work of Farmingdale Road Company will be suspended."

"Does that mean further blockades, threats from your men and attacks?"

White bear said nothing.

Ryan heard Wolf Shield gasping angrily next to him.

Fox went on: "The men of the company know the contract and they have a damn tight schedule. If the road is not handed over by the agreed date, each additional day will cost thousands of dollars. Farmingdale has requested military protection for the road construction. Their workers are afraid of further raids. There were already injured employees. And I'll make damn sure things don't escalate. And I have every authority."

"This street can't cross the street of the bear and cut off its path. If Nanuk doesn't find the way to his holy land anymore, he dies", the old man spoke slowly and emphasizing every word. "You, Lakota, understand. Can you make this man understandable?"

"I understand", Ryan replied.

Then he looked directly at White Bear.

"There are people who do not want to understand and who have no respect for Nanuk. They will point the rifles at him when he crosses their street and are not afraid of him."

"Hm!", Wolf Shield made. "You don't even want to try it!"

"I'm just a US Air Force Sergeant and I'm under their command."

Fox grinned subtly.

Wolf Shield jumped up.

"I should have known, traitor!", he hissed bitterly and left the room.

"A fatal mistake", Fox noted.

"I don't care if you cut off each other's throats to straighten your sense of honor. But as long as the Lakota is a member of the Air Force, I will not allow that."

Ryan stared at his feet. He could no longer bear the disappointed look of the White Bear.

Even in the evening, when he was alone in his quarters, he couldn't get it out of his head. Ryan tried to explain in his mind that he couldn't refuse the order. White Bear wouldn't understand that any more than Slim Fox the spirit of the Nanuk.

*****

Even before the new morning sent its blazing light into the day, the first task force, led by the young sergeant, moved out. The helicopter almost touched the tree tops, dropped the team on the construction site and immediately disappeared again. Ryan and the seven men who were subordinate to him first inspected the construction site to find out about the current situation.

A little later, the men from the Farmingdale Road Company moved in and started their work. The use of headlights on the construction site was unavoidable and generator sets buzzed. The men thus worked in the spotlight and were visible from afar while they themselves could not see what was going on around the construction site. Ryan shook his head barely noticeably. Despite the peculiarities, the work progressed quickly. The deadline pressure became noticeable and the workers now felt safe from the raids. Eight US Army personnel had to protect twelve construction workers or keep a handful of rebels away from them.

Ryan posted four of his armed men directly to the construction site. He distributed three in the forest. He was always roaming around looking for traces. The task force consisted mainly of helicopter pilots, which Forner had equipped with automatic rifles.

Ryan had intentionally left the rifle he had been given at the base. He had no intention of shooting the Inuit. He justified his refusal by saying that he had been trained for close combat and a rifle was only a hindrance. He encountered distrust with Fox and Forner. Finally, they approved it. Ryan carried his service pistol and knife with him. That was enough. He knew exactly that Wolf Shield and his men were nearby. This time he wanted to be faster. These Inuit were masters at leaving hardly any traces even in the snow. Ryan had stripped off the hood of the white snow jumpsuit and listened attentively to every sound he filtered out of the noise of the construction site. Slowly and with care he moved forward. Nevertheless, he did not cover his own tracks. For Wolf Shield it was definitely easy to find it. Ryan stayed calm. He felt the proximity of the Inuit, although he had not yet found any trace of them.

Ryan's face twisted into a mocking grin when he heard someone's pounding feet coming towards him. He leaned against a tree, waiting. Just a few steps away, one of his men put the rifle on the tree and relieved himself. Ryan had left his place. when the man tried to pick up his rifle again, he grasped at nothing.

"Damned!", he swore softly and looked around nervously.

It was quiet.

The man looked at several footprints in the snow, which led around in a confusing circle. He wasn't sure if they were his own. Finally, he crouched down to take a closer look at the footprints. But the fine powder snow had made her collapse like a dried up sandcastle. The man got up again and opened the zipper of his overalls a little bit. He looked around helplessly and reached for his radio. Before he could use it, he winced. A few birds fluttered out of the brushwood.

"Are you looking for something?"

Obviously startled, the man turned and stared at the Indian, who was suddenly standing behind him. Then he smiled in relief.

"Man! Sergeant Hawk! Damn, you scared me. I thought …", he didn't finish the sentence.

Ryan held the man's rifle in his hand.

"Is this yours?"

"Yes, damn it", he growled.

"You better watch out!"

"Hm", the other muttered dejectedly.

"Yes, Sir. I'm a helicopter pilot, not a warrior."

"It's not a war either", Ryan replied. "Follow the tracks in this direction. If you notice anything suspicious, report it."

"At your command."

The pilot trudged away through the high snow.

Ryan stood still for a moment, looked around and listened attentively. It was still silent. The pilot's footprints and his own were more than clear. Finally, Ryan climbed onto one of the fir trees. Wolf Shield was here. Ryan was sure of that. The striking traces had to lead the Inuit to the tree. Ryan waited. Moderate, monotonous noise came from the construction site.

Like ghosts scurried some figures. Hardly to be seen, they were already gone. Maybe he could have believed in a delusion if he didn't know better. The Inuit came invisibly, quickly and silently from different directions and met under the tree. They only communicated by gesturing. The amount and clarity of the tracks seemed to amuse them. Nobody had looked up yet.

Ryan grinned.

Then he took measurements and jumped. The noise he made, made the men snap around immediately. But Ryan was faster. He had already knocked the first man down with him. He remained unconscious in the snow while Ryan jumped on his feet. He seized the moment of surprise and grabbed the next man. It surrendered without resistance. The knife blade flashed as he pulled his head back on his hair with his left hand. Ryan used him as a shield.

"Freeze or I will be a second time faster. Hold your men back, Wolf Shield!", ordered Ryan.

All Inuit stopped.

"If we cannot achieve anything with law and order, we will go this way", he replied.

"That's the wrong way."

"Who says that?", Wolf Shield asked sarcastically. "A Lakota or a bought traitor!"

"You know it!"

Wolf Shield eyed Ryan suspiciously.

Ryan met his eyes with determination.

"Will you cut his throat if we overwhelm you? Without you it is easy to drive the construction workers out of here. The first vehicle is already out of service."

"In this way you will neither stop construction nor move anything else. Catch the right one next time. One who can make a difference."

"Fox?"

"No. Not Fox. The one who gave the order to change the plan and forgot to inform you."

"The one who signed the contract with us will come in three days. White Bear has agreed to this. Until then we stop construction."

"Not as long as I have the command to prevent it."

Ryan was still holding the man and pressing the blade of his knife against his throat. The Inuit dared not move.

"Lakota, do you want to know what we found out?"

"Well, let's talk. As long as we do that there is a cease-fire."

"I agree. You have my word."

Ryan let go of the man and put the knife away.

"The infrastructure is good. The only question is for

whom", Wolf Shield began. "There will soon be a landfill at Tower Rock. Garbage that nobody wants near him. Somebody will make a hell of a lot of dollars with it, only we won't see any of it. We get sick of it and will perish. For this you also need a larger airfield. The Air Force will know for sure. They hide the truth from us. And that's just the tip of the iceberg, we think."

"You won't be able to prevent it", Ryan replied.

The Inuit snorted contemptuously.

"Then the country of the bear will no longer exist here. If Nanuk dies, we die too. But maybe it's not too late. I, we will not stand by and watch them lie, run over and kill us."

Ryan nodded slowly. "I understand you well. But if you continue to fight the Road Company workers on your own, even though Whiter Bear has signed the contract, you will be dead even faster than Nanuk."

Wolf Shield remained silent.

Ryan waited.

"You may be right, Lakota", said Wolf Shield after a while. "Those who fight risk losing. But if you don't even try, you've already lost from the start."

Ryan shook his head.

"They will not fight with you or with you all. They have a lot of money and a lot of power. They will bustle you with a few killers to get the problem out of the world quickly and easily", Ryan said.

Wolf Shield shook his head angrily

"But I can't stand by. I don't want it and I won't look away either. It is our life."

Ryan nodded.

Then he pulled out a packet of cigarettes and offered it to Wolf Shield and the men. He took a deep drag and looked over at the construction workers.

"Are you a pilot?", asked Wolf Shield

"No. Driver."

The men grinned.

While they stood together smoking and talking, the helicopter pilot came back. He had followed the tracks on his tour. The Inuit paused when they heard him. Ryan already see him coming. He came closer and slowly raised his rifle.

"Oh, that's how it works!", he shouted and through his radio he said: "I have found them. Sergeant Hawk is in cahoots with the rebels."

Wolf Shield clutched a short, thick branch with his right hand. The pilot put the rifle on. At the same time the Inuit hurled the branch against the snow-covered branches by the tree above him. The snow fell and enveloped the pilot, taking away the air and sight. When he got rid of it, he looked around. All Inuit were gone, silent and quick. Only Ryan was still there.

The pilot points his gun at him.

Ryan took his hands up and waited. Three more men from his task force appeared. They captured their own sergeant and led him away. Ryan let himself be brought to Fox without resistance.

*****

Fox was crouched on a wooden crate in the storeroom while Ryan stood with his back to the door. They were alone after Forner blowing off steam. The dim light from the ceiling lamp cast large shadows. Slim Fox had stayed calm. Even now he was studying the Lakota in silence

before asking softly: "What the hell did you think?"
"As long as men talk and smoke, they do nothing else." Fox grinned.
"That's true, however. At least there was no significant disturbance and no more delay today. What were you talking about?"
"I told the men, that there is no point in doing what they do."
"Have they finally understood now?"
"No."
"Then we will keep the few of rebels in custody until the road is ready. And they, Hawk, you will bring them to me."
"These men think that in three days the man will come who has made the contract with them and talks to White Bear about changing the route. As long as they want to stop working. Only after that they will accept it and let this go."
Fox raised his eyebrows.
"You don't believe that yourselves."
"No, Sir. But the Inuit believe it."
Fox made a thoughtful face and considered.
"You know your command, Sergeant Hawk. I don't want gun fighting, fighting or any hassle."
"At your command, Major General Fox", Ryan replied harshly.
"Qualms of conscience?"
"No, Sir!"
"Good. You can step away."
Ryan left the room with his command and with a bad feeling. On the way to his quarters he met Lone Wolf. Ryan greeted him in silence, even though he should have been greeted first. Their looks met. He hadn't missed

Ryan's condition. The old Inuit had been able to read the soul of the Lakota in a moment. He stopped.
Ryan too.
"The louse in the fur of the bear won't stop him on his way", said Lone Wolf softly.
"Yes. He has to go his way. Even if he got it. He will have no choice."
Lone Wolf nodded and went on.
Ryan turned to the canteen to get his dinner.

Forner had sent a couple of his men to the construction site as guards. When Ryan replaced the night shift with his men the following morning. He first ordered all vehicles to be checked carefully. Then he spoke to Fox via radio.
"He was here before us. All construction vehicles are disabled. Gas, Oil, Hydraulics and brake lines destroyed, Sir."
"Bastard!", Fox screamed angrily. "How could that happen?"
"Wolf Shield and his men are warriors. Forner's men are helicopter pilots, Sir."
Fox grumbled.
"Arrest them all. Immediately", Fox ordered.
"They have achieved their goal, Sir. They are no longer here."
"Find them, Hawk!"
"They will be at home in the village of White Bear. We can pick them up there."
There was a momentary silence. Ryan only heard the breaths. Fox seemed to be considering.
"Come back to the base with the men straight away", he finally said.

"At your command, Sir."

Ryan grinned, leaned against one of the giant wheels, and pulled a cigarette out of his box. Calmly he lit it and took a deep breath. Then he slowly blew the smoke that mixed with that of his breath into the air and followed him with his eyes. The other men gathered around him in a semicircle.

"These idiots must have slept on guard", one said grumpily and also pulled out his cigarette.

"I can't believe that. In the cold, they were out all night. Otherwise they would have frozen to death", said another.

"It's beyond me that they have not noticed."

"Hm", grumbled the one who spoke first.

"But they said at the handover that everything is okay..." another replied.

"What do you say, Sergeant?"

"Maybe it was their ghosts", Ryan said.

Someone tapped his forehead with his finger.

"We have the order to retreat", said Ryan stubbornly. He took the last puff of his cigarette and stamped it out.

"Have you found any traces, Sergeant Hawk?"

"Yes, I have."

"Shouldn't we chase the guys?"

"What for? We have a command."

The helicopter could already be heard. Ryan got off the tire and went ahead to get in.

The small Air Force base resembled a wasp nest this morning. Everybody was on its feet and buzzed around. Ryan had to report to Fox. He did it immediately.

Fox was in an eager discussion with Forner when Ryan entered the room.

"And you, Hawk!", Forner hurled angrily at him. "You

should have known that! Why the hell weren't you in your post?"
"Sir, because your men arrested me and I was pulled out of there, Sir."
"Fox!"
"I tried to explain it to you", Fox snapped back. "Your men have no nerves! You call in specialists and your team becomes unreliable at the first opportunity. They acted like a flock of sheep to Master Sergeant Hawk."
Forner snorted.
"Damn it! They are pilots."
"Yes, but no snops in white suits that drive United customers from A to B. They are US Air Force pilots flying helicopter gunships and know how to use a weapon, or at least they should know it, Forner. Maybe you should have prepared them better", Fox countered.
Forner gave Fox a scathing look.
"You two, you and Hawk, will bring me the gang. They belong under lock and key."
Fox raised his eyebrows, pulled the corners of his mouth down, and shook his head.
"Our job ends here. If you really want to arrest these men, do it." Then Fox laughed with amusement as he continued. "Only as long as the machines are standing until the work can continue your friends will not show up again."
Ryan couldn't suppress his grin anymore. Forner pressed his lips together and snorted. He seemed to have no arguments and swallowed hard at his defeat.
"If you ever need a professional again, my friend, please let me know."
"The damage can be repaired within two days."
"It's up to Farmingdale. By the way, have you already

informed them?"

"Yes, I did", Forner growled. "Wait Slim! Only two days. When work resumes, they come back. Then we are at the same point."

Fox took a deep breath.

"Only two days!", he approved annoyed.

"What do you say, Hawk?"

Ryan was surprised that Fox actually asked his opinion. He nodded.

"That's the way it's happened, Sir."

"Okay. We have to keep our head down for two days. Then access or return to South Dakota."

Ryan nodded.

"At your command, Sir."

Ryan was not allowed to leave the base for two days. He lay on his bed for hours reading. When he was looking for movement, he went down into the garage complex. The snowmobiles had a magical attraction.

"You wanna ride it again, right?", asked Lone Wolf, who spent most of the time down here.

"A dream", Ryan smiled.

"You are like a wolf that has been locked in a cage. You run back and forth on the bars."

"You know where they are", Ryan said.

The Inuit nodded.

"I know more than you think."

Ryan looked questioningly at the old man.

The old one smiled. "If the bear has to wait too long for the salmon, it will starve."

"Then another bear caught and ate the salmon before he could come to him", Ryan ruminated.

"That's the way it is."

"Tell the bear, that I won't wait for the salmon to starve."

Lone Wolfe nodded in satisfaction.

Ryan took out some kind of amulet and gave it to the Inuit.

"Give it to him. It's our Medicine Wheel. Even if we have different rituals, the same blood flows in us."

Lone Wolf looked at it carefully before putting it in his pocket.

"Thank you. I will do that. Wolf Shield is my grandson", the old man smiled proudly, nodded to Ryan and left.

Ryan regretted that he would no longer be able to drive one of the snowmobiles. But the fronts between which he was caught had vanished. He smiled contentedly and shoved his hands into the back pockets of his pants. Ryan looked at the parked snowmobile one last time before leaving.

Fox himself did not show any emotion when the news came that the Road Company had not received its spare parts delivery on the second day.

"Pack your things!", he ordered Ryan.

Thirty minutes later, they took off. It was only after about ten minutes Fox turned to Ryan. First he eyed him, squinting his eyes a little.

"I could bet you knew", he said finally quietly.

"Sir, what, Sir?"

"That this rogue of Wolf Shield intercepted the delivery with his men."

"Sir, no Sir."

"Wouldn't you have done it in his place?"

"Not without your order, Major General Fox."

Ryan avoided smiling. He didn't look at Fox either. But Ryan grinned triumphantly inside himself.

Fox had outdone himself.

He hardly talked to Ryan that much in the following months. Fox seemed to distrust him. Ryan followed his orders correctly and without contradiction. He stood behind Fox like a shadow. The cool rejection never broke.

After five months, Ryan was placed under a new commander. The driver's reputation for exceptional abilities preceded him. Officers and Generals, to whom he was assigned as personal protection and driver, changed constantly. Because of the many requests Taylor was sometimes in distress. Vacation was out of the question.

Chapter 5
Betrayal

In the few hours of vacation he was granted, Ryan visited his sister or Baxter took him over. Another year had flown by. Ryan knew the other world well, in all its facets. At least that's what he believed. He was now twenty-three years old and had a great deal of life experience that he could never have dreamed of. And he was rightly proud of it. He had been promoted to Command Chief Master Sergeant by now, which was unusual for someone who did not fly at the US Air Force. Only once, when he dreamed of his family, of the horses and Samantha Crying Crow, desire tortured him. It reminded him of how far he was from the Lakota in him. Then he also knew that he still existed. Old Raven had said to him that he had to go his way, which would one day lead him back home. The belief in it gave Ryan the strength he needed.

*****

Baxter sang loudly and devotedly. He overruled his radio music and the sizzling of the steaks in the pan.
After turning the steaks, he took a sip from the beer can and poured some of it into the pan. With a loud 'zshsss' he found himself enveloped in a cloud of smoke. Baxter cursed in a choking voice and opened the window. The cloud of smoke slowly evaporated. As Baxter worked with the pepper mill over the pan, he heard the knock on the door clearly.

"I'm coming!"
He hurriedly put the pepper mill down so that it fell over and jumped to the door and tore it open.
"Hi Goodman. The taxi service is here", greeted the expected guest.
Baxter laughed.
"I haven't ordered one, but come in."
Ryan grinned, entered, and closed the door behind him. His eyes caught on Baxter's pan.
"Hm! Smells good. What's that?"
"Real T-bone steaks and the potatoes are in the oven", Baxter replied proudly. "I bought and arranged everything myself! You're amazed, right?"
Ryan nodded.
"Made by Kraft", he said skeptically.
"Hey, hey! If you start to bitch, then ..." Baxter grumbled and waved wildly his meat fork threateningly.
Then he laughed. Baxter had already set the table long ago and in the middle was the big red bottle.
"Sit down, my friend. It will be served soon."
Ryan sat in one of the two chairs that Baxter owned. There was not much space in his apartment. There was a living room with sofa bed, single kitchen included and a door that led to the bathroom.
"Small, compact and far too expensive. But furnished and much more comfortable than the sleeping boxes at the Air Force", said Baxter not without pride.
Ryan crossed his arms and watched his friend.
"You could go into business with your taxi company", Baxter said, while shoveling the food onto the plates.
"I looked at your schedule for this week. Taylor must think of you as a robot or something. Oops!"
Baxter caught a few potatoes flying around and threw

them on the plate. "Uhh .. damn hot!"
Baxter laughed and came to the table with the plates.
"Dig in. Enjoy, my friend!"
"Thanks", Ryan replied.
Baxter reached for the ketchup bottle and wasn't stingy with it. Ryan shook his head barely noticeably and pricked a piece of potato. Baxter must have hidden the steak somewhere under this hill. Ryan hoped to find the meat before his stomach was full of potatoes. He grinned at the thought.
"What's up?", Baxter asked, chewing.
"Something wrong?"
"The potatoes usually grow among the cattle."
"Oh!"
Baxter jumped up.
"Wait!"
He took a fresh plate from his kitchen cupboard and put it on Ryan's plate like a lid. Then he turned it over with nothing falling and took the top plate away.
"You crazy dog", Ryan laughed.
"Old-age magic trick", said Baxter and stuffed his mouth full. "Much better than the Army canned food. What are you saying?", he finally asked expectantly.
"Definitely, Baxter. Your pepper steak is by far the best I've ever had."
Baxter grinned triumphantly.
"Black Hawk taxi company. Fly to your destinations safely", giggled Baxter.
"We put that as advertising on the Chrysler."
"No advertising, Bax! Business is booming at the moment."
"Then we will have to raise the prices. I can manage you too."

"You'd better stay my mechanic, Baxter."

"Nonsense. Don't be so pessimistic. We open our own company! I can do that with left and umpteen Alaska killer viruses."

Baxter laughed, choked and coughed tortured.

"But maybe not me, Bax. From Alaska to Tierra del Fuego and back and possibly even to China."

"Well my friend. So you've already got to know our civilized stress."

Ryan nodded. "Fast sometimes is not fast enough."

"At least, Do they pay well?"

"Taylor says I'm one of the highest paid drivers in the Air Force."

"I sure hope so! Your part-time job alone, playing the nanny for these bastards, is priceless. I'm serious. You could drive on your own account."

Ryan shook his head.

"Stop it, Baxter!"

Baxter took a deep breath.

"I can neither lead you to the water nor convince you to drink. Stubborn ass!" Baxter growled.

Ryan grinned.

Baxter opened a beer can and put it on. He belched loudly when he put her down.

"You my drink this piss with an easy mind. Not even an ant gets drunk of it."

"No Baxter."

"Okay, let's have a Whiskey. I have good one."

"Without me, Baxter", Ryan smiled and declined.

"Something is wrong with you ...", Baxter ruminated.

"It's all right with me."

"Hey. Why are you press yourself like this?"

Ryan took a deep breath.

"Alright. I want to tell you. I haven't touched a drop in five years. The brandy and bad marihuana had forced me to the ground and I was afraid of being sober. I had lost respect for my father and myself. Two of my friends were drunk when they were killed in a car accident. There was not much left of them. That was the point where I got up and swore to go another way."

Baxter nodded. "Understand."

He got up and got a bottle of Coke from the fridge.

"I will no longer bother you with my Whiskey. You could have said that to me earlier. I hope you don't mind if I drink one."

"No." Ryan drank from the bottle. When he put the bottle down, he smiled. "Your food makes me thirsty."

"Well. Was maybe a little bit too much pepper", Baxter admitted sheepishly.

Ryan's smile turned into a broad grin.

"How are you and Rice doing? As I heard you let him live."

Baxter disgracefully distorted the face.

"I thought a lot about what you said to me, about his eyes and stuff. They are not dead when his tongue speaks, but they say otherwise."

"Then you understood my warning."

"I saw through him. Rice is unpredictable and I'm proud when he circled around me. This idiot tried to make me bad with the men and shot himself." Baxter laughed contentedly. "Now he knows what they think of him. I recently had to show up in Taylors office and make various statements. Peanuts. Is only a matter of time before Taylor figures it out."

"I think Taylor appreciates what he has in you.

"Yes. But sometimes I'm not so sure about that either.

For him it is important that everything runs smoothly. As soon as serious difficulties arise, he sits on his tail."
"He's not the only one", Ryan said.

*****

When Ryan and Baxter met outside the garage the next morning, Baxter said softly: "Beware of this Barkley. His eyes are more dangerous than his poisonous words."
Ryan nodded.
"Yes, I know. But I can't choose the people."
"Could you if you were self-employed…", Baxter hissed and broke off when his friend's eyes flashed sharply.
"All right. The subject is closed", he appeased, raising his hands. "Well, scrap and wrinkle-free flight, Falcon!"
Baxter slapped Ryan's shoulder amicably.
"See you later", Ryan answered.
Barkley, General of the Air Force, also liked to have cars and drivers in private. It was not unusual for him to be picked up from home. Ryan stayed in the car and waited in front of the entrance. Barkley was not as punctual as his predecessors. The sun was shining and the sky was almost cloudless. It promised to be a hot day. At the moment, thanks to the automatic climate control, it was much more pleasant inside than outside. Ryan listened to the radio and read the daily newspaper. Barkley came out the door with his wife and grandchild twenty minutes later than agreed. Ryan got out to open the car door. He greeted in a militarily correct manner and nodded to the lady and the estimated ten-year-old girl. The little girl eyed him suspiciously.

"Grandpa!" She called out loud. "Is that an Indian?"
"Yes, Darling. Get in! We are late."
"Can he drive us at all?"
Ryan didn't move. He waited.
"Of course he can, Synthia. He learned it from the Air Force. And now get in!"
Reluctantly, she did.
Finally, Ryan got in and fastened the seat belt.
"Take me to the office first. Then drop the two ladies off at the regional airport and come back."
"Yes, Sir", Ryan replied shortly and started.
When he had dropped Barkley, he turned the car and drove towards Rapid City Regional Airport.
"Hey! Can you engage the second gear? The plane doesn't wait", he heard the snappy voice of the child.
"When does the plane start?" asked Ryan.
"An hour from now, Mr. Hawk", answered Mrs. Barkley.
"Then we can do it easily."
Ryan looked in the rearview mirror and watched the child. Synthia snorted, grimacing her pretty face, and chewed a chewing gum with a smack. Her blonde curls were spiraling over her crossed arms. She looked out the side window and made chewing gum bubbles. After a while she tapped the driver on the shoulder.
"Stop the car!", she ordered.
"Synthia, honey, what's the matter for god's sake?", Mrs. Barkley asked worriedly while Ryan stopped the car.
"I feel sick", she moaned and pushed open the door.
Mrs. Barkley also jumped out and tried to help her.
"Oh little one, I told you not to eat too many pancakes. And the sweet chocolate, but you didn't want to listen."
"Everything is already out again, granny", growled Synthia.

"We should rather postpone our trip to another time. The holidays have just started", said the grandmother concerned.

"No way! But I won't get on the plane with this dress! The Indian will drive us home immediately."

Since Ryan didn't respond, Mrs. Barkley asked: "Would you please take us home, Mr. Hawk?"

"No, Mrs. Barkley, unfortunately impossible. That would be refusal to obey orders."

"But you see for yourself. The child is dirty."

"That is unfortunate."

"My father will make sure you lose your job. He has so much money that he could buy an entire airport."

"Synthia, please!", warned Mrs. Barkley.

She opened the purse and held out a hundred dollar bill to Ryan, who was still sitting motionless in his seat.

"Please, Mr. Hawk", she pleaded.

"I am under the orders of the U.S. Air Force, Mrs. Barkley. You should take a taxi for the money."

"That is... unbelievable! My husband, General Paul Isaak Barkley, ordered you to drive us!"

"My order is to drop you both off at the regional airport. That's exactly what I'm going to do."

"Grandma! You don't think I'll show myself like this among people. The dress stinks!"

Annoyed, Mrs. Barkley pulled out a second bill and held them out to Ryan.

"What's it going to be? This is an emergency and I offer you double."

Ryan smiled kindly at the lady.

"Put the money away and get in."

When the two were back in their seats, he closed the door on the central locking system.

"What's this all about?"

"Just for your safety", Ryan replied and continued to the airport, only faster than before.

"Fucking redskin!", the girl yelled.

Ryan ignored that.

"Mr. Hawk, please!"

Ryan said nothing. Undeterred by the female protests in the rear, he only stopped in front of the entrance to the airport building. He got out to open the doors for the ladies.

"Get out, Grandma! The idiot is crazy! I'm sick again", Synthia snapped.

"Did you want to kill us? You have a very aggressive driving style. I have to say that!"

"All I had to do was catch up time and I kept to the speed limit, Mrs. Barkley", Ryan replied, grimacing at the corners of his mouth with a smile.

"I will have to inform my husband of this. Maybe it is better to hire another driver. Have a good day!"

Mrs. Barkley slammed the door and hurriedly disappeared into the airport building with Synthia by the hand. Ryan's smile widened as he got back into the car.

"Do that, Mrs. Barkley. It's not a bad idea at all", he said softly to himself and started the car.

In front of the Air Force Base office building, Ryan waited patiently for Barkley. He enjoyed the rest, leaned back and closed his eyes. After half an hour the cell phone rang.

"Major General Taylor here. Sergeant Hawk, I have an urgent order. Come to my office immediately."

"Yes, Sir!", Ryan replied shortly and made his way to Taylor.

He knocked and entered.

"Ah, Sergeant Hawk. General Barkley has a few hours left in his office and doesn't need you for the time being. In five minutes a Cessna will land at our base. An FBI agent, Mitchell, has an important witness to protect in a murder case. You will take the two men to a secret location that Mitchell will tell you on the way. The Rapid City Regional airport was too unsafe for him and he asked me for a good and reliable driver."
"Why doesn't the FBI take their own drivers, Sir?"
"Because Mitchell doesn't trust anyone and not even the FBI in Rapid has been informed. So: top secret."
Ryan raised his eyebrows skeptically.
"An order, Sir?"
Taylor looked at Ryan in surprise.
"Yes of course! And hurry up now!"
"Sir. I cannot guarantee that I will be ready for Barkley again on time", Ryan argued.
"You can do it. I'm sure of it", Taylor grinned confidently.
Ryan pressed his lips together and sucked in the air sharply through his nose.
"I'll let the general know if you're not back in time", Taylor nodded.
"You may step away."
Ryan left the office and drove out to the runways. The Cessna was approaching. Ryan headed for it and stopped at about the same time as the small plane. He got out and waited at the back door of the black sedan.
Someone opened the door of the Cessna and lowered the little stairs. A man, in his mid-thirties, got out. He was wearing jeans and an orange shirt. An older man wearing a dark gray suit followed. Immediately it seemed strange to Ryan that the younger man was handcuffed. Ryan watched the two suspiciously. The man in

the suit introduced himself.

"Hello, Sergeant. My name is Mitchell. Have you been informed in detail?"

"Yes, sir. Get in the car."

Ryan opened the door.

The witness that was supposed to be protected got in first. He was wearing an inmate's shirt and Mitchell treated him that way. He quickly took a seat next to him. He did not take the handcuffs off the man. Ryan tried to get an idea of these inconsistencies, which swirled like jigsaw pieces through his head and laced his mistrust.

The black Chrysler left Air Force Base.

"Tell me where to go."

"Right and then right again", Mitchell said.

That was all. The two men in the back seat didn't talk to each other. He did not take the handcuffs off the man. Ryan tried to get an idea of these inconsistencies, which swirled like jigsaw pieces through his head and intensified his mistrust.

The black Chrysler left Air Force Base.

"Tell me where to go."

"Right and then right again", Mitchell said.

That was all. The two men in the back seat didn't talk to each other.

Ryan kept looking in the rearview mirror to watch the men. The man who was wearing the handcuffs looked out the side window. Ryan immediately noticed that his lip had chapped. The blood was already crusted. The right cheek was also bluish. The guy might have been beaten up or he'd been beaten up.

A little later Ryan had to turn off Highway 90. The path led directly into the Black Hills. Then Mitchell ordered to turn left into the mountains. Ryan continued his thou-

ghts during the silent ride, why Mitchell treated the man like a prisoner. The man next to Mitchell didn't seem to want to be protected by him.

He had to be Mexican, Ryan thought.

He had not missed the fact that the man was becoming increasingly restless and was eyeing all sides.

He looked like a wild animal that had been drove into a corner, Ryan thought further.

When Mitchell finally ordered to turn left into a narrow path that was going uphill, Ryan became increasingly suspicious. Asking Mitchell, however, seemed unwise to him. Ryan did not trust the FBI people, nor did he believe that he would be told. When Ryan looked in the rearview mirror, his eyes met those of the prisoner. Ryan thought he saw pure fear in the man's eyes. Ryan tried in vain to suppress his uneasy feeling. It was quite common for such important people to be taken to remote hiding places to protect them. He himself observed the area around him very carefully. Ryan was looking for a hut or something. The narrow road seemed to lead nowhere. The undergrowth to the right and left of the path was a brushwood. Mitchell ordered Ryan to stop the car.

Without losing another word, he got out, looked around and looked for a tree nearby. Ryan stayed seated and watched the stranger.

"Step on it!", said he hastily. "They will kill me. My name is Miguel Rodriguez and I know too much about Mitchell's business. He wanted to blackmail me, do you hear? Help me, brother", he pressed out almost without an accent. Since Ryan made no move to start the car, Rodriguez pushed open the door and fled into the thicket like a deer. Mitchell turned slowly, drew his pistol, and fired into the thicket twice in quick succession.

"Stop! Freeze!", he yelled after the fleeting one. "Damn it!"

Mitchell opened the driver's door.

Ryan already had his pistol in his hand, only covered by the uniform jacket.

"Sergeant, come quick! We have to find him before they catch him."

Ryan remained seated, apparently looking past Mitchell, watching his every move.

"Who are THEY and why are THEY here before us?"

"Hit men. I don't know how they found out that we're here."

Hence the man's orange shirt, Ryan thought. So Rodriguez was a good target in the forest. He had told the truth. Branches cracked in the undergrowth. A male voice was heard from afar.

"They chase him. They will kill him", Mitchell noted.

"Get in", Ryan said unperturbed.

"No. We have to get him back."

"My command has been carried out. I brought you here."

Mitchell seemed momentarily baffled. It was quiet. No voice, no crack and no shot. Then a voice came to Ryan's ears.

"Hands up and no move!", ordered someone who was in the bush behind Mitchell.

Mitchell obeyed and took two steps to the side. At that moment a bullet whistled almost silently towards the Chrysler and clicked dully on the door post.

Muffler! Ryan thought.

Ryan started the Chrysler. Mitchell seemed to lose his nerve and dragged him out of the open car door. Ryan got rid of this clumsy man surprisingly quickly, without engaging in a duel with him. Now he jumped into the thicket like a fleeing deer.

Idiot! Ryan thought and paused.

A low whistle hissed over his head. Tree bark splintered. Ryan was exposed to killers like Rodriguez.

How many?

Ryan carefully crawled on the floor, almost without moving branches that might have betrayed him. He heard soft voices all around, but didn't understand a word. Ryan wasn't particularly surprised when he heard Mitchell's voice very clearly.

"He can't have got far. Combing the thicket. He must be gone in this direction. He carries a pistol."

Ryan carefully raised his head. Four men stood by Mitchell and nodded. They immediately started to move. They were away only a few feet from Ryan. He had put the pistol away. A shot would have betrayed him. He also heard the Chrysler start. Someone was driving and accelerating rapidly. Then there was the crash of the impact. Ryan winced slightly. He took one last look back. Mitchell himself was out of the car he had driven into a tree.

If Baxter knew he would kill you by hand, Mitchell, Ryan thought.

A rustle ripped Ryan's mind. Lying flat on the ground he saw black boots between the branches. His heart was pounding strongly and quickly. Ryan opened his mouth to keep his quick breath silent. With the knife in hand, he waited. The one to which the boots belonged went on slowly. The man moved dangerously close to Ryan without noticing him. Ryan pressed his lips together, jumped up and stabbed his knife in the kidney before the guy could react. He slumped to the floor silently.

Ryan took the pistol, which had a muffler, briefly he thrust the knife into the earth to clean it of the blood. Then he pocketed both. The uniform jacket was more than a hindrance. Since the other men would soon discover the dead man, Ryan took them off and also threw the striking white shirt on the floor. He disappeared quickly and silently, like a snake, deeper in the thicket. A few seconds later he heard a man scream.
"Come here!"
One turned the dead man over and swore. A second man came along.
"This is a damn different handwriting than that of a chauffeur. Mitch brought the wrong driver with him. And the guy took the pistol with him."!
They looked around searching. They had no idea that they were being watched.
Ryan pushed further into the bush without knowing exactly where he was. A small clearing appeared in front of him. He had not yet given up hope of getting the Chrysler. A little further down the slope something caught his eye. Someone lay inconspicuous and motionless. The orange shirt stood out clearly from the forest floor.
Miguel Rodriguez!
Ryan listened. Nothing but silence.
He crawled carefully out of the thicket. Crouched and with a few quick steps Ryan was with him. He knelt down to Rodriguez and looked at the entry points of the bullets. Two between the shoulder blades, a bullet in the head. Rodriguez was face down. He had been caught on the run, shot, executed. The man had no chance.
Hands stretched forward, still handcuffed. He had been an important witness. But no one had protected him.

A suspicious whistle shot through the air at Ryan, who immediately threw himself flat on the floor. He felt a hot burn on the skin on his left upper arm. The smell of burnt meat crept into his nose. Ryan squinted at his arm. The bullet had grazed him and shredded the flesh. The pain that came up wanted to rob him of his senses. Ryan turned black in front of his eyes. He gritted his teeth hard and inhaled sharply through his nose. He lay motionless.

The wolves shredded my flesh, he thought, *but they won't get me*.

Slowly and hot the blood seeped out of the wound and dripped to the floor. Ryan thought for a moment to take a piece of the shirt's fabric to cover the wound, but didn't dare move. The shot had come from behind. They knew exactly where he was. They might think he was dead. The wolves would come to see. They would not talk. They would shoot immediately. Ryan decided not to wait for it. Today was not the day to die.

As expected, the shooter came to check. He ignored all caution, because he actually believed he had a dead man in front of him. He kicked at Ryan. He took advantage of the instant of surprise, turned and fired. The killer sank to the floor, moaning. The shot was fatal.

As the ring around the two dead and Ryan closed, Ryan gathered his strength and climbed into the protective canopy of an elm tree. He had only left a few drops of blood. Three of the five wolves now stood under the elm and examined the two dead. Ryan had killed two of the killers. Mitchell was missing. He paused motionless between the branches of the tree. He pressed his left, injured arm against the branch. In between was a piece of moss. With his right hand he held onto the branch. He was dizzy. The pistols were stuck in the belt. The pain of the wound radiated over the shoulder and made the left arm practically unusable. Ryan pressed his lips tightly together and breathed evenly, out and in. It started pounding in the head. He closed his eyes for a few seconds. No one had noticed him yet.

One of the men picked up the walkie-talkie, submitted the management report and seemed to be receiving a new order.

"OK!", Ryan heard him answer.

"Spread out and turn every branch, each leaf individually. Mitch has to report to the company. They will be here soon. So hurry up and watch out! The Indsman is a professional, even if he is injured."

Two of the killers set off in different directions. The third who had spoken examined the place for traces. Ryan took aim and pulled the trigger. The man immediately fell to the ground. Ryan secured the weapon and put it away. He slowly climbed down. From the last branch he dropped to the ground. He landed on his feet and fell forward. The dead man was only three feet in front of him. Ryan crawled to him and took the walkie-talkie and gun. Then he sat up and examined the wound. Without further ado he tore a shred of cloth from the dead man's shirt and wrapped it around his arm. With his right hand and the help of his teeth, he pulled the knot tight. Then he examined the walkie-talkie. Maybe he could hear the men. There was silence at the moment. Ryan listened and looked around. He had no time to waste. He had to get out of here. Soon FBI agents would be swarming here. He pushed the walkie-talkie deep into his pocket and stuck the third pistol in his waistband. Then he disappeared in the direction from which he had come.

There was his car and possibly Mitchell.

Ryan hadn't been wrong. He watched what was going on. Mitchell was at Chrysler when a strange GMC appeared behind him. Another car followed. The crew immediately jumped out and gathered around Mitchell. He reported gesturing and pointing into the thicket of the forest. An armed man stayed with Mitchell by the off-road vehicle. Everyone else started combing the forest area. While Mitchell lit a cigarette, the engine noise of the GMC made him drive around. The car that came last was set back at a rapid pace.

"Damned Crap!", Mitchell shouted angrily and immediately stubbed out the cigarette. He drew his pistol and fired several times at the car that was leaving. The off-road vehicle disappeared from view. Mitchell cursed and jumped into the other car, started and stepped on the accelerator. The GMC bumped a few feet backwards with a yelping noise and stopped. Mitchell angrily jumped out of the car and kicked the flat tire violently.

"You bastard!", he screamed like mad.

Mitchell requested reinforcements and issued the search for the fleeing killer. A U.S. Air Force Sergeant had killed Rodriguez and three of his men.

*****

There was a knock on the door to Barkley's office. Taylor entered immediately. He greeted General P.I. Barkley, who was very angry with his driver.

"Did you order him to go away?", he roared. "I have ordered to be picked up here. Where are we here? In the madhouse?"

Barkley tried in vain to keep one's cool. Taylor felt a lot of heat. He swallowed before answering.

"Sir, he should be back long ago. We could trust in Sergeant Hawk all the time."

"Only not today! That's inadmissible, damn it. Doesn't he have a cell phone?"

"But. Yes. Naturally. But he is currently unavailable."

"Maybe he takes a nap after lunch and doesn't want to be disturbed", Barkley hissed sarcastically.

"He will be here soon. The schedule is very tight", soothed Taylor.

"Either he will be available to me in ten minutes or you will bring me another driver. If you can't get it right, Major General Taylor, you will drive me! I am not traveling for my pleasure."

Barkley's words sounded like someone had slammed a door. He didn't expect an answer.

"Yes, Sir", Taylor said, and left Barkley's office.

The phone was already adamantly ringing in his own. On the way from the door to the desk he took a deep breath and picked it up. The voice at the other end belonged to Mitchell.

"Your driver, Taylor, has put his company car against a tree. The damn Indsman killed the witness and three of my men. And he stole an FBI off-road vehicle he's currently fleeing with. I have requested reinforcements."

Taylor slowly opened the mouth.

"No, I don't believe it", he said stunned into the receiver. He heard Mitchell snort at the other end. "It might make sense to help us with the search. After all, Sergeant Hawk is a member of the military. What the hell is that man you sent me there? Taylor, damn it, get him back

under control. Write down the vehicle and license plate data."
Taylor tried to understand what he had just heard. He still couldn't believe it. He reached for paper and pen.
"I assume that you will inform me immediately if he shows up with you, Major General Taylor!"
Before Taylor could have answered anything, Mitchell hung up. Taylor took a deep breath and also hung up.

*****

The sun had peaked and was burning on Carry's skin. She winced in shock when someone spoke to her and touched her shoulder. She dropped the towel and turned around, startled.
"Ryan!"
Her eyes were wide open, staring at her brother.
"Carry, help me", Ryan pleaded. "The GMC has to get out of here, quick. Where are the children?"
Ryan spoke softly, hastily and constantly looking around.
Carry pushed the duvet on the clothesline aside.
"There. They play in the sand."
Carry eyed Ryan worriedly. Her gaze slid over the battered, naked upper body, the dirty trousers and the bloody scraps of fabric on his arm. Then their looks met. She noticed the despair that lay in it and that scared her.
"What should I do?", she asked softly.
"Do you have a car for me?"
Carry nodded.
"Follow me to the airport car park. There I park the GMC. Then I drive on with your car. You go back by taxi. I

have money."
Carry shook her head.
"Wait. I'll get the keys."
"Hurry up! If someone stops me, just keep driving!" Ryan became increasingly restless. He looked around again and again. Carry was back in a short time, grabbed the children and put them in their car.
Ryan was already in the FBI's off-road vehicle and drove off. They left the district at the permitted speed. The sunlight was blinding. Ryan narrowed his eyes and looked for sunglasses until he finally found one. He kept looking in the rearview mirror and watched Carry's car following him. They brought the news on the radio. Ryan turned louder. He clearly heard the speaker's words.
"Just now, three dead men have been found in the thicket in the northern Black Hills, south of Interstate 14, towards Galena. The fugitive is known to the FBI. A Lakota Indian named Ryan Black Hawk is searched for. He is a U.S. Air Force Base Rapid City Sergeant and is currently escaping in a black GMC. The FBI urges caution because the fugitive is heavily armed and dangerous. Whoever sees the GMC with said license plate should immediately call the following number ...."
Ryan turned off the radio. Deep in his gut he felt a mixture of anger and fear. Anger at the lies and fear because nobody would believe him. His life was forfeited.
The airport appeared. Ryan turned and stopped in an open parking lot. Carry stopped right next to him.
"I keep driving. Get in", she said.
Ryan had no time to waste. The loss of blood had weakened him. Without a word of contradiction, he sat down exhausted in the passenger seat.

"Jo, give me the shirt", asked Carry.

Joan Crowman threw it over her uncle's shoulder.

"It is still damp. Put it on."

It took some effort, but Ryan crawled in, groaning.

"Did you hear the news?", he asked softly.

Carry nodded.

"What are you planning now? Where do you want to go?"

"Initially to Old Raven. The wound is bothering me. I've already lost too much blood. You drop me down on the way and drive back immediately. When they stop you, you say you were with the children at the grandparents."

"Okay."

Ryan was silent and sank to the side on the seat. He slept. Charry glanced at her younger brother from time to time. His face was turned ashen and the cheeks were sunken so that the bones came out more. When they passed Senic's few houses, Carry was overtaken by two black limousines and a police car. Carry took the gas back and slowed down. She watched the cars stop within sight. Carry was afraid and braked. She felt her brother twitch slightly when she touched him. Blinking, he looked around.

"They put up a roadblock", she noted with concern.

"Drive very close to the roadside. I let myself out of the car. On the other side, if you don't see them anymore, you are waiting for me."

Carry's hands trembled as she did what he asked for. As she drove on slowly she moved her lips. She prayed for her brother. Whatever happened, she believed in his innocence. The children, six-year-old Joan and her ten-month-old brother Mason were quiet as a mouse. Carry's car slowly rolled toward the roadblock. One of

the men stepped in the way in front of her and unmistakably motioned for her to stop. Carry lowered the side window.
"Hi there. Get out!", he ordered.
Carry obeyed and stood by the open door to watch her children.
"Your papers! Where do you want to go?"
"To see my parents-in-law."
"Where is your husband?"
"At work."
The man carefully examined the inside of the car. Even under the seats. Then he opened the trunk. Carry tried to hide her agitation. She didn't quite succeed.
"No baggage?"
"I want to be back home today."
"Where does your husband work?"
"In Rapid City. Home Woods and more."
"Okay. Go on!", he ordered.
Carry got in and started. She continued driving slowly until the roadblock had disappeared from view. Then she stopped, turned off the engine and let the arms slide off the steering wheel with a sigh. Mason had sunk into his sister's arms and blinked wearily.
Joan looked at her mother anxiously. "Will he come back?" she asked.
"I hope so, Jo."
Carry looked around. The time seemed infinite. She breathed a sigh of relief when the shadowy figure of the brother appeared at the passenger door. Ryan slipped in through the little open door. Even more exhausted, more dusty, and more sweaty than he was anyway, he breathed violently through his open mouth.
"Do you have something to drink?", he asked hoarsely.

"No, I have not."
A small hand tapped Ryan on the shoulder. Joan held out a bottle and smiled.
"Here. I took Mason's tea with me."
"Thank you Jo", said Ryan, turning his head to her and smiled tired.
The tea was lukewarm, but extinguished the burn in the dry throat. Ryan collapsed with the bottle in hand and fell asleep seconds later. With Carry, the children and in the reservation, he felt safe, at least for the time being, and let his exhaustion be allowed. After all, he still had a path that should not be underestimated. When Carry stopped and turned off the engine, Ryan woke up. Their looks met when he opened his eyes. Carry still hadn't asked.
"Thank you, sister. Do what I told you to do."
"They may come to your house and ask questions."
"They will nothing hear from me. Not even from Jo."
Ryan nodded. "I couldn't have done it without you."
He opened the door.
"Uncle Ryan, are they all real?", Jo asked, pointing to the weapons that were still in his belt.
"Yes, Jo, they are."
"That's good. Then they will not dare to harm you."
Ryan smiled wearily.
"Travel home safely", he said
Then he went alone to Old Raven.
Carry immediately started her car and went home.

*****

Ryan couldn't suppress the moaning as Old Raven cleaned his wound. Hila helped him. He sat in the tent and watched each of her hand movements until he became dizzy and blacked out. Old Raven smiled as Ryan sank into his arm.

"He lost a lot of fluid", Hila said.

Old Raven nodded.

"It's better this way. As long as he is passed out, I will cut open the wound and burn it out so that there is no infection. It looks bad. Give me the alcohol."

Ryan groaned painfully again without becoming conscious. He woke up hours later. He was on fire. He still felt the burn in his throat. When he tried to sit up, a terrible pain reminded him of what had happened. Old Raven gave him something to drink. Ryan drank. He was thirsty. The water ran pleasantly cool down his neck. He finally lay back weak, looked around and at the bandage on his arm. The burning and throbbing pain tormented him. The pain relentlessly stretched over his shoulder to his back. When Ryan wanted to look at his watch, it was no longer on his wrist. He heard Old Raven laugh softly.

"How long have I been out?"

"The sun comes up. You had bad dreams."

"Before the sun goes down I will be gone."

"You have become very impatient, my grandson. Everything will take time."

Ryan chewed on the chapped lower lip.

"It's too dangerous for you if I stay. The FBI is looking for me."

"Does the injury come from such a weapon that you carry with you?"

"Yes."

Ryan groped into the empty space and looked questioningly at Old Raven. He nodded to Hila.

"She cooked chicken broth. Drink it."

Ryan looked into Old Raven's eyes, revealing his fear. The old man looked at him intently. Then he took the big cup from Hila.

"Drink", he just said.

Ryan drank slowly and carefully. The broth was hot. The heat flowed through his body and drove sweat out of his pores. The heat spread from the scalp to the feet. When Old Raven returned the cup, he had it filled again and handed it to Ryan. "Drink!" He obeyed the old man. Old Raven knew exactly what he was doing. The inner heat became unbearable to Ryan. He would have loved to throw the blanket off and crawl out. He thought longingly of the cool morning air. But Ryan was like paralyzed, unable to move.

"The fire! Grandfather lit the fire. I will be able to walk again. But where ... where ... where do I have to ...?"

Ryan was talking like in a fever and fell into a deep sleep again. Only when the sun had reached its highest point did he open his eyes again and look around. He was alone in the tent. Excruciating thirst drove him up. A water bottle stood next to him. With a light 'tshh', he opened the large plastic bottle and drank it half empty. He was looking for his things in vain. It would have shaken him to wear it again. Barefoot, wearing a black short, Ryan went to the stream and washed himself. The old woman watched him and smiled. The sun dried his skin. He sat down in the shade of the tree, leaned back against the trunk and looked at the ponies. Lost in thought, Ryan pulled out a long, tough blade of grass and began to chew on it. He stared steadily at a spot in the stream. Ryan considered what had happened. No.

He couldn't have prevented anything. Ryan didn't know how long he had been sitting when someone stepped up next to him and finally settled down. The other man was silent too, staring at the water. Ryan recognized his friend, Two Moon.

"I'll go back to Air Force Base and turn myself in", Ryan said softly.

Two Moon looked worriedly at Ryan without saying anything.

"I will go to Taylor. I'll only talk to him", Ryan said. He heard his friend's deep breaths.

"They have built roadblocks around the reservation. The airport, city and all arterial roads are monitored. They comb everything, turn everything upside down. They searched Carry's apartment. They will be here soon, my friend."

"I'm going out tonight."

Ojeda Two Moon pushed a package over to Ryan. "You need some-thing to wear and something to smoke."

Ryan turned his head to him and took it.

"Thank you."

"My sister is waiting for you on the street with my car. She will drive over Potato Creek and then straight to the highway. In the middle of the day with a woman it's not as suspicious as if I drive you or you alone. There is only one roadblock."

"What would we be without our sisters ..." said Ryan and smiled. "You should be able to fly like an eagle."

Old Raven came and stopped in front of the two young men.

"Are you ready?", he asked.

"Yes, I am."

"Is there a man you can talk to?"

"Yes, the Major General. He gave me the order. He trusts me and knows I would never do anything like that."
Old Raven smiled mysteriously.
"Talk to the black dog that looks like a wolf. He made you believe."
"Did you have a vision?", asked Ryan.
Old Raven grinned.
"Where can I find him?"
"He will find you", the old man replied.

*****

Major Taylor had not been home for two days and had hardly slept for the past two nights. Barkley gave him hell. The manhunt went into full swing and still had brought nothing. They only secured the getaway car they were looking for, which belonged to the FBI, at the airport. Based on this fact, the FBI had extended the search to all states. There was no trace of Sergeant Hawk. He seemed as if swallowed by the earth. Even in the reservation someone claims to have seen him. At home he had not shown up and no doctor confirmed that he had attended him.

Taylor hadn't gone to bed in a ready room until well after midnight. Now he shuffled to his office, not necessarily more awake, but with a large cup of hot coffee and two sandwiches from the canteen. He was no longer sure he hadn't locked his door. His head was full of a thousand important things. Only when he closed the door with his back and his gaze wandered to the desk he was suddenly wide awake. Taylor froze, eyes and mouth wide open. The young man sitting in his office chair looked at him as he rose and greeted in a militarily correct manner.

Taylor gasped. Only when he had put down his breakfast with trembling hands that he returned the greeting. His eyes wandered over the pistols, which were equipped with silencers and a walkie-talkie. Everything was in a line on his desk.

"Sit down", Taylor said in a low voice.

Then he sat down on his chair. He pulled the cup towards him weakly. Ryan took a seat across from him.

"I can't believe it, Sergeant Hawk", Taylor started, staring at Ryan with tired eyes. Ryan was wearing dark blue jeans and a black shirt. Unlike Taylor, he made a very alert impression. Ryan avoided looking directly at the Major General and waited silently for questions. Taylor immediately noticed the white bandage, which clearly withdrew from the brown skin and the black shirt.

"Are you hurt?"

"Yes, Sir, I am."

"Where the hell have you been in the past two days? You just scared the hell out of me."

"I attended the wound, Sir."

"But not in the hospital."

Ryan said nothing.

Taylor took a deep breath.

"I'd rather not ask how you got into my office unnoticed, Hawk. Assuming that you came to me to report, speak in God's name."

"Is Agent Mitchell still at the Air Base, Sir?"

"No, he isn`t. He was withdrawn from the case. Another man came."

"Agent Mitchell led us into a trap, Sir. The killers were

already in the ambush. Rodriguez should not be protected, but should be killed. I was inevitably witness and had to fight back to safe my skin."

Then Ryan started his full and detailed report until he escaped. Taylor listened attentively and sipped his coffee. He hadn't touched the sandwiches. He stunned shook his head.

"That's unbelievable! Why didn't you come to me first? With your escape, Hawk, you made things worse."

"Mitchell certainly came here first. You should have handed me over. Then I would be dead now, just like Rodriguez."

"You might be right about that, Sergeant. But there is someone from the FBI that I have to report. In this case he will talk to you. But you are still subject to military law."

Ryan just nodded.

Taylor sat up and placed the empty coffee cup next to the guns.

"Supporting evidence?"

"Maybe. But I used it. I must have blurred all the other fingerprints with it."

Taylor played with his lips. He did not say anything. Then he picked up the phone and dialed a number that he read from a slip of paper on his desk.

"Good morning, Superintentent Thompson. I hope you slept well."

Taylor paused and listened. Then he continued: "Yes, he is with me. Please come to my office." Taylor waited for the answer and hung up.

Ryan stared at the floor and didn't move. He would never reveal his thoughts and fear. Neither Taylor nor this Thompson, nor anyone else. Ryan had chosen this path and not a life in constant flight. One day he wanted to go home, breed horses, have a wife and children. But this path could also put him in prison for the rest of his life. Ryan didn't trust anyone, especially the FBI. He was terrified and hid proudly behind an immovable mask to protect himself.

Steps could be heard outside the door. It just seemed like a single man. Ryan's heart beat faster. Cold crept up on him. The door opened and closed quietly without anyone knocking. This 'anyone' came to the desk and grabbed a chair.

"Good Morning. My name is Thompson."

The man sat at the front of the desk between Taylor and Ryan. The room was filled with silence. Ryan remained rigid. He hadn't looked at Thompson at once, nor had returned the greeting. However, it did not seem to bother him in any way. Undeterred he began to speak.

"So you are Sergeant Black Hawk, who kept us busy for two days and deprived us of sleep for two nights." Thompson laughed softly. "I have the greatest respect for you. You survived the hunt, killed three killers and escaped with our company car. The other one incapacitated to thwart the persecution. Somebody has to do that first. I would have loved to see Mitchell's face."

Thompson laughed again, amused. That irritated Ryan and made his mistrust only grow. This way these people used not to conduct interrogations. Ryan said nothing. He still hadn't looked up at the man with the deep, full voice. He now turned to Taylor.

"Can you please call for coffee? I have not had breakfast yet. This could take a little longer. So let's make ourselves comfortable."

Taylor nodded and called the canteen.

"Are you Sioux, Sergeant?", asked Thompson.

"Yes, Sir", Ryan replied.

"What's your name?"

"Ryan Black Hawk", he finally answered.

"Well, Ryan Black Hawk. I want you to tell me what happened, in all the details and in the correct order. Please mention everything, including inconspicuous details that may not seem important to you. For you, it all depends."

Silence filled the room. In this silence, there was a knock at the door. Thompson jumped up and opened it. He returned to the desk with a large tray full of sandwiches, fruit, muffins and three large cups of coffee.

"Major Taylor, please make sure no one bothers us."

"Okay. I lock up", he said, and did it.

Thompson placed the tray in the middle of Taylor's desk, ignoring what was underneath. He had previously ignored the weapons. Then the dishes rattled. The strange man put a cup right in front of Ryan's nose.

"Milk, sugar or black?", he asked.

Ryan looked at the hand on the cup and said: "black."

He usually drank his coffee in black and black was also the hand that put it down.

"Thank you, Sir", he added, and started eyeing Thompson unobtrusively.

A black man in a gray suit. Thompson's gray hair revealed that he was older than he might seem. Glasses with golden frames shone on his nose. With every move he made, the man exuded calm and security. Thompson's features appeared rather harsh. But when he reached for a muffin and sat back on the chair with it, he smiled contentedly and bit into it.

Taylor also helped oneself.

Ryan stared at the coffee mug and began to tell where Thompson wanted it to be. He ended up fleeing the forest in the GMC. Then he was silent. Thompson seemed to be working on it at length. Major Taylor held back.
Then Thompson asked: "And then?"
Ryan looked at Thompson for the first time. Then he lowered his eyes again.
"Your coffee is getting cold, Ryan. Don't you want to eat something too?"
"No thanks."
Ryan reached for the cup and only sipped it briefly. Then he put it back. Thompson grinned broadly, leaned back in his chair and crossed his legs.
"You are very suspicious. I understand that very well in your situation. The coffee is okay. Nothing in it that doesn't belong in it." Calmly, Thompson finally pulled out a cigarette and asked, turning to Taylor, "don't you mind?"
"No Sir."
Thompson lit it, took a deep breath and put the lighter back. Taylor was a non-smoker, he had found out and Hawk would have refused, Thompson was sure of that.
"Why did you park the GMC at the airport?"
Ryan said nothing.
"From there you were driven on or driven in a car. You were shot and your strength was weakening. So you needed help. You could not go to a doctor or to a hospital. You would have been reported immediately."
Thompson paused in his remarks. He wanted to give Ryan a chance to talk. Ryan said nothing. Thompson kept talking.
"I would have visited a medicine man in your situation. I might have found it in the reservation. I just don't know how I would have got through the roadblocks unnoti-

ced."
Ryan said nothing.
"Major General Taylor, would you please leave us alone. I know I'm in your stomping ground, but I want to save us from having to take the Sergeant out in handcuffs."
Taylor nodded. "Okay."
He got up and left his office.
Thompson closed the door behind him. Without losing another word, he sat back on his chair. Casual and loutish. He waited and smoked another cigarette. He ate another muffin and snapped a crumb from his jacket with his finger. This black man in gray wolf fur amazed Ryan. He was different than he expected. It had to be the man who had made to believe him. Although Ryan's suspicion had not given way, he had realized that Thompson might be his only chance.
"My sister took me to the medicine man. I had lost too much blood. And he knows what to do about infections. I was passed out for many hours."
"Did he advise you to give oneself up?"
"No, that was my decision."
"Did your sister bring you here?"
"No. A friend helped me."
Thompson lit the third cigarette.
"When did you break into Taylor's office?", he asked.
"Two o'clock this morning, Sir."
Thompson nodded acknowledging.
"You are crazy, daring and brazen. A professional through and through. You were sent to special training before being used as a driver. But you, Ryan Black Hawk, have, as far as I know, even taken the professionals for a ride." Thompson laughed amused.
"Stealing the FBI's own company car from under their

butt ...", Thompson chuckled softly. "Even the story of blowing up your examiner with a magnetic bomb dummy was not hidden from me. You are exceptional."
There was admiration in Thompson's voice.
"Will you take me to prison?", Ryan asked firmly.
Thompson became instantly serious and waited as if he seemed to think carefully about his answer.
"Your statement is against Agent Mitchell's statement. Both sound believable. That Rodriguez was still handcuffed was a mistake. He tried to explain it. That you escaped him was also a mistake. You can testify against Mitchell. However, he doesn't think it is possible to believe an Indian more than him, an FBI special agent. I have the authority to issue an arrest warrant for shooting three of Mitchell's men. But then the cat bites his tail. Mitchell told you they were killers targeting Rodriguez. Then it turned out that Mitchell knew the killers and gave them orders. The only one who knows is you, Ryan. In the search for you, Mitchell stated that the three dead were men from the FBI. Rodriguez lost his nerve and fled the car. On this escape you shot him from behind. With exactly the same pistols, the same caliber as they are on the table here. Why do the killers, who knew exactly when Rodriguez was coming, use the same weapons as Mitchell's men?" Thompson took a deep breath and pulled his cigarette for a long time.
"Because they were the same", Ryan replied, looking Thompson straight in the eye.
Thompson nodded slowly.
"I agree! And Mitchell tries to cover this up with all means by throwing you to the lions. The pistols are full of your fingerprints. Maybe the forensic experts will find something useful in the laboratory. I have a few special-

ists in my team who use a few crumbs of mummy dust to reconstruct a life-size wax doll." Thompson took another cigarette. "I will conduct the investigation and make Mitchell believe that I do not know anything."
"What will become of me, Sir?"
For me you have witness status without hesitation. I will not take you to the trial. You just have to write down your statement. This leaves you a free man and left to the Air Force. Taylor will tell you what to do next."
"Yes, Sir", Ryan replied.
Thompson stubbed out the cigarette.
"If you ever need a shitty job that nobody wants to do, get in touch with me, Ryan Black Hawk. The risk allowance is about twenty to fifty thousand dollars per order", Thompson casually mentioned.
"I don't work for the FBI!"
Thompson smiled as he got up.
"Not for the FBI. For me." Without expecting an answer, Thompson turned and left the office.

Taylor didn't come back alone. General P.I. Barkley entered the office in front of him. Ryan immediately got up and greeted. Barkley replied shortly and eyed him suspiciously. He and Taylor stood up in front of Ryan.
"Sergeant Hawk", Barkley started. "You acted absolutely irresponsible. Your unreliability is unworthy of a U.S. Air Force Sergeant. I accuse you of refusing to issue orders. My order exactly two days ago. Without exception, my order has priority over that of a major general and it would have been your duty to inform me immediately! Instead, you disappeared without a trace for two days and were not available to me, their operations manager, or the U.S. Air Force. Do you know what it's called?

Desertion!"

Barkley had talked himself into rage and was growing red in the face.

Ryan said nothing.

"Do you have anything to tell me about this?", Barkley asked when he gasped.

Ryan swallowed hard, pressed his lips together and said nothing.

"Answer me! That's an order", Barkley said harder.

"No Sir. I have nothing to say about it, Sir", Ryan replied loudly and clearly.

Barkley seemed happy with it. Taylor stood next to him like a decorative accessory. He was silent too. It was he who had brought his Sergeant into this situation and he couldn't bring him out of there. Messing with Barkley was a delicate thing.

"I will deal with you in more detail today. You'll be acquainted with one of our cells till tomorrow, Sergeant Hawk", Barkley decided.

Then he called the men to take the sergeant away. He ordered tougher terms of liability because he knew what Hawk was capable of.

They brought Ryan away, handcuffed. Some men at the base crossed their path and watched the spectacle in surprise. But one came right up to Ryan and the escort. So close that he could have looked his friend in the eye and stubbornly stopped.

Ryan didn't look anywhere, not even to Baxter.

Indian Cowboy - Volume 2
The Hunter

Dark clouds loomed over the land around the Black Hills. No sunbeam could penetrate them. Dawn dominated the day. Oppressive sultry, without any draft, announced the approaching thunderstorm. It was incredibly quiet. Not a bird sang and the thick air swallowed the engine noise of Highway 90.

A young man came from there on foot. He didn't seem to be in a hurry, but he didn't stroll. A black bag hung over his shoulder and although it wasn't necessary, he wore sunglasses. No road, no path, led in this direction, in which he walked purposefully. It seemed as he knew where he was going. He had put the shirt in his belt. It dangled in time with his steps. Ryan Black Hawk knew exactly where he was going. He knew the way. Not the first time he put it back on foot. After about two hours he had reached the edge of the forest in the Back Hills. In the mountains he would find shelter from the thunderstorm that was coming up very quickly. The jeans stuck to the skin and the tongue to the palate. Even the dark forest offered no cooling relief. A fire seemed to be burning in his sneakers. Ryan ignored all of this. His face looked petrified and his thoughts tormented him. Finally, he put the glasses away. It was dark in the thick forest. Here, too, the Lakota did not follow any track. His feet touched the soft mixed forest floor, rotting needles, withered leaves, moss and branches. It smelled of it. A barely audible sound that didn't belong here made Ryan stop and listen.

He clearly heard a human groan. Ryan grinned at the corners of his mouth and waited.

Silence.

Then someone groaned again. It came from above, from the slope. Ryan left the bag behind, crawled up and finally lay on the floor. His grin widened when he realized the cause. Another miserable moan came to his ears. Ryan got up.

Although the Lakota always avoided interfering in other people's affairs, it seemed extremely necessary here. A white-haired man, wearing only his underpants, was hanging upside down on the lowest branch of a tree. His head hovered above the ground, while his arms hung in a large anthill. The animals bravely defended their dwelling and did not agree with the intruder. Ryan took out his knife and cut the rope. The old man flopped in the crawling pile and croaked. He swore weakly and tried unsuccessfully to get up. The old man waved awkwardly. Ryan grinned mockingly at the strange, ridiculous creature and turned to go.

"Hey you!", the old man suddenly snorted. "You can't..." He groaned as he laboriously tried to get on his legs, "...leave me here. goddam!"

Ryan paused and looked back.

"Maybe you didn't deserve it any other way", he replied unaffectedly.

"I'll kill those cursed skunks! Ungrateful people!"

The old man had enough air in his lungs to swear heavily. On all fours he crawled out of the bunch of brave little animals and kept stroking his fiery red arms. Some dead bodies fell to the ground. When he thought he was safe, he leaned against a tree and took a first look at his rescuer. The little old grinned, coughed and said in a hoarse voice: "Thank you! I owe you something."

Wind came up and drove into the leaves of the trees. It

rustled. Ryan looked up.

"I can feel something prowling. I noticed it last night in my old, rotten bones. I'm Samuel Gabriel Anthony Williams by the way. For you, Sam. If you give me your name?"

Ryan looked down at him skeptically and eyed him. He was small, stocky and had short, crooked legs. His white hair stuck in all directions from his head. But the beard made an extremely meticulously groomed impression. His big nose was reminiscent of a potato and his eyes blinked curiously at Ryan.

"Ryan", he finally said.

Sam laughed in a smoky voice.

"I like you, fellow. You're Indian. Looks like an Air Force cut on vacation. No one else would have had the stupid idea to roam through this godforsaken piece of forest. My luck. Otherwise the ants would have gnawed off my bones."

Old Sam changed his mood from an unfriendly snarling to an idiosyncratic humor. He laughed and beckoned to Ryan.

"Come on boy! Help an old man get on his feet. My skull is humming from the twisted world."

Ryan took a step forward and held out his hand. The old man grabbed his wrist and pulled himself up. Then he took the first stiff steps.

The wind grew to a storm.

The thunder rumbled.

It was high time for Ryan to go to the cave. Again he turned to go.

"The lightning should hit me, that I drop dead immediately, if I'm a liar. I am a businessman and have always been honest with everyone!", Sam screamed through the loud roar of the storm.

Branches cracked menacingly. One fell to the ground. Ryan remained indifferent and continued on his way.

"Why should our creator send you to me on your way? To save my life! He didn't want me up there yet!", the old man shouted after him.

"Ever heard of hell?", Ryan shouted back without stopping.

He heard the old man croak behind him.

"The devil is afraid of me!" ...

German language:
„Indian Cowboy" Band 1-6,
„Maggie Yellow Cloud" Band 1-2
„Die Farben der Sonne"
„Sheloquins Vermächtnis"

English language:
„The Indian Cowboy" Part 1
Comming soon:
„The Indian Cowboy" Part 2

Buy now:
Twenty-Six-Verlag Online Shop
Amazon
Thalia, Weltbild, Hugendubel and
all online-book-shops in all formats

www.brita-rose-billert.de

More than just a book...